T0285322

Death on Dartmoor Edge

By Stephanie Austin

Dead in Devon
Dead on Dartmoor
From Devon with Death
The Dartmoor Murders
A Devon Night's Death
Death Comes to Dartmoor
A Devon Midwinter Murder
Death on Dartmoor Edge

a&b

Death on Dartmoor Edge

STEPHANIE AUSTIN

Allison & Busby Limited
11 Wardour Mews
London W1F 8AN
allisonandbusby.com

First published in Great Britain by Allison & Busby in 2024.

A CIP catalogue record for this book is available from
the British Library.

First Edition

ISBN 978-0-7490-3118-3

Typeset in 11.5/16.5 pt Sabon LT Pro by
Allison & Busby Ltd.

By choosing this product, you help take care of the world's forests.
Learn more: www.fsc.org.

FSC
www.fsc.org
MIX
Paper | Supporting
responsible forestry
FSC® C171272

Printed and bound by
CPI Group (UK) Ltd, Croydon, CR0 4YY

For all my theatre friends, on stage and off

CHAPTER ONE

On the morning that all the trouble started, I decided to leave my van at home and go to *Old Nick's* on foot. I'd just come back from walking the Tribe in the woods and had returned the five of them to their various homes, so it wasn't as if I needed the exercise. But I wouldn't be able to park. The little town of Ashburton was in chaos, thanks to the gas company's decision to dig a big hole at the junction between East Street and North Street, thus severing the town's main artery and making it impossible to drive from one end of town to the other. It also reduced the available on-street parking, put two bus stops out of action and obliged all drivers to puzzle out their own route to the town hall car park. Ashburton was never built for motor cars. But we needed new gas pipes, apparently.

I shrugged my coat tight around me as I walked, stuffing all my hair inside my hood. An icy wind was coming straight off Dartmoor. It might be March, yellow daffodils glowing in the window-boxes, but the sky was the colour of concrete and it was colder than

February, or even January when Ashburton had been briefly visited by snow. March had come in like a lion, as the saying goes, and was still roaring. The idea that it might go out like a lamb seemed remote.

I stopped on North Street, gazing into the window of one of the many rival antique shops, lusting after the kind of items I could never afford to buy for *Old Nick's*. I was twisting my neck around in an owl-like fashion, trying to read the price label of a mahogany console table, the wood polished to such a high gloss that it glowed, and the gleaming silver samovar sitting on the top of it, when a movement caught the corner of my eye. I turned, momentarily stunned, to see a chunky figure in grey sweats pounding the pavement towards me – Detective Constable Dean Collins, puffing and red in the face. Scowling, he flipped a palm upward in greeting. I got the impression I was someone he would rather not have met under the circumstances. I couldn't help it, I laughed.

'Don't you start,' he panted, pausing in front of me. 'I'm getting enough grief from everyone at the station.'

'I think it's laudable,' I told him, trying to look serious, 'levels of fitness in the police force and all that.' If anyone needed to improve his level of fitness, it was Dean. He'd been piling on the pounds recently.

'Gemma's been having a go at me about losing weight,' he grumbled, 'and so has the boss.' He began doing that jog on the spot that runners do to prove they have bundles of energy left and they're not just stopping for a rest.

'Does this mean my biscuit tin is off-limits?' I enquired sunnily.

'When we're having one of our cosy chats about criminal matters, d'you mean?' He grinned. 'That depends on the level of police co-operation you might require, Miss Marple.'

He knows I hate him calling me that. I tried not to grind my teeth. 'Well, as long as you're still open to bribery.' I patted him on the arm. 'Keep up the good work.'

He muttered something rude under his breath and resumed punishing the pavement. I turned off down Shadow Lane, the stone walls of old buildings closing in around me, offering me shelter from the wind. It's only possible to drive so far before the lane narrows to a pedestrian passageway, but I can usually park here without any problem. Today, several desperate drivers had wedged their vehicles between the gutter and the wall, probably the last free parking places to be found anywhere. I was glad I'd left Van Blanc at home.

As I picked my way between the parked cars, a green blob landed on the pavement beside me. I looked up. A family of jackdaws were in the gutter above me, flicking their beaks through lumps of moss in the hunt for insects and tiny worms. Unlike the rooks which roost on the church tower and take off at daybreak to look for food in the surrounding fields, jackdaws are stay-at-home types and like to gather on the town's mossy rooftops. At this time of year, the pavements of Ashburton are spotted with little green lumps the jackdaws have tossed aside. I love to listen to their softly murmured conversations. They pair for life, I've heard.

Ahead of me I could see *Old Nick's*, the shop that used to belong to a client of mine, Mr Nikolai, until he left it to me in his will. I re-named it in his honour because, despite the fact he was an evil old sod whose greed got the better of him and got him murdered, I still remembered him fondly. In his day, the shop was run-down, dark and shabby. Now, its fresh green paintwork picked out in gold, it looked bright and welcoming, enticing even, assuming anyone could be encouraged to stray down the narrow ginnel of Shadow Lane in the first place. I have a café-board propped optimistically at one end of it, pointing the way – *Old Nick's: Arts, Crafts, Books, Antiques and Collectibles*. It worked, sometimes.

A man was staring in the window, shoulders hunched against the cold, peering intently through the glass, shading his eyes with one hand. Something about the way he was lurking started my antennae twitching. He glanced my way, saw me coming and hurried off up the lane. Great, I thought, my first potential customer of the day and I've scared him off.

Despite the freezing weather, an upstairs window in what would once have been Old Nick's living room was flung wide open and an arm was waving about. The hand at the end of the arm was clutching a mobile phone, which could only mean that it belonged to Sophie Child, desperately seeking a signal.

Sophie minded the shop for me in return for free working and selling space, an arrangement that suited us both, giving me time to attend to my other business, the one I was engaged on when I first met Old Nick– *Juno Browne, Domestic Goddess* – housework, gardening, shopping, dog-walking, etc. Since he was murdered, I've been able to add amateur sleuthing and accidental corpse finding to my CV. I'm not sure it's a good look.

Sophie lived at home with her mum because she couldn't afford to move out. She used to spend all day studiously hunched over her drawing board or at her easel, working on the current stunning wildlife painting or meticulously detailed study of the hedgerow. But her activities had changed in recent months. She'd begun to spend half her time on the phone talking to her new boyfriend, who was away studying in Wales. I watched that arm waving about at the upstairs window and sighed. She'd never get a signal up there and she knew it.

Because we could never get a decent signal, I told her that she was welcome to use the landline in the shop. But she ran me up such a horrific bill in the first month that it frightened us both and she stopped using it. Since then, she's often missing for parts of the day, whispering sweet nothings into her phone on whatever corner or in whichever café she can find that will give her a decent signal. She is also missing at weekends when she takes trips to Wales that she can't afford, or Seth comes down to see her and she wants the day off.

It's my own fault. I was the one who introduced Seth to Sophie. I'd met him at a talk about astrology, given by one of my cousin Cordelia's old friends. I'm not that interested in the subject myself, but Cordelia, who'd helped to bring me up, and is now sadly no longer with us, was an astrologer by profession. Anyway, Seth had popped into the shop next day for a chat and that's how the great romance got started.

I was happy for Sophie. No one looking at her shining eyes and glowing little face could not be happy for her, but her new-found love life was proving just a little inconvenient. Juggling the shop with my Domestic Goddess business was difficult enough as it was. Especially on a day like today when she could only stay for a couple of hours before she caught her train; and Pat, who minded the shop under the same arrangement as she did, couldn't come in either. I'd been forced to put off the client whose house I should have been cleaning so I could mind the shop myself. I don't like letting clients down; but I don't like closing the shop either, especially on a day when it was usually open.

I waved at Sophie and she grinned weakly, embarrassed at being caught out and hastily slammed down the window. By the time I reached the shop door she was already downstairs, seated at her worktable as if she'd been there all the time.

'Hi Juno,' she called out breezily as I came in, closing the door behind me and shutting out the cold.

'Hello.' I stared down at her painting of a dormouse

sleeping in its nest among the brambles. 'How's it going?'

'Oh, fine,' she responded, her long-lashed gaze flickering just for a moment.

I wasn't sure it was fine. Her work, as always, was exquisite, each stem and leaf, each tiny claw and quivering whisker rendered in meticulous detail. But it wasn't progressing very fast. And Sophie had a deadline. She had been commissioned to illustrate a book on the Devon hedgerow, to deliver a series of full colour paintings and drawings. It could be her big break. But she wouldn't see a penny until she had delivered the complete package. And she was already spending the money on trips back and forth to Wales. Despite her happiness and excitement, I could sense a growing nervousness in her, the slightest falter in her confidence.

'I didn't think you were coming in today,' she admitted.

'I wasn't, but Pat can't make it. She's taking in a lot of new waifs and strays.'

Sophie gave a nod of her neat, dark head and I caught myself running a hand through my own hair, a red tangle maddened by the wind. 'What time's your train?'

She pulled a face. 'I'm going on the coach this time. It's cheaper. I've got to change at Bristol.' She brightened suddenly. 'Seth is picking me up from Cardiff.'

'You can go now if you want, Soph,' I offered. She'd start to get twitchy about time soon.

'I don't need to leave for another hour,' she assured me. 'Mum's going to drop me off at the coach stop.'

But suddenly I wanted her to be gone, to be alone in the shop. I tried hard not to let it get to me, but sometimes her new-found love stabbed me with the memory of the love I'd lost. I hadn't seen or heard from Daniel for months. He'd disappeared. The firm he used to work for wouldn't talk to me. The only way that I knew he was still alive was that work had recommenced on the renovation of his aunt's old farmhouse on Halsanger Common. I'd been up there a few times, watching the progress on replacing the roof, rebuilding the chimney, repointing old walls with lime mortar. But the caravan he had bought to live in while work was going on remained cold and empty. The builder told me that he still got his instructions from Mr Thorncroft via text, and the work was paid for; but that's all he would tell me. I knew I shouldn't keep returning there. It was like picking at a wound. If I didn't leave it alone it would never heal. And it was my own fault. I was the one who told Daniel to go away.

'Are you all right, Juno?'

I must have been silent for too long. Sophie was watching me with anxious eyes. I smiled at her, putting away dark thoughts. 'Of course. But go on, I don't want you to miss that bus. Thanks for opening up.'

'Well, if you're sure,' she responded, trying to look reluctant to go.

'I'll cope.'

She gave a delighted giggle and rinsed out her paintbrush. Then she stood up and threw her arms around me in a hug. 'Thank you.'

I'm a lot taller than she is and she barely came up to my shoulder. 'Get going,' I told her. She shrugged on her coat, pulled a red beanie hat over that shiny dark hair, and headed for the door.

'Got your inhaler?' I yelled after her.

She stopped, checked her pocket and grinned. 'You're worse than my mum.'

'I wonder why. Give my love to Seth,' I added as she danced out of the door.

The shop bell jangled a farewell, then there was silence.

I looked around the shop, gazed for a moment at walls hung with Sophie's paintings, and photos of Pat's animals at Honeysuckle Farm waiting for new homes. She runs an animal sanctuary, along with her sister and brother-in-law. Today they were taking in animals from another shelter up on the moor, forced to close because the owner couldn't afford to keep it running. They couldn't afford to take in more animals either, but they were too good-hearted to refuse. *Bouncer, looking for his forever home,* I read under the picture of a Bull Terrier – *good with children but needs a home with no other dogs. Or cats.* I bet he does.

As customers were rare this early in the morning, I nipped upstairs to the kitchen to make a cup of tea and see if I could drag a comb through the tangled mass of my hair. While the kettle boiled, I gave in to the craving to look on my phone. No messages. Nothing from Daniel. I thumbed through some photos of him I'd taken last year. I've tried to delete them so many times, but just can't bring myself to do it. Just as I can't bear to burn his letters, addressed to *Miss Browne with an e. My dear Miss B,* he would always start. He stared back at me, lean, dark and hawkish, a quizzical look in his grey eyes, an ironic twist at the corner of his mouth. The second photo was different; all loving smiles. There was even a selfie of the two of us together, pulling idiotic faces. Just as the kettle came to a boil, I heard the jangle of the shop bell downstairs, pocketed my phone, and hurried down.

A man was standing in front of the counter, hands in the pockets of his jacket, staring around him uncertainly, the same man I'd seen peering in the window a little earlier. He was about fifty, I suppose, with greying sandy hair, parted low on one side, and large spectacles. He seemed nervous, his fingers jingling change in his pocket. If my antennae had started twitching when I'd seen him out in the street, at close quarters they started whirring like hornets' wings. There was something about him that was just creepy.

'Can I help you?' I asked, trying not to stare at his comb-over.

'Is Mrs Hunter in today?'

'Mrs Hunter?' I repeated, frowning. I didn't know who he meant.

'She works in here on certain days, I believe.'

'I think you've got the wrong shop,' I told him.

'There's no Mrs Hunter working here.'

He smiled hesitantly, an uncertain gleam in his eyes, as if he was trying to work out whether I was lying to him. 'There's only Sophie and Pat,' I went on. 'Sometimes Elizabeth comes in. But none of them is called Hunter.'

He nodded in a smug way that made me feel I'd said too much.

'Perhaps,' he went on slyly, 'she goes by another name.'

I got it then. It clicked. I knew who he was talking about. 'I really can't give out personal information about the people who work here,' I said, adopting a brisker tone. 'Do you mind telling me your name and what you want.'

'I'm Colin.' He turned towards the door. 'Tell Mrs Hunter I called, will you?'

'Colin?' I repeated.

He nodded. 'That's right. Colin from Moorland View. She'll know who you mean.' He gave a knowing wink and left.

'Shit,' I muttered, reaching for the phone on the counter. *Shit. Shit. Shit.* I dialled Elizabeth's number. I wished I hadn't mentioned her name. In Ashburton, she's known as Ms Knollys, Olly's great-aunt. She is supposed to be his only remaining relative, and to have come from afar to look after the teenage boy when his great-grandmother died. Apart from Elizabeth herself, only Olly and I knew that was not her real identity. Her phone was engaged. Shit again.

I realised that I'd never known her married name. If it wasn't Hunter, then no harm had been done. Colin, whoever he was, was clearly barking up the wrong tree; or just plain barking. But if it was Hunter, then someone else knew her true identity. And that wasn't good. She'd mentioned that she might pop into the shop later as she knew I was short-handed. I'd told her not to bother but now I hoped she would come. The phone rang, making me jump. I swept up the receiver.

'Elizabeth?'

But the voice at the other end wasn't hers. It was cracked with age and trembling with emotion. 'Juno?' it croaked.

'Maisie?' I wasn't due to see her today. 'Are you alright?'

'I'm on the floor,' she responded tearfully. 'Can you come and help me?'

Maisie, aged ninety-seven, had fallen over.

'Are you hurt?'

'I don't think so. But I can't get up. Can you come?'

'I'll be there, Maisie,' I assured her. 'But it'll take me a few minutes to get to you, so sit tight. Don't worry, I'll be there as soon as I can.' I put the phone down with a sigh. I'd have to shut the shop now. If only I'd driven here and not left the van at home. I grabbed my keys and locked up, flicking off the lights as I went. Should I ring an ambulance? With the road up, would that get to Maisie any quicker than I could? And if she wasn't hurt, I could be diverting a crew from something more urgent. All this was reeling through my mind as

I hurried up the street, dodging pedestrians and their dogs on the narrow pavement.

I thought about going straight to her place, and not bothering to fetch the van. But if she needed medical attention, we would want the transport.

I can't have been many minutes fetching Van Blanc from outside my house and driving to Brook Cottage, but it felt like an age. I let myself in with Maisie's spare key and was immediately challenged by a snarling Jacko, barrelling up the hall towards me.

'It's me, you stupid dog!' I yelled before he could launch an attack on my ankles. I've walked him three times a week for years now but he still treats me like a burglar whenever I come through the door. Reassured by my dulcet tones, he backed off and went to stick his snout in his food bowl.

I could see Maisie's thin legs sticking out from behind an armchair. She was sitting on the floor, her tiny body propped against the back of it. In her hand was a small greasy frying pan, while on the gas hob of the cooker in her tiny kitchenette, blue flames blazed away unhindered.

'Hello, Juno,' she called out cheerily as I reached out for the knob on the burner and turned it off. Luckily, she'd clung on to the frying pan as she fell, or the kitchen might have been on fire by now. The pan was empty, its contents almost certainly wolfed down and obligingly licked clean by Jacko.

'What were you doing?'

'I fancied a fried egg.'

Maisie might be all smiles now but I could see the snail-trail of a tear on her raddled cheek. She'd knocked a table over in her fall. Fortunately, it was the one with the phone on it, which was how she'd been able to make the call. I righted the table and sat down on the floor next to her, removing the frying pan from her gnarled grasp and encasing her hand in mine.

'How long had you been sitting here before you phoned?' I asked.

'Only a few minutes.'

A bit longer than that, I was willing to bet. I've been through this kind of thing with her before. At least it was warm in here. 'You haven't hurt yourself?'

She rubbed her knee. 'My knee's hurting a bit, but it's nothing. I just can't get up, that's all.'

'Let's try, shall we?' I stood up, manoeuvred myself into position, put my hands under her armpits, braced myself and hauled her to her feet. She weighed next to nothing, which, I suppose, was how she has managed to escape injury so far. Women much younger than her ninety-seven years have shattered their hip bones on impact with the floor. I checked her over for bruising, examined the suspect knee, made sure she could stand unaided, and fetched her walking frame, which, as so often on these occasions, wasn't where it needed to be.

'And how did you come to fall over?' I asked. 'You weren't dizzy or anything?'

'Oh, no,' she answered evasively. 'It was Jacko's fault. He got under my feet.'

We both turned to look at him, sitting rooting in

his groin. Jacko is in many ways a revolting little dog, smelly, greedy, disobedient and aggressive. But I doubt if he was the real culprit in this case. It was far more likely that Maisie had tripped over her own slippers, or simply had a wobble.

'So, next question,' I began. 'Where is your pendant alarm?'

Her daughter, Our Janet, who lives up north, had set Maisie up with a home alarm system the last time she had visited, a pendant she could press if she got into trouble, which put her through to a call-centre. She should have been wearing it around her neck.

'I forgot to put it on.' She's not a good liar. I could see the pendant discarded among the cushions on the sofa. The agency carer who came in every morning to help Maisie dress would certainly have made sure she was wearing it before she left. She'd taken it off herself, probably the moment Maria was out of the door.

'I don't like it,' she admitted irritably, seeing the direction of my gaze. 'And Jacko doesn't like that thing.' She gestured at the speaker mounted on the wall, a white box with a glowing green light signalling that it was switched on. When the pendant was activated, the reassuring voice of a call-centre operative should talk to her through that speaker and send help if necessary. 'He starts barking when that voice comes out of it.' Jacko was getting the blame for everything this morning. Maisie hunched a shoulder. 'I don't like using it.'

No, you'd rather call me, I thought.

'Juno,' she went on, her voice wheedling, 'we don't need to tell Our Janet I fell over, do we?'

I sighed. It was Our Janet who paid my wages and once a week I phoned her to keep her informed of Maisie's welfare.

'She wants to put me in that place up north with a lot of old people. Northern old people,' she finished in disgust.

That place was a comfortable care home where Maisie would be safe and near enough for her family members to visit. I sympathised with Janet's desire to take care of her mother properly. But Maisie was determined not to leave Brook Cottage except in her coffin and I sympathised with that too.

'I don't want to go into a home,' she went on, her face crumpling. 'I don't, I don't!' and she began to cry. 'They won't let me keep Jacko.'

I was horrified. Usually, whenever we have this conversation, Maisie is feisty and belligerent, not tearful. I put an arm around her thin shoulders and gave her a squeeze. Jacko, sensing perhaps that his future was at stake, waddled over and licked her hand.

'You put me in a very awkward position,' I told her. 'I won't say anything to Janet this time, but you've got to promise me you'll wear this,' I reached out for the pendant and,' I added, stabbing with a finger at her walking frame, 'you won't go wandering about in here without it.'

'I promise,' she murmured, patting my arm with a veined hand.

I hung the pendant around her neck. 'I'm awarding you this gold medal for bad behaviour.' She gave a watery chuckle. I made her a cup of tea and, after thoroughly scouring the pan, fried her the egg she'd fancied. That's about the limit of my culinary skills. I left her sitting in her armchair watching the telly. I'd prepared sandwiches for her lunch. The ready meal for her supper was in the microwave, all she had to do was turn the dial. I'd phone her later to check up on her and Maria would be along in the evening to help her get into bed. Between us all, we kept her going. *Ninety-seven*, I muttered to myself as I let myself out of her cottage. How much longer could we keep on getting away with it?

CHAPTER TWO

When I got back to *Old Nick's*, about an hour and a half after I'd locked it up, the shop seemed to have magically re-opened itself. The lights were on and the sign on the door was turned to *Open*. My first thought was that Pat had finished with her waifs and strays and come in after all, or, perish the thought, that Sophie had come back because she'd missed her bus. But as I let myself in, there was no sign of either of them. The place seemed deserted. I was just about to call out when a voice from the back room stopped me.

'What exactly is it that you want?' It was Elizabeth's voice, precise as always, beautifully articulated, and at this moment, sounding quietly furious. It stopped me in my tracks.

'Well, Mrs Hunter . . .' the other voice belonged to Colin, the man who had been asking for her. 'Or may I call you Elizabeth?'

'You most certainly may not,' came the clipped reply.

'Oh?' he sounded surprised. 'I thought you might prefer it to being called Mrs Hunter around here.'

'Get to the point.'

'You must understand my dilemma, Mrs Hunter,' he went on, 'what with the rise in the cost of living and everything . . .'

'I understand you're after money.'

'Well, the two gentlemen who came to Moorland View enquiring after your whereabouts are most certainly after money, aren't they? Quite a lot of it, from what I can gather. They're offering me a very generous sum to discover those whereabouts, Mrs Hunter. And in order not to reveal the fact that I *already* know where you are, I feel a little renumeration is in order.'

'This is blackmail.'

'Nasty word, Mrs Hunter.' Colin seemed determined to use her name with every breath. 'After all, I'm only a humble care assistant, I don't get paid much. And I would have thought, a mere half of what these gentlemen are offering me in order for me to stay silent, would be perfectly fair in the circumstances.'

I crept a few steps nearer to the door into the corridor and peered cautiously around the frame. I could see Colin in the back room, where I display my antiques and collectibles, standing in front of a pine dresser. I could see only the back of Elizabeth, her silver-blonde hair, as always, swept up into an immaculate chignon, her white blouse pressed.

'What if I go straight to the police?' she demanded.

I saw Colin smile. 'What if you do, Mrs Hunter? I should think very carefully about the consequences of doing that if I were you. Living under an assumed name, sharing a house with a minor. What will the police think of that? And teenage boys are so vulnerable, aren't they? Emotionally I mean. And I understand young Oliver is about to take his exams . . .'

'You come anywhere near Olly and I will kill you,' she promised in a fierce undertone. Colin laughed. He wouldn't be laughing if he knew as much about Elizabeth as I did.

'If you're going to make threats,' he retorted, 'then you might like to consider Joan's welfare. After all, some nights I'm the only care staff on duty at Moorland View. And I can't be everywhere at once.'

'Get out!' Elizabeth came towards him, stepping into my line of sight. She picked up a native African club that was lying on a nearby table. It was made from ironwood and a blow on the head would certainly prove fatal. But Colin just laughed. Perhaps it was the price label tied around its neck that struck him as comical. He pointed at it as he backed away. Then he glanced in my direction and his smile vanished.

'It seems we have an eavesdropper present, Mrs Hunter.'

'You have a witness,' I told him, walking down the corridor towards him. I glanced at Elizabeth. She was white-faced, her steely grey eyes blazing with fury, her mouth frozen in a tight line. 'This is my shop,' I told Colin. 'And I want you out of it, right now.' I stood aside to let him pass. 'Go on, get out.'

He looked me up and down. 'The famous Juno Browne,' he gave a mocking chuckle. 'No doubt about who *you* are, is there?'

I could feel my gorge rise as the odious little man passed close by me. He stank of cheap aftershave. 'I'll give you a little time to think about things, Mrs Hunter,' he added generously. 'I'm sure this has come as a bit of a shock.'

I didn't look at him again as he let himself out. My eyes were on Elizabeth. We heard the bell jangle as he closed the door. She dropped the club with a groan and collapsed into the nearest chair. She was trembling, but with rage, not fear.

'Elizabeth, what on earth . . . ?'

'I knew they'd catch up with me one day.' She gazed up at me and her usual steely resolve had left her eyes. She looked as if she were staring down the barrel of a gun. 'Juno,' she breathed in a long sigh. 'I think it's time I told you the truth.'

I closed the shop. This was more important. Elizabeth and I went upstairs to *Old Nick's* kitchen where I made us a cup of tea. We would both have preferred something stronger but I don't keep spirits on the premises.

'You remember when we first met?' she began.

'Of course.' After the death of her husband, George, who turned out to have been a secret gambler, Elizabeth had left her old life behind, surrendered the keys of her much-mortgaged house to the bank and gone on the road to escape his loan sharks. When I met her, she'd been living in her car with her cat. She'd also been carrying a pistol in her handbag.

'I didn't tell you the whole truth,' she went on, meeting my gaze squarely. 'I told you I had no particular reason for coming here, to this part of Devon.'

I nodded. 'You said you just liked the area.'

'I lied. I did have a reason for wanting to be here.' She paused a moment. 'I have a sister, Joan, living in a care home in Bovey Tracey. She and her husband retired there some time ago, but shortly after they moved, he was diagnosed with cancer and he didn't live out the year. They had no children. Joan used to be very active, very fit, swam at her local spa every morning. About seven years ago, while she was alone in the pool, she suffered a stroke. It was some time, perhaps half an hour, before anyone realised what had happened to her. By that time, a lot of damage had been done. Now Joan cannot walk or speak and doesn't know who I am.'

'That's terrible.' Words, as always, seemed inadequate. 'I'm so sorry.'

She smiled sadly. 'I've been visiting her at Moorland View for years. So, when I was forced to leave my home, I came to this area so that I could be close enough to still visit, but not so close that anyone could trace me through her. Of course, by this time, the staff already knew me by my married name, Hunter.'

I could see why she'd been attracted to Ashburton. Just a few miles from Bovey Tracey, she could visit her sister easily, but still retain distance, anonymity.

'I thought I'd got away with it,' she went on dryly, 'until today. It seems that some of the people George owed money to aren't prepared to let it go so easily.'

'And they've managed to track you to your sister's care home?'

'It seems so.'

'Do you know how?'

She gave a helpless shrug. 'I suppose if they came up with some plausible reason for making enquiries, they might have learnt something from our old neighbours, from people who lived in the street where George and I lived. They all knew Joan and what had happened to her, long before I disappeared. I believe one of them still sends her a Christmas card.'

I have never heard Elizabeth complain, but leaving all her friends behind, slamming the door on the life she had known, must have been hard. 'Anyway, whoever these two are, they've traced her to Moorland View and have been there enquiring about me, according to Colin. And they've offered him money if he can tell them where I am, so he's made it his business to find out.'

'Does anyone else there know where you live, apart from Colin?'

'The home has my mobile number of course, in case they need to contact me in an emergency, but they don't have an address. In any case, Mrs MacDonald, who runs the place, would never give out personal information of any kind. I'm certain I can rely on her discretion.'

'So, how did Colin find out where you are?'

'I can only assume he must have followed me back to Olly's house. He seems to be well-informed. He must have been snooping around Ashburton, asking questions.'

'He's been stalking you. Now he's trying to blackmail you. Why don't you go to the police?'

'And tell them what? That I've been living under an assumed name . . .'

'That's not a crime.'

'And that, although I claim to be his aunt,' she went on, 'I am *not* related to the underage boy whose house I've moved into? I'm not sure they'd consider me a suitable person to continue looking after him. And do I tell them that I'm on the run from my husband's creditors? And by the way, George and I had some bank accounts set up in joint names, which means, legally, I probably am liable for his debts.'

It didn't seem fair. She'd already lost everything she owned because of her husband's gambling. 'Did George owe a lot of money?'

She gave a rueful smile. 'A horrific amount, and to some very unpleasant people.'

'Does Olly know you've got a sister?'

She shook her head. 'I've told him as little about my past as possible. The less he knows, the better. I have to protect him.' Her jaw tightened. 'That's all that matters. I have to protect Olly. And my sister.'

'What are you going to do?'

'I don't know. But I'm not giving any money to that bloody awful man. I can't, I haven't got it to give.'

'How much is he asking for?'

'Ten thousand pounds.'

'What!' I was gobsmacked. 'So, if Colin is telling the truth, these men who came to your sister's home are offering him *twenty* thousand just to find out where you are.' I puffed out my cheeks. 'Which means George must have owed them a lot.'

'His debts ran just short of two hundred thousand, spread about among a number of these . . . creditors,' Elizabeth said bitterly. 'And those are just the debts I know about. Of course, most of that money owed is interest on the original loan and until it's paid, that keeps on rising.'

'Do you think Colin is telling the truth? He might have found out about George's debts somehow and have invented these two loan sharks, just to frighten you into giving him money.'

Elizabeth was silent a moment, thoughtful. 'I don't see how he could have found out. Joan couldn't have told him anything, poor darling.'

'But when you go to visit her . . .'

'I talk to her of course. Tell her all the latest news. Just because she can't speak doesn't mean she can't hear. I don't know whether or not she can understand me but it's important to keep her stimulated. I tell her about Olly and his exams coming up . . . Oh God,' she moaned. 'That foul little man must have been eavesdropping, picking up clues.'

I was still thinking about the two loan sharks, the men Colin claimed to have spoken to. 'I wonder if they've approached the owner of Moorland View.'

'Mrs MacDonald?'

'She'd be the obvious person to ask. And if they'd made enquiries among any of the other staff she'd know, surely, and she'd tell you someone had been asking for you. They must have left contact details of some sort.'

'She hasn't been in touch.'

'You could go to her and complain. Tell her that Colin has turned up here and you think he's been stalking you.'

Elizabeth raised an eyebrow. 'And lose him his job? He'd be even more in need of money then, not to mention nursing a grudge.'

'That's true,' I admitted. 'But if Mrs MacDonald knows nothing, then at least we can be reasonably sure that it's only Colin we have to deal with.'

'We?'

'Well, it's none of my business obviously, but . . .'

She reached across the table and took my hand. 'I don't want to drag you into this business, Juno. I don't want to get you involved.'

'I am involved,' I told her. 'If that creep thinks he can come into my shop, threatening my friends . . .'

She laughed, shaking her head. 'You are priceless!'

I ignored this because I wasn't quite sure what she meant. 'If we could find a way of putting pressure on Colin,' I carried on, 'turn the tables on him somehow.'

Elizabeth was nodding, that steely glint of determination back in her eye. 'Then I might not have to murder him after all,' she said lightly.

I thought about this later, in bed. I'd been telling Bill about it but he wasn't any help, just purred at the sound of my voice. He was curled up now, a furry black blob on the duvet. How much did I really know about

Elizabeth? When I met her that evening in the town hall car park, she'd been homeless and on the run. She'd resisted all overtures of friendship until the night she'd saved me from an attacker by calmly pulling a pistol from her handbag and just as calmly, pulling the trigger. It had dampened his ardour somewhat and he'd run off howling, a bullet hole in his hand. She's always claimed she was a music teacher before she retired, and I'm sure that at some point in her life, she was. She helps to coach Olly on the bassoon, accompanying his practice on the piano. But at the time she arrived, he was being bullied at school and she taught him some useful self-defence moves. I think that in the past she might have been in the military, whatever that means.

All I did know was that she was a force for good in Olly's life. Somehow, he had slipped through the social services' net. At fourteen, he'd been living alone in his great-grandmother's house, so terrified of being taken into care that he'd kept the old woman's death a secret. Elizabeth's arrival had been a godsend. She'd moved in, taking on responsibility for Olly, pretending to be a family member. This had also solved the problem of her homelessness. And while it might not exactly have been a marriage made in heaven, she and Olly got along. And they had grown fond of each other, fond enough to carry on with the arrangement and to keep each other's secrets.

Another person Elizabeth had grown fond of was Tom Carter, an old client of mine. She'd met him when she'd joined the church choir. Initially, they'd been held back from full-on romance by Tom's need for a replacement hip. But since the operation, who knew? Whatever was going on, they were discreet about it. He was teaching Elizabeth fly-fishing. That was about as much as she'd admit to. Of course, none of us at *Old Nick's* believe their romance hasn't gone further. But I can't help wondering just how much Tom knows about his new lady friend and her interesting past.

CHAPTER THREE

The next day was Saturday so I was in the shop anyway. I only work on Domestic Goddess jobs during the week, although I had called in on Maisie on my way in that morning. She was back on form, her usual cantankerous self; still not wearing her pendant alarm, I noticed.

'You promised,' I reminded her, slipping it around her neck. She scowled but didn't argue. She was being taken out to lunch with the pensioners' association so at least I didn't have to worry about leaving her on her own. I wasn't expecting Pat, still busy with her waifs and strays, and she didn't usually come into the shop at weekends anyway. The only person I was expecting was Elizabeth.

She didn't disappoint, slipping in through the shop door about half-way through the morning as I was busy unpacking a box of plate stands that I had ordered online. They came packed in a cardboard box, with a mile of heavy-duty sticky tape wound around it, like the wrappings on a mummified corpse. I was hunting in the counter drawer for my slicing tool, a cunning little blade concealed between two discs of plastic about the size of a fifty pence piece. The blade is pushed out by a little slider on the side. I don't know if this object has a name. I call it my snipe. The whole device fits neatly into the palm of my hand and is one of my favourite objects. There's something very satisfying about the way it slices through sticky tape. But then, I'm funny like that.

I abandoned my search for it when Elizabeth came in. Her concession to the weekend was to braid her hair in a complicated plait and wear jeans with a padded body warmer. She still managed to look effortlessly elegant and make me feel bedraggled, as if I'd just fallen out of bed. She grabbed the back of Sophie's chair, wheeled it over to the counter and sat down opposite me, her face serious and intent.

'Well?' I asked.

'I phoned Moorland View and spoke to Mrs MacDonald,' she began. 'I enquired after Joan, and asked if she'd had any visitors recently. Mrs MacDonald said she thought not, but she'd check amongst the staff. She rang me back a little while later.'

I sensed something significant was coming and leant forward over the counter. 'And?'

'It seems there was an *incident* involving Joan two weeks ago, and she'd only just learnt about it. She was very apologetic. Apparently, there was a junior member of staff on duty at reception at the time who hadn't written a report about it because she was scared of getting into trouble. But it must have been worrying her because when Mrs Macdonald asked about Joan's visitors, she burst into tears and confessed all.'

'So, what had happened?'

'It seems Joan did receive visitors, two men, who came to reception and asked to see her. They claimed to be cousins, even arrived with a bunch of flowers, and the receptionist let them in to her room.'

'I take it they weren't really cousins?'

'No. Joan doesn't have any. And they clearly didn't know the seriousness of her condition because when the receptionist went by, she heard them asking her questions. "Where is she?" they kept repeating. "Tell us where she is."'

'They didn't know that she couldn't speak?'

'Apparently not. When the receptionist looked into Joan's room, she saw that they had dragged her to her feet and were shaking her. She was obviously distressed. The girl asked them to leave, threatening to phone the police. Eventually she was forced to call for a male member of staff to show them off the premises.'

'Let me guess.'

Elizabeth nodded. 'It was Colin. That must have been when they approached him.'

'He'll have some questions to answer when he goes back on duty.'

She shrugged. 'He'll say he didn't report the incident because he was protecting the junior member of staff.'

'But surely visitors to Moorland View have to sign in and out?'

'They do. But when Mrs MacDonald checked the names in the visitors' book, Joan had been visited by a

Mr Smith and a Mr Jones.' She gave a bitter laugh. 'Not exactly original. The receptionist described them as both well-dressed, wearing expensive suits and overcoats. They arrived in a brand-new Audi, she noticed. One was young, and quite good-looking apparently, the other was older and taller. He wore gold cuff-links, she remembered. They looked respectable and they were very polite. She had no reason to suspect they weren't who they said they were. Except that what she *should* have done is to check Joan's file to see who her permitted visitors are. Anyone not on that list should have been checked with Mrs MacDonald.'

'Does Joan receive any genuine visitors?' I asked.

'Neighbours who knew her before she suffered her stroke used to come at first. But once they realised that she couldn't recognise them anymore, they gradually gave up. You can't really blame them,' she added sadly, 'it's a long way for them to come.'

'Have you visited Joan since this incident happened?'

'Once.' A frown puckered Elizabeth's brow. 'And you know, when I arrived, she squeezed my hand so tightly, it hurt. I realise now that perhaps she was trying to tell me something.'

'Was Colin on duty on the day you visited?'

'I only saw him once, in the car park, getting into his car as I was about to leave.'

'So that could have been the day he followed you home.'

She fiddled pensively with a gold earring. 'It could, yes.'

'It seems that Mr Smith and Mr Jones aren't prepared to hang around Bovey Tracey waiting for you to appear.'

'If they are George's creditors, they will have come from London. Which is why, presumably, they've employed the services of Colin. It's also possible that they don't know what I look like. After all,' she added with a wry smile, 'we've never been introduced.'

'I still can't believe they've offered him twenty thousand pounds just to find you.'

'No,' she agreed. 'It's more likely to be a fraction of that. He's just trying to screw as much as he can out of me.' She tapped the counter with a manicured fingernail. 'And I suspect he still intends to collect from Messrs Smith and Jones, whatever I pay him.'

'So, what next?' I asked.

'A visit to Moorland View tomorrow, I think, and a serious chat with Mrs MacDonald about tightening up security.'

'Did she call the police about the incident?'

'She called them as soon as she found out what happened, but it was already too long after the event. A police officer called this morning apparently, and the girl on reception was asked to try to identify the two men from photographs of suspected conmen – criminals who've been known to worm their way into care homes in order to steal – but with no success. She's currently helping them put together two photofit pictures, which Mrs Macdonald assures me will be pinned up on the noticeboard in reception so that these men don't gain entry a second time.'

'I wonder if Colin will be on duty when you visit tomorrow.'

'I didn't ask.' She shrugged. 'I won't know that now until I get there.'

'I could phone,' I suggested. 'No one at Moorland View will recognise my voice.'

An amused twinkle crept into Elizabeth's eyes. She took out her phone and scrolled down. I took it from her to see the number but used the shop phone to call.

'Hello?' I bellowed as soon as the phone was picked up. I tried to sound ancient and deaf, like Maisie. 'Is that Colin?'

'This is Moorland View Residential Home,' a well-rehearsed voice said at the other end. 'Charelle speaking. How many I help you today?'

'What? I want to speak to Colin. Is he there?'

'I'm afraid Colin Smethurst isn't on duty until tomorrow.' Charelle sounded a little less like she was talking from a script. 'Who's speaking, please?'

I ignored the request to identify myself. 'Sorry, I can't hear you. What shift's he doing tomorrow?'

'Um . . . he's on ten till six. If I can tell him who's calling . . .'

I put the phone down. 'Did you hear that?'

She nodded, smothering a laugh. 'I'll get there at around four, talk to Mrs MacDonald and spend a couple of hours with Joan.'

'You must leave before six,' I told her. 'Before Colin gets off. If he's finished his shift when he sees you leaving, he might try to follow you again. We want him to go home. I'll wait outside the place in my van and watch for him to come out. I can follow him and find out where he lives.'

Elizabeth frowned. 'It's a bit risky.'

'Why? Van Blanc is anonymous, it's just a white van. Colin won't recognise it.' It was a good job I still didn't drive my old van, bright yellow with advertising all over it. But that vehicle had perished in a fire. 'The important thing is that he doesn't catch you following him. When you leave, you must go straight home to Olly's.'

'Agreed, but . . .'

'We need to find out all we can about him, remember.'

At that moment the shop bell rang, and in came sexy seventy-something, Tom Carter. It was good to see him walking so well, no longer in pain or having to lean on a stick.

'Now, who'd have thought you'd find the two most beautiful maids in Devon, sitting together in the same shop?' he asked, grinning.

'Hello Tom,' Elizabeth smiled, standing up. She flicked a glance at me. 'It's time I made us all a coffee, I think.'

CHAPTER FOUR

The Dartmoor town of Bovey Tracey, or simply *Buvvy*, as it is known to everyone who lives around here, is a mere nine miles from Ashburton, and has many delights to recommend it. As well as a new library and a fascinating glass marble factory, it boasts its own whisky distillery, a cheese emporium, and extensive riverside park. The mill by the river from which the town takes its name, is filled with fine crafts for sale and there are several delightful teashops. But this was a Sunday in March, it was nearly six o'clock and all of these establishments were closed. Sadly, so was the cheese shop and just then I could have murdered a nugget of cheddar.

I swept up the hill of Fore Street. At least it was still light. I'd lost an hour's sleep that morning with the clock's going forward for British Summer Time but at least I hadn't needed to get up early to walk the dogs I take out on weekdays. Once past the shops, the road levelled out between some fine houses and allowed me occasional glimpses of Dartmoor. At the top of the hill, I passed the medieval church, the grandly named Church of St Peter, St Paul and St Thomas of Canterbury – known to the locals as PPT. It's a lovely church, full of interesting stuff and I rather regretted I was on a mission and couldn't stop for a look around. Rumour has it that the dedication to St Thomas was made by the lord of the manor in penance for the sins of his cousin, sir William de Tracy, one of the four knights who murdered archbishop Thomas Becket in Canterbury Cathedral. Unfortunately, there is no evidence to support this, or even that the two knights were related, but it makes a good story.

I passed the church as bells were ringing for evensong and drove out towards the edge of town, where a turning opened up to my right and a sign in curling script pointed me towards Moorland View. It was a substantial, white-painted villa with gardens and a conservatory, and a visitors' car park separating it from the road. I glanced at my watch. It was ten to six. There was no sign of Elizabeth's car. She'd already gone and I only had ten minutes to wait until Colin reached the end of his shift. Just to be on the safe side, I didn't stop in the car park where Van Blanc would be clearly seen but turned around and tucked myself onto a verge a few yards down the lane, at a spot where I could see all the vehicles exiting the gates. Colin drove a dark grey Honda estate, Elizabeth told me, so I only had to settle down and wait.

It was about twenty minutes before I saw his car nose out of the gates and he drove past. He surprised me by not taking the road back down the hill into

Bovey but heading out towards the moor. I followed him to the edge of Yarner Wood and the pretty village of Ilsington. We passed the Carpenters Arms and were on our way out of the village again heading for Higher Sigford. We were working our way south west down narrow country roads, the sun setting ahead of us in the pale evening sky. Was Colin heading back to Ashburton? He must be aware that a white van was on the road behind him, I just hoped he hadn't realised it was mine. I was trying to give him as much distance as I could without losing sight of him. But before we reached Sigford, he turned, just after a junction marked Birchanger Cross, his car bumping down a narrow lane that didn't look as if it led anywhere. High hedges enclosed it on either side and a scree of muddy gravel spread down the middle. I drove on past the turning, then pulled in on the verge and consulted the map. The lane looked like a dead end. I'd give Colin a minute before I drove after him. After a few seconds of tapping my fingers on the steering wheel in deliberation, I decided to get out and follow on foot.

The sun had almost sunk behind the horizon now, lighting up thin ribbons of cloud from beneath, turning them pink and gold. Darkness and shadow lurked between the hedges in the lane, the first light evening of the summer quickly fading to an indigo dusk. I jogged along for about a quarter of a mile until the hedges opened out to show me fields, distant woods and a small gathering of houses by the road that looked as if they had once been farm buildings. There was no sign of

Colin's car anywhere. I cursed at the thought that I might have lost him. But another few yards brought me to a modest looking house with a painted sign by the front door. Dartmoor Edge, it proclaimed, the words picked out in flowers. There was his grey Honda, parked on the verge by the garden wall. There was also a powerful motorbike that looked too expensive to belong to him.

As I drew level with the front gate, a light flicked on in a window downstairs. I crouched down behind the cover of the wall and dared a peek over the top. Colin was standing in the lighted room, and another man, about the same height, but younger, darker, in white T-shirt and leather jacket. The owner of the motorbike, no doubt. The younger man was talking and he didn't look happy. Bending almost double, I ran across the front of the property, sheltered by the stone wall, and once out of sight of the windows, scrambled over it into the garden, scraping the heel of one hand on the rough stones as I put my weight on the top. I stumbled inelegantly through a bed of scruffy flowers till I reached the corner of the house where I leant against the wall, a few inches from the window, sucking my stinging hand and straining my ears to hear what was being said inside.

'You've had three weeks,' the younger man's voice was raised in anger.

'It's not my fault.' Colin's voice was softer, slightly plaintive, more difficult to hear. 'She doesn't visit every week, and she never comes on the same day twice. Today she left before the end of visiting time.

I couldn't just break off and leave before the end of my shift.'

'They must have family records, her address or something.'

'Anything like that is locked in MacDonald's office.'

'Well, get yourself in there for God's sake. It can't be that difficult.'

I didn't hear what Colin answered; it sounded like a weak protest. But whatever he said detonated an explosion of impatience in the younger man. 'If you're messing us about . . .'

Colin's voice came back loud in alarm, and I wondered if the younger man had raised a fist. 'No! No, I swear . . . I'll find out.'

'You'd better. Mr Shaw is looking to expand his business operation down here in the south west and that takes a lot of investment. A lot of capital. He's been forced to move the current operation away from the coast, near to the moor. And that could be a great opportunity for you, Colin. Know what I mean?'

'Yes. Yes. And I do appreciate the opportunity.'

'He's looking to recoup some of his earlier losses. And this where you come in. He won't take kindly to failure.'

'Yes. Yes. I promise I will find her. I will.'

'Make sure you do. You can either be a part of this, Colin, or you can be out of it. It's up to you.'

'Yes, well, I — '

'I'll give you another week. After that, our agreement is terminated.'

'Don't worry,' Colin's voice came back in a rush. 'You can promise Mr Shaw that I'll have the information he needs.'

'Oh, I'm not worried, Colin. As for promising Mr Shaw anything, that's a dangerous game, that is. You don't want to make him promises unless you're sure you can keep them. Know what I mean?' After a moment's pause, he spoke again. 'This is a nice little place you've got here. Live here by yourself, do you?'

'Yes. It was my mother's.'

'Expensive to run though, these old houses, aren't they? What you need is a lodger.'

Colin gave an uncertain laugh. 'Oh, I don't think so.'

'Perhaps I should get one of the lads to move in with you. One of Mr Shaw's boys. Keep you company, keep an eye on you. See what you're up to. Know what I mean?'

'No!' Colin cried out in alarm. Then added more softly. 'No, that won't be necessary.'

'Glad to hear it. I'll say goodbye then. See you next week.'

I heard the front door swing open and I dodged back out of sight. I dared a glance around the corner of the house as I heard the motorbike growl. By then its owner had already donned his helmet, and I watched the powerful machine roar away into the almost dark.

Colin must have been watching too, because it was only then that I heard the front door close. I hoped he'd go back into the room and draw the curtains, giving me a chance to nip across the front garden, but instead, a light came on at the back of the house, which meant presumably, that he'd gone into the kitchen. I waited for a few moments, just to be on the safe side. Then a small enquiring voice behind me made me stifle a shriek. I wheeled around to see a white cat standing on the lid of a water butt. She meowed again, arching her back towards my reaching hand. I shushed her softly, but she obviously wanted in out of the dark and cold, and kept telling me about it. When I heard the scraping of the back door bolts, I fled around the side of the house.

Colin's voice was calling 'Snowdrop?' as I scrambled back over the garden wall and more or less fell into the lane. Then I picked myself up and jogged back to the car. I'd head home to Ashburton and tell Elizabeth what I'd heard.

As I drove back, the scene in the house kept replaying in my head, the brief glimpse I'd had of that lighted room. All flowered wallpaper and dark furniture, it looked as if it belonged to an old person. Colin obviously hadn't bothered to redecorate since the demise of his mother. As for the young man who'd been standing in the room, he was dark, tanned, with thick eyebrows and white teeth. The receptionist at Moorland View had described one of the two men who had visited as young and good-looking. This might be him. And expensive looking, she'd said. That gleaming motorbike didn't come cheap. Was he Mr Smith or Mr Jones? And whichever one he was, was his older companion the sinister-sounding Mr Shaw?

'Colin certainly felt threatened,' I told Elizabeth, once Olly had gone up to his room to complete the homework that had been hanging around all weekend, 'frightened even.' I didn't add so frightened that I'd almost felt sorry for him. 'But he still didn't tell Smith-or-Jones where you are.'

'There can only be one reason for that.' Elizabeth poured a glass of Sauvignon Blanc with a steady hand and pushed it across the table towards me. We were sitting in the kitchen. It might officially be the first day of spring but it was still chilly and we were glad of the warmth spreading out from the kitchen range. 'He's still hoping to get money out of me before he collects his payment from this Mr Shaw or whatever he's called.'

'He's been given another week,' I told her, 'So that gives us time to think of something.'

Elizabeth smiled ironically as she poured herself a glass. 'Yes, but what? I can't think what pressure I could bring to bear that would make Colin prepared to disappoint Mr Shaw. From what you overheard, it sounds as if that might be a dangerous thing to do and I don't see Colin as the noble or heroic type.'

'Have you told Tom about any of this?'

She frowned at me, mystified. 'No, of course not.'

'Why not?'

'Because he would want to protect me and anyone attempting to do that is likely to get hurt.' She nodded in my direction. 'You've already taken too many risks today, finding out where Colin lives.'

'But now we know. Shouldn't we try to break into his place, have a poke around?'

She gave me the kind of look she would have given Olly if he'd suggested the same thing. 'Definitely not.'

'So, what will you do? Run? Hide?'

'I think I've done enough of that. Besides, I can't abandon Olly.'

'Then what?'

She shrugged. 'Let's not panic. As you say, we've got a few more days. I made discreet enquiries of my own this afternoon. Not that I found out much. I asked Mrs MacDonald how long Colin Smethurst had been working for her. He certainly wasn't on the staff when Joan first went to Moorland View. It's about four years apparently. Of course, she wanted to know why I asked, whether there was a problem?'

'What did you say?'

'Oh, I praised him to the skies, told him how wonderful I thought he was with Joan – which, ironically, he is. But I added that I was old-fashioned enough to find men wanting to work in care a little strange. Surely, he could pursue another profession that would bring him a better income? She told me that Colin had always looked after his mother, so caring came naturally to him. And of course, there was nothing like the satisfaction of working in the care sector.'

I gave a snort of laughter. 'I wonder what the rest of the staff would say about that.' I looked at Elizabeth, sitting there so calmly, and a thought came into my head. 'There isn't anything you haven't told me, is there?'

She raised her slender eyebrows. 'What do you mean?'

'This *is* about the money George owes, isn't it? It's not something else? This Mr Shaw, you don't know him, do you? Personally?'

'Is he some character from my mysterious past, you mean?' She laughed softly. 'My past is not nearly as mysterious or exciting as you seem to believe it is.'

Her amusement made me feel foolish. 'What about all the self-defence?'

'I used to be a physical fitness instructor in the army. That was about a hundred years ago.'

'And the gun in your handbag?'

'I've told you. It was a war-time souvenir of my father's. Shooting was my hobby. I used to compete at international level.' She gave an elegant shrug. 'Old habits die hard, that's all.'

'And where is the pistol now?'

'In pieces, each one hidden separately,' she responded softly. 'Do you think I want Olly to find it? As for this Mr Shaw . . . *if* that's his real name . . . no, to my knowledge, I have never made the gentleman's acquaintance.'

'Just checking.'

Elizabeth eyed me cynically as she took a sip from her wine glass. 'Hmmm,' was all she uttered.

'So, what did his young friend mean today when he talked about Mr Shaw expanding his business operations here in the South West?' I asked her. 'What business is he in, d'you think?'

She raised her eyebrows. 'In addition to being a loan-shark?'

'It's what he suggested about forcing a lodger on Colin, that's making me think. It sounds like something that drugs gangs do. They move in with vulnerable people so that they can take total control of their lives, force them to do their bidding.'

Elizabeth was nodding. 'I believe it's called cuckooing.'

'They've offered Colin money to find you,' I went on. 'I wonder if they have any other kind of hold on him.'

'Other than turning nasty if he doesn't find me?'

'It's a pity Colin knows who I am.' I mused, frowning. 'Or I could have gone to Moorland View claiming I was looking around the place on behalf of an elderly relative and had a snoop about.'

'I don't know what you think you'd find out,' Elizabeth gave a quiet laugh. 'You could take Maisie.'

'Kicking and screaming all the way? No thanks!' I gave my brain cells the benefit of another sip of wine. 'It's a pity that we don't know anyone who . . .' I stopped as inspiration struck me. Who did I know who would accept an undercover mission to visit a care home on the pretence of looking around for an ancient relative and try to dig up information on one of the staff?

I smiled.

'What?' Elizabeth asked, immediately suspicious. 'Juno, I've seen that smile before. What are you thinking?'

'I've thought of the perfect couple,' I told her. I was

sure I could persuade them to do it.

'Juno, if you're thinking what I think you're thinking,' she said, voice raised in alarm, 'believe me, it is not a good idea.'

I shrugged. 'Just a thought.' The difficult part would be coming up with a reason for wanting to find out about Colin Smethurst without revealing Elizabeth's part in the story. I picked up my wine glass and leant back in my chair. I was sure I could think of something.

CHAPTER FIVE

Ricky swung back the grand front door of Druid Lodge and looked at me in surprise. 'Hello, Princess! To what do we owe the honour?'

'I found myself with a spare afternoon,' I lied as I strolled past him, conveniently forgetting the complicated juggling with clients I'd been forced to do to scrape a few hours off. I took off my jacket and looked about me at the large wicker laundry hampers cluttering up the hall. 'I remembered you had a show coming back today. I thought perhaps you could do with a hand with the unpacking.'

Morris's bald head suddenly appeared at the top of the sweeping staircase. 'That's very kind of you, Juno, my love,' he said, bustling down towards me. 'We certainly could.'

Ricky and Morris run a theatrical hire company, and the grand house they live in, on a hill overlooking the town of Ashburton, is home to several thousand theatrical costumes. They hire out to companies all over the country. The two of them should have retired years ago, but can't bring themselves to give it up. The hampers now standing in the hall, contained costumes returned from a recent production of *Kiss Me, Kate*, by a theatre in London. They had travelled down to Devon by courier.

'Bloody lorry driver got lost again,' Ricky complained bitterly. 'I keep telling them, don't get off the A38 at Linhay, get off at Peartree, by the garage. It's only straight up the hill from there. Then they don't have to try and negotiate a bloody great wagon through the narrow streets of Ashburton. Especially at the moment with the road up. But they never listen.'

'Different drivers each time, probably.' Morris reached up on tiptoe to give me a kiss on the cheek. Ricky just muttered. He and Morris are very different, physically as well as emotionally. Ricky is tall, silver-haired and distinguished, still handsome despite being ancient. Morris is short, fat and bald with gold-framed specs. He took them off to polish the lenses on his sweater. *He's in a bad mood,* he mouthed at me silently, nodding at the back of Ricky's head as he stooped to unbuckle the straps of a hamper.

Why? I mouthed back.

He beckoned me a little closer. 'Waiting for these hospital tests,' he whispered, 'it's getting on his nerves . . .'

'What are you muttering about, *Maurice*?' Ricky demanded, without turning his head.

And mine, Morris added soundlessly.

Ricky, as many elderly gentlemen do, was experiencing problems with his bladder, and was waiting to undergo a scan on his prostate.

'How are you?' I asked, trying to be tactful.

'Perfectly fine.' Ricky swung back the lid of the hamper. 'Don't listen to that stupid old woman.'

Morris tutted as he took my jacket and hung it up for me. 'He's getting so rude.'

He disappeared from the hall for a moment and came back wheeling a clothes rail. 'We'll unpack them all straight on to this for the moment, Juno, love. And sort them out later.'

The wicker hamper creaked as Ricky leant into it to pick up a costume. 'My God, they've just chucked 'em in here!' He held up a long, velvet dress with trailing sleeves which should have been carefully laid flat in the hamper, sheathed in its own polythene bag; instead, it was creased and crumpled.

'It's not even on a hanger,' Morris complained. 'I don't suppose they've sent any of our hangers back. Who's in charge of wardrobe at this theatre?'

'I don't know,' Ricky responded, still holding the dress up and peering back down into the hamper. 'But if the rest of the costumes are in this mess, they'll be getting a phone call.'

'I'll have to go upstairs and fetch some hangers.'

'I'll go,' I volunteered. As I reached the turn of the stairs I stopped and sniffed as an unexpected aroma reached my nostrils. 'Is it my imagination, or can I smell whisky?'

Ricky sniffed at the dress he was holding. 'It's not coming off this one.'

'I can smell it,' Morris waved a hand at the hampers. 'It's coming out of one of these.' He wrinkled his nose. 'Phew! Someone must have spilt half a bottle. Well, we'll be sending them the dry-cleaning bill.'

After we'd unpacked the first three hampers, we stopped for a cup of tea. The costumes were a mess, clothes, hats, gloves and shoes just chucked in anyhow, with no attempt to match pairs or keep the different components of the costumes together. It looked as if whoever had packed them had done it in a real hurry, with very little care for the contents, which were made mostly of velvets and silks, and weren't going to be easy to clean. Coming from a professional theatre, this was a bit dispiriting. As yet though, we hadn't located the offending source of the whisky.

'They're going to have to buck their ideas up if they expect to hire costumes from us again,' Ricky complained bitterly. 'I bet the cast wore 'em all to their last night party. That's what will have happened.'

Morris, as always in charge of the teapot, was nodding as he poured, in the way of someone who had seen it all before. 'And then the wardrobe department will have been panicking because the courier van was coming to collect them first thing next morning, and they will have thrown them all in the baskets in a rush.' He passed me a mug of tea. 'There you are, Juno love.'

'So,' Ricky sniffed as he lit up his customary tea-break cigarette, 'how's things with you, Princess?'

Now was the moment for me to launch into my plan, to ask the two of them if they would go to Moorland View, pretending to look around the place on behalf of an elderly relative, in their case extremely elderly, and see if they could dig up anything on Colin Smethurst. 'Elizabeth has a friend who's a resident there,' I explained, 'and she has suspicions about one of the staff.'

'What kind of suspicions?' Morris's eyes grew round with horror. 'You don't mean abuse?'

'Something like that,' I hedged evasively. 'I don't think she's totally sure . . . you see, this friend has had a stroke. She can't speak for herself.'

'But something must've made Elizabeth suspicious.' Ricky stopped and slanted a keen glance towards Morris. 'What's up with you?'

'What do you mean, what's up with me?' he responded, baffled. 'I never said anything.'

'What was that great sigh about?'

'What sigh? I didn't sigh.'

'You did. A great big heartbroken sigh. I heard you.'

'I did not,' he protested, getting indignant.

'Juno,' Ricky turned to me, 'didn't you hear him give a sigh like a flipping great walrus breaking the surface?'

I had heard a sigh actually but I didn't want to mention the fact. I wanted them to stop bickering. Morris was growing red in the face. 'You're hearing things,' he accused Ricky.

I heard it again then. 'Shut up, the pair of you!' I

held up a warning finger. 'Listen!'

We all fell silent. The sound came from one of the hampers in the hall. A sigh. We stared at as it came again, and with it, the unmistakeable creak of wicker. 'There's something in one of the hampers.' Morris blinked nervously, his voice dropping to a whisper. We listened; the creaking came again. 'Perhaps it's a cat or something.'

A few moments later came a long and obviously human snore.

'Not something, *someone*,' Ricky muttered, clamping his cigarette tightly between his lips and rising to his feet.

We followed him into the hall. There were four wicker hampers waiting to be unpacked. One of them creaked and rocked slightly on its wheels. Another long snore emanated from it and an exhalation of whisky-sodden breath, as if someone had thrown open the door of a distillery. Ricky bent to unbuckle the leather straps that kept the lid in place and flung it back dramatically.

There, lying in a nest of velvet and crushed lace, was curled a sleeping figure, a bit like Sophie's dormouse in its nest but minus the enchantment. It was a man, an empty whisky bottle clutched to his chest, and a considerable quantity of the contents dribbled down his waistcoat. He wore a striped blazer, cravat, flannel trousers and spats; his hair, though tousled, had once been parted and smoothed down with hair-oil. He had clearly not come from medieval Padua or wherever *Kiss Me, Kate* is set, unless the wardrobe department had thrown in a free Bertie Wooster. As we stared, the figure slept on oblivious, a monocle hanging on a twisted ribbon around his neck.

'Freddy!' Ricky snarled in a low voice, long practice keeping the fag in place as his lips moved. 'It's bloody Freddy!'

Before I could enquire who bloody Freddy might be, he grabbed a broom that had been propped up against the wall and prodded the unfortunate sleeper in the buttock with the handle. The sleeper muttered and jerked awake, blinking around him in confusion. Ricky prodded him again, even more fiercely. 'Wake up, you little bastard!'

'Ow!' Freddy protested indignantly, rubbing his backside. He stared around him, his pale blue eyes looking slightly unfocussed, until he spotted Ricky standing over him and broke into a broad grin. 'Hello Uncle Ricky!' He tried to sit up and fell back, making the basket creak alarmingly.

'Don't you Uncle Ricky me, you abominable little turd,' Ricky growled in response, 'where's my five hundred quid?'

The grin vanished. 'Ah! well, you see, the thing is, I—'

'Never mind that for the minute,' Morris broke in. 'What are you doing in there?' Freddy blinked as if he wasn't quite sure. 'How did you get in there?'

'And more to the point,' Ricky added, eyes narrowed in suspicion. 'Why?'

'Ah! Well, it's rather a long . . . I say, it's jolly

cramped in here. Do you mind if I get out?' His voice was light and jovial, pure public schoolboy. He handed the empty whisky bottle to Morris, gripped the edge of the hamper and tried to stand up. The basket rolled forwards on its little wheels. Ricky stamped on the wheel-brake with his foot, halting its progress and forcing the unfortunate Freddy to sit down heavily among the costumes. Morris lent him his arm, allowing him to clamber out.

'I've got this most ghastly headache,' he moaned, swaying slightly as he stood up. 'Is there any chance of a cup of . . . oh, by Jove!' he grinned again, registering my presence for the first time. 'Freddy Carstairs,' he said, rolling a lascivious eye over me. 'How do you do?' Unconsciously he slicked back the lock of brown hair that had fallen across his forehead. If he'd struck me as young at first glance, on closer inspection, he was probably in his fifties. A sudden look of alarm creased his brow. 'Look, I've been in that damned basket a long time.' He turned to look at Ricky. 'Do you think I could use your, er . . . ?'

'Down the hall,' Ricky muttered ungraciously, jabbing a pointing finger and Freddy fled to the downstairs cloakroom.

'Is he really your nephew?' I asked, watching him go. He didn't look remotely like Ricky.

'God, no!' Ricky sneered. 'His father and I go way back and I've known him since he was a kid. He'd always called me uncle when he was growing up but we're not related.'

Morris, still holding the empty whisky bottle, began heading back to the kitchen. 'I'd better make coffee,' he sighed. 'Strong black coffee.'

'So, what's the story?' Ricky demanded, after a white-faced and slightly trembling Freddy had been drooping at the table with his head in his hands for about ten minutes, now and again taking sips of scalding black coffee.

'Well, the fact is, Uncle Ricky, I've got myself into a bit of a scrape.'

'Stop calling me Uncle Ricky!' he ordered. 'It's nauseating coming from a man of your age. And stop talking as if you're acting the idiot in some Wodehouse farce. Although looking at how you're dressed,' he added scathingly, 'that's exactly what you have been doing.'

Freddy flushed scarlet. When he spoke next his voice was an octave lower and had lost its silly-ass quality.

'In fact, it's a rather good play,' he said sulkily. 'It's quite a hit.'

'What's it called?' Morris enquired.

'*Murder Weekend*. I suppose you'd call it a comic thriller. It's a sort of a mash-up between Wodehouse and Christie.'

I could imagine Freddy appearing in one of those Agatha Christie-style thrillers where the suspects get picked off one-by-one. He'd be the one who got murdered first.

'It's actually jolly amusing . . . sorry,' he corrected

himself, 'but it is very funny. My first job in a long time, as a matter of fact,' he admitted with a grimace. 'Quite a decent part too. I've been doing it about four months now, and the play's set to run and run. I had to take over at short notice. The previous actor – a chap called Steven Spendlow – did a bunk,' he added, lapsing back into Woodhousian. He flicked a nervous glance at a thunderous looking Ricky. 'Well, he did!' he added defiantly. 'He disappeared, not been seen or heard of since.'

He took another sip of coffee. I could see that he might have been good-looking in his youth, but there was a pouchy look about his eyes and a paunch under that waistcoat, that suggested lack of exercise or too much high living. But perhaps it's not fair to judge someone in the throes of a hangover.

'No one minded much. Steven was unreliable. Kept changing his lines apparently.'

'Changing them?' Morris frowned, taking off his specs and polishing them on his jumper. 'You mean, forgetting them?'

'No, no, changing them.' Freddy insisted, putting down his cup with a heavy sigh. 'I don't suppose you've got any aspirin, have you?' Ricky leant back in his chair, reached out a long arm, grabbed a packet from the drawer of the dresser and threw them on the table.

'Thanks awfully, Uncle . . . I mean . . . um, thanks,' he added, fumbling with the packet. 'Anyway, I hadn't been in the job more than a week or two, when a man came around to see me in the dressing room after the show. The doorman let him in, thinking the fellow was a friend. I'd never laid eyes on him in my life. Rather a rum-looking cove. Sorry,' he corrected himself again, 'a suspicious looking individual. You know the sort – beard shadow, foreign accent, Serbian or something like that. Well, to cut a long story short, he offered to pay me two hundred smackeroos – I mean, pounds – per week, if I would do the same as my predecessor had done.' He paused, looking around at us to see if we understood. 'If I would start altering some of my lines.'

'Why?' I asked.

He shrugged. 'I asked the same question obviously, but he told me that there was no need for me to know. All I needed to know, was that every Tuesday evening I would receive my two hundred quid in an envelope, together with the re-written lines, and that all I had to do was to make sure I put them in on the Wednesday matinee. That was the only performance each week where I had to do it, and it would always be the same scene every time and only three lines that would be affected. It sounded painless, so I thought I'd give it go. I mean, what harm could it do? And I would get paid every week, whether I had to alter the lines or not. Free boodle! How could I resist? To be honest, as the weeks wore on and I heard nothing more, I began to wonder if the whole thing hadn't been some kind of silly practical joke, except of course that I was already getting the money. But then, one Tuesday evening, there was my envelope with my name on it, pinned on the back-stage noticeboard, with the usual two hundred quid in twenties, and this time a slip of paper with new lines written inside.

'What were they?' Morris asked, fascinated.

'Well, I'm in a scene with this other actor, a chap called Hugh Winterbourne. Now, in the script, Hugh says the line "Where is your aunt taking her holiday this year?" And I am supposed to say, "You mean, my Aunt Drusilla?" And Hugh answers, "Yes." Then I am supposed to say, "she's staying in Scarborough." But in this newly-written version, instead of Aunt Drusilla, I had to call her Aunt Persephone. And instead of Scarborough, she was staying in Brixham.'

'Is that all?' Morris sounded disappointed. I think we were all expecting something more dramatic.

Freddy was nodding. 'Well, the first week I got away with it. I managed to convince Hugh that I'd forgotten the old girl's name and where she was staying and just improvised. But I could see he wasn't happy. He said to me, straight after the show, "You're not messing around like Steve did, are you? Only the old girl who wrote this damn thing is a stickler for every word, and if she pops in to see the show, it's likely to be on a Wednesday matinee." Anyway, I forgot all about it until the following Tuesday evening, when there's another envelope full of cash, and another revision to the script. This time, I have to call my Aunt Melinda and say she's staying in Dartmouth. Hugh was furious. He said if the writer or director came, they'd think it was some private joke going on between the two of us and that he'd get the blame for not taking the play seriously, as well as me. Beryl wasn't too happy about it either.'

'Who's Beryl?' I asked.

'Beryl Macintyre. She plays the housekeeper.'

Ricky cackled. 'Beryl Macintyre? Is she still alive?'

'Very much so. And as you know, old Beryl is a real sport.' Freddy kept slipping in and out of his silly-ass voice, as if he'd been using it so long, he couldn't shake it off. It had become a part of him. 'But she has to refer to this aunt and her holiday later in the show, and now every Wednesday she has to listen out for my lines, just to find out what to call her. And let me tell you, this aunt has been called some very peculiar things. One week she was called Puffling.'

'Puffling?' Ricky repeated. 'You mean, that's some place where she was supposed to be staying?'

'No! *She* was called Puffling.

'A puffling is a baby puffin,' I said.

'Is it?' Freddy grimaced. 'What sort of name is that for an aunt? She was holidaying somewhere called Branscombe that time. I don't even know where that is.'

'It's near Sidmouth,' I told him, although he didn't look any the wiser.

'Anyway,' he went on, 'the next week she was back to being Persephone again.'

'And you never discovered what it was all about?' I asked.

'Well, no,' he admitted. 'This went on for months. Some weeks I would get the money with no lines and Aunt Drusilla would go to Scarborough as usual. The money kept coming, but I never laid eyes on the fella who had come to my dressing room again until last Wednesday.' He rolled his eyes dramatically. 'You see, the Wednesday before, the inevitable happened and the writer finally came in to watch the matinee. Worse, the director came with her.' He shrugged. 'I didn't know they were out there. I'd received my usual envelope and so when we got to the crucial scene, I came out with the fact that Aunt Kiwi was staying at a hotel in Salcombe. Well, after the show, I got the most terrible roasting. They thought I was messing about and threatened me with the sack if I did it again.' He took a breath. 'I guessed the director might be sitting in the matinee again this week, just to make sure I behaved. So, I ignored what was written in the envelope and stuck to the script. I knew there'd be trouble. I didn't go back to my dressing room when the show ended, but slipped out of the theatre straight after the curtain call, just in time to see our foreign friend heading for the stage door. He didn't look happy. In fact, he had a face like thunder. He was hanging around for ages. Eventually he gave up and I crept back in for the evening performance. Well, I thought, if I do run into him, I shall have to explain, that's all, and offer him his two hundred quid back. But I didn't get the chance. When I came off stage at the end of the evening, there was another envelope pinned on the noticeboard, and this time there was just a note inside. All it said was . . .' Freddy gave an involuntary shudder, 'You're dead.'

'Hold on a minute,' Ricky interrupted. 'Who pinned these envelopes on the noticeboard each week?'

'It was the stage doorman. He found them in the letterbox each Tuesday morning among all the other post – mostly cards and fan mail and stuff – and pinned them up with the rest.'

'So, no one ever saw them being delivered to the stage door?' I asked.

Freddy nodded. 'After that, he was hanging around outside the stage door after every show. Well, you know what a rabbit-warren it is backstage at the Davenport. I managed to keep dodging him, making my escape through Fire Exits and so on, until Saturday's matinee, when I went back to my dressing room in the interval, and there he was, sitting in a chair, waiting for me. And what's more,' he added, his pale eyes bulging at the memory, 'he had a gun in his hand, pointing it right at me!' He looked around us to see if this revelation had had the intended dramatic effect. It had. 'Well, I didn't hang around to make conversation, I just shot off like a jack-rabbit. He came after me, of course. I managed to give him the slip but I knew he couldn't be far behind. The scenery dock of the Palace Theatre next door was open, so I hid in there. I could see our friend wandering about in the alleyway outside, and I wondered if he'd spot the scenery dock shutter was raised and come looking for me. I was going to hide in a dressing room or something when I saw a couple of stagehands wheeling these costume hampers out to the back door. I followed them and found there were several baskets lined up outside the dressing rooms, in various stages of being filled, and they had *Druid Lodge* return labels on. Uncle Ricky's place, I thought. What a stroke of luck! I also spotted an empty dressing room with the door open and a bottle of whisky on the dressing table, so I clambered into the nearest basket, with the aforementioned whisky, to wait until our friend had given up and gone home.'

He stopped a moment to draw breath. 'Well, I'd only been in it for few minutes when someone came along and did up the leather straps of the basket. So, I couldn't have got out if I'd wanted to. I thought about shouting for help, because I didn't have a phone in my pocket. We're not allowed to take them on stage for obvious reasons, so I always leave mine in the dressing room. But I had to keep quiet in case the fella with the gun was still hanging around outside. And then I realised,' he went on, eyes rounding in horror, 'that I couldn't go back and do the second half of the show! *Freddy old fella*, I thought, *you'll probably never work in the West End again.*' He rubbed his face with his hands and sighed. They were pale and pudgy, I noticed, unused to any manual labour.

'Next thing I know, the jolly old hamper is on the move, being wheeled into a lorry. Nothing for it but to drink the whisky and enjoy the ride down to Devon. Mind you, I think I slept most of the way. Woke up once, still in a lorry, I think. Moving, anyway.'

'Wasn't it uncomfortable in there?' I asked.

He grinned. 'Snug as a bug in a rug.'

'But what happened when you didn't go on stage for the second half of the performance?'

He rubbed the side of his nose pensively. 'Well, I imagine that after the stage manager had been rushing around like a blue-arsed fly trying to find me, she'd have put the understudy on. Young Lucas is our swing. He understudies me, Hugh and the juvenile lead. He'd have been thrilled to bits.'

'But what was it all about?' Morris asked. 'All this changing of lines, didn't you ever find out what it was for?'

Freddy puffed out his cheeks. 'I suppose I was passing some kind of message to someone out there in the Wednesday matinee audience.'

Ricky scowled, unconvinced. 'It's a bit bleedin' cold war, isn't it? Like two spies meeting on a park bench. It's old-fashioned. These days you can just send an email.'

'Emails can be hacked,' I pointed out. 'So can phones. All electronic messages can be traced back to their source, if you know how. You might want to avoid that if you're up to something you shouldn't be. Especially if you've been hacked before. But this way . . .' I stopped and looked at Freddy. 'Didn't you ever find out what was going on?'

He shrugged. 'Once I'd made the bargain, I never saw our friend again until he turned up with a gun in his hand. How was I supposed to find out anything?'

I was disgusted by his lack of curiosity. 'But you must have realised that your predecessor . . . what's his name?'

'Stephen,' Freddy supplied helpfully. 'Stephen Spendlow.'

'He had made the same bargain and had disappeared. Never been seen since, according to you. Didn't you wonder if the two things might be connected? Weren't you worried?'

He shook his head vaguely. 'Not really.'

'You never thought of contacting the police?'

Ricky stubbed out his fag and nodded in Freddy's direction. 'I think you're assuming that there's a brain in that head, Princess. Well, there isn't, not much.'

Freddy protested with a weak giggle, quelled by the look of loathing Ricky cast him. I could understand Ricky's exasperation. Freddy was irritating.

'I expect you'd like a shower, or a nice hot bath,' Morris suggested, before Ricky could speak again. 'Why don't you clean up and I'll cook us all some supper? You must be hungry.'

'That's most awfully kind of you, Morris. I was hoping,' he added, with a furtive glance at Ricky, 'that perhaps I might stay here for a few nights, you know, until everything blows over and I could sneak back to London.'

'Why don't I show you where everything is.' Morris suggested soothingly and guided him towards the stairs.

Ricky was shaking his head in despair. 'What a twerp! He's spent a lifetime playing the hapless idiot on stage and now he's turned into one.'

'He can't just go back to London, can he?' I asked. 'Whatever this is all about, someone is prepared to shoot him for it. They're not just going to forget about it and leave him alone.'

'No, they're not, which means we're stuck with him,' Ricky muttered in disgust. 'I just hope whoever's after him doesn't realise how he escaped and follow him down here.'

Morris came back in, carrying Freddy's soiled clothes and heading for the washing machine. 'He'll have to go to the police,' he said, shaking his head. He turned to me. 'You will stay for supper, won't you, Juno?'

'As long as you'll let me help.'

The three of us set to in the kitchen, accompanied by the gurgling of bathroom pipes and some rather tuneless singing coming from upstairs. Freddy's unexpected appearance had made me forget why I'd come to see Ricky and Morris in the first place. But Morris, apparently concentrating on rolling a pastry lid onto a chicken pie, suddenly reminded me of it.

'This home in Bovey Tracey that you want us to visit, Juno, what was it called again?'

'Moorland View,' I told him, selecting another potato to peel.

'I thought that's what you said,' he responded, scoring lines in the pastry with a sharp knife.

'Trouble is, they know us there.'

Ricky stopped chopping cabbage. 'They do?'

'We did a concert there one afternoon, for the residents.'

'You went as Sauce and Slander?' I would have thought that the material of their double act was a bit risqué for an elderly audience.

'Oh, we kept it very genteel,' Morris assured me, winking. 'We can, you know.'

'So what if we did?' Ricky responded. 'Just because we performed there once, doesn't mean we can't have some toothless old aunt in need of care.'

'No,' Morris admitted, inclining his head. 'But I think it would be better if the visit was from someone completely unknown.'

'So do I.' I watched him stroking beaten egg on his pie crust with a pastry brush. 'So, who could we ask?' I had a sudden brainwave. 'What about Digby and Amanda?' They were retired actors and Digby owed me a favour for keeping quiet about Amanda's latest shop-lifting activities. He always swore if there was anything he could do for me, I only had to say.

'They're away on holiday,' Ricky pointed out. 'Lanzarote.'

'Oh,' I moaned, spirits dashed.

For a moment there was silence as we all pondered. Then came the banging of the bathroom door, followed by the aroma of scented steam, and Freddy came down the stairs arrayed in one of Ricky's silk dressing gowns, whistling as if he hadn't a care in the world.

'That feels better,' he declared, grinning. 'I feel like a new man.' After a moment of looking at each of us in turn, his smile flickered uncertainly. 'Am I missing something?' he asked innocently. 'Why are you all staring at me like that?'

'Because a new man,' Ricky answered him with a sly grin, 'is precisely what we need.'

CHAPTER SIX

I decided not to tell Elizabeth what we were up to. I phoned her later to see if she had received any more contact from Colin, or come up with any ideas about what to do about him. No, she said. She seemed so relaxed about the situation I began to suspect that she might have some secret plan she intended to put into action without telling me. That would be like her. I challenged her but she denied it. She was considering going to the police after all, she said. That would be the sensible thing to do, but I wasn't sure I believed her. In the meantime, there was no reason why I shouldn't put my own plan into action.

It had been decided over dinner the night before that Freddy and I should go to Moorland View alone. At first, Ricky and Morris insisted on coming but I managed to talk them out of it. I didn't want this developing into a family party. Besides, as Freddy would be the only one of us going inside, it was pointless for all three of us to wait in the car. Freddy had rung the home that morning.

Mrs MacDonald would be delighted to show him around at 11 a.m. This gave me time to take the Tribe for their usual scramble along the muddy lanes, check in at the shop, pick Freddy up and drive him to Moorland View in time for his appointment. I'd drop him off and collect him later. He shouldn't be more than an hour. This would give me enough time to drive back down the hill into Bovey and do a few errands.

Freddy had been primed with a list of questions to ask about security and staff CRB checks, as well as standards of care and the level of comfort his elderly aunt would be living in, should she choose to settle at Moorland View. He had been provided with clothes by Ricky and Morris and warned not to use expressions like *spiffing, by Jove* or *jolly good show!* He would, he assured us, be serious and dull, the very soul of a concerned nephew, wanting nothing more than to secure Auntie's security and comfort. I have to say he looked a lot better without the central parting and hair slicked down with oil. A lot greyer too. I dropped him off at the appointed time.

'I'll pick you up,' I told him. 'I won't bring the van into the car park. I'll be waiting just up the lane there, on the verge.'

'Righto!' he beamed.

I gave him a warning look and his face fell. 'Sorry.'

Just before he got out of the car, I laid a hand on his arm to stop him. 'Look, there's something I want you to do for me while you're in there.' I took my phone out of my pocket and handed it to him. 'If you get the chance, will you take a photo of a picture that's on the wall behind the reception desk? It's a police photofit of two men. They're local conmen and the picture is there to alert staff if they try to come into the home.'

Freddy looked baffled. 'And you want a photo of them?'

'Yes. You see, we think they may be linked to Colin Smethurst, the member of staff my friend is worried about. Which is why I can't just go in and take the picture. Colin knows me and the last thing we want is to arouse his suspicions.'

Freddy slid my phone into his pocket. 'Leave it to me, Juno,' he said and gave me a jaunty wink that made my heart sink into my boots. I wasn't convinced I could trust him at all. But as soon as I saw him disappear into the entrance of Moorland View, I set off down the hill, back into Bovey and parked.

I'd been charged with buying some cheese for Morris from the emporium, or The Cheese Shed, as it's really called. He's particularly fond of a certain local brand that's only sold there, and I was willing to sacrifice myself, trying out samples of cheese from among their vast selection as I struggled to remembered the name of the cheese he had written on the piece of paper in my pocket.

There's a cave-like coolness inside the shop, and the air feels slightly damp. The racks of cheeses maturing on the shelves must be kept at a constant temperature of eleven degrees, so the Big Cheese behind the counter told me.

I sampled slivers of Cave Aged Cheddar, Cornish Gouda with Honey and Clover, Dartmoor Chilli and Wild Garlic Yarg, before I allowed myself to remember that the cheese Morris wanted was Extra Mature Wyfe of Bath. After serving me with a goodly chunk, some evil-smelling goats' cheese for Ricky, and some Smoked Wedmore for myself, I came out of the shop with a full carrier, and as per Morris's instructions, some posh-looking crackers and a good bottle of red to wash it all down with. Actually, I was feeling a bit sick by then.

I drove back up to Moorland View, hoping Freddy had finished his tour of the establishment by now; and that he'd remembered to take that photograph.

There was no sign of him outside. I pulled in and glanced at my watch. I had a few minutes in hand. He'd be out soon. Ten minutes passed, then fifteen. The tour must have taken longer than I thought. I just hoped he was asking some worthwhile questions. Half an hour went by. He must really have got into the part, I decided, and was probably enjoying himself rotten, playing the role of concerned nephew.

After three quarters of an hour, I began to feel concerned. Had the silly fool misunderstood where I was picking him up? I drove into the car park and backed up, ready to turn around, when suddenly he appeared, peering through the shrubbery at the edge of the tarmac, looking both right and left before he tiptoed out, as if he were performing in a pantomime.

'What's the matter?' I asked as he slid into the seat next to me. 'What are you doing?'

'Just drive us away from here, dear girl,' he told me. 'And I'll fill you in.'

'Not so much of the *dear girl*,' I warned him. 'It's Juno to you.'

After a few hundred yards, I turned the van down a lane and pulled over. 'Now then,' I said firmly, turning to Freddy. 'Tell me, what have you doing all this time?'

'Well, I got the grand tour, as arranged.' He began quite sensibly, despite looking immensely pleased with himself, 'and had a long chat about Auntie with Mrs MacDonald and then about fees and the like. I made sure to ask about security and staff and what-not – all the stuff you told me to ask. There was no sign of this chap, Colin. So, I asked if it would be alright if I just wandered about by myself for a bit and take a few photos to show Auntie, you know, just to give her a feel of the place. Well, the boss lady wasn't happy to let me roam about unaccompanied, but had no objection to my taking photographs.' He dug about in his pocket and pulled out the phone. 'So, I snapped away, including a few of the little charmer on reception, making sure I got the wall with the picture of your two villains in the frame.'

He began scrolling through his pictures without letting me see the screen, which I found infuriating.

'Anyway,' he chattered on blithely, 'suddenly, this Colin appears. I knew it was him because of his name badge. And he went out into the garden. I told the receptionist I would like a stroll outside and she told me to feel free.'

'You followed him?' I wished Freddy would get to the point.

He nodded, his pale eyes wide with excitement. 'Well, the chap goes down the lawns into a rose garden, and he definitely looked shifty. He kept turning around to look behind him, obliging yours truly to keep dodging behind rosebushes. He comes to this arbour affair with a fountain and statues and hangs about for a few minutes, obviously waiting for someone. Then this other fellow, thick-set sort of character in an overcoat, steps out from among the bushes, and they have a chat. Not a very happy chat, by the look of things. I couldn't hear what they were saying but I didn't dare creep any closer.'

'Were you still hiding behind rosebushes?' I asked.

'No, no. By now I was lurking behind a conveniently place nymph. As I say, I really couldn't get any closer without being seen, but,' he held up his scrolling finger triumphantly, 'I did manage to take a picture.'

At last, he showed me the screen. Beyond the curved breast of the stone nymph, I could see two men having what looked like a heated conversation – Colin, and the rather heavy looking man in an overcoat.

'Unfortunately, I stepped on a twig at this moment. It went off like a firecracker. Which is why they're both looking in my direction. I scuttled off into the shrubbery.'

'Did they see you?'

'Don't think so. But that's why I hung about. I didn't

want to break cover too soon in case they'd spotted me.'

'Thanks, Freddy.' I took my phone from him. 'You've done a great job.'

'Anything I can do to help,' he assured me smugly and patted me on the knee.

CHAPTER SEVEN

Freddy was surprised when I dropped him off at the door of Druid Lodge.

'Aren't you coming in?'

'No. Tell Ricky and Morris I'll be up later,' I passed him the carrier bag full of cheese and other goodies. 'There's something that I've got to do.'

I headed home. I wanted to take a closer look at those pictures. As I parked the van, I could hear baby Noah screaming from inside Kate and Adam's flat on the ground floor. At rising six months, he was starting to teethe and was letting everyone know how he felt about it. As I let myself in through the front door, Kate was in the hall, holding him in her arms and jiggling him up and down. She looked as exhausted as any first-time mother is supposed to look, shadows like bruises under her beautiful dark eyes.

I gave her a sympathetic smile. Not that I know anything about motherhood.

Noah, cheeks mottled red and tear-sploshed, distracted himself by biting into the long dark plait of hair that hung down over his mother's shoulder.

'That's right. Have a chew on that,' I recommended, smoothing down a tuft of dark hair sticking up on his head. 'Okay?' I asked his harassed-looking mum. 'Anything I can do?' I added, hoping the answer was no.

She shook her head. 'No, thanks Juno. I'm trying to get him off to sleep. None of us got much last night. Did he disturb you?'

'No. I didn't hear him,' I told her, only slightly lying. 'How are things at *Sunflowers*? Is Adam busy?' Despite serving great food, the café had struggled to keep going over the last couple of years. At one point, Kate and Adam had even considered selling the business, but I'm glad to say they had decided to keep going; although the arrival of Noah had restricted Kate's working hours and Adam was having to work much harder, especially as his usual helpmate, student Chris, wouldn't be around until Easter.

'Actually, it's quite busy at the moment,' she told me. 'Adam thinks that having the main road closed to traffic has been a good thing. It's meant people driving down past the café who wouldn't usually come along that road. It's made people more aware of us.'

Well, it's an ill-wind, I thought.

'He brought some of that curried vegetable pie you like home last night,' she went on. 'I've left it up there outside your door.'

'Fantastic,' I said. 'Thanks.' There is nothing like having café owners for landlords. The left-overs

alone are worth the cost of rent. I grabbed the two
foil-wrapped portions from the table by my front
door and hurried inside. It was past lunchtime and
my stomach was rumbling. I ate the first piece cold,
straight from the foil, while I waited for the kettle to
boil, then reluctantly put the other piece in the fridge
for later.

Armed with a mug of tea, I sat down in front of
my laptop and uploaded the photos Freddy had taken
from my phone. I wanted a closer look at this man
Colin had been talking to in the garden. Freddy is not
the best photographer. Some of his pictures were badly
framed and out of focus, particularly those taken on
the move out in the garden. The clearest shot was the
one that he had taken from behind the stone nymph,
the ample curve of her breast blotting out a section
of sky. But Colin's face was clear, and so was the face
of the man he was talking to – tall, thickset with a
double chin, his dark brown hair clearly receding.
Whatever the conversation between the two of them,
neither of them looked happy. The stranger looked
angry; Colin looked scared. I scrolled back through
the other photos – uninspiring shots of the residents'
lounge and communal dining room – until I found
several pictures of the reception area. Behind the desk
stood a smiling young woman, possibly the Charelle
I had spoken to on the phone. On the wall behind
her head, I could see the white rectangle of the police
photofit of the two men who had threatened Joan. To
be fair to Freddy, he had taken several of these shots,

and made sure they were all in focus. I magnified the clearest, cropping out everything but the men's faces.

It was obvious that the older of the two was the man I'd just seen in the garden – thickset, double-chin, incipient hair-loss. And the other one, younger, handsome with dark eyebrows – I had seen him before, at Colin's house. And I'd heard him speak. *Know what I mean?*

My first thought was to warn Elizabeth. The men who were trying to find her had not gone away. They were close by, talking to Colin. Both she and Joan were still in danger. I got no answer from her phone, but sent her the pictures with a brief message, saying that I would see her later. I had an hour before my next client, just time to drive up to Druid Lodge and see Freddy.

'But why do I have to go back there?' he protested when I told him what I wanted him to do.

'Because you were the one there earlier today, idiot,' Ricky told him unkindly. 'You took the photos.'

'Yes, but can't I just send . . . ?'

'I want you to show these photos to Mrs MacDonald in person, tell her how concerned you are,' I insisted. 'Tell her you were just showing them to Auntie, when you noticed the similarity between the man in the photofit displayed in reception and the man that a member of her staff was talking to in the garden. Tell her you think she should call the police.'

'Police?' he repeated, turning pale.

'Demand that she does. She can hardly do nothing if you're standing there in front of her.'

'But what if the police want to speak to me?' he faltered.

'Well, what if they do?' Ricky demanded, narrowing his eyes. 'Problem, is it?'

'Well, I'd rather not . . .'

'Look, they are only going to be interested in these photographs,' I told him as Morris quietly placed a tea mug by my elbow. 'That's if they bother to follow it up at all.'

'Why don't we print out the relevant photos?' Morris suggested. 'Then you can leave them with Mrs MacDonald to show to the police. You don't have to wait about until they come.'

'Oh, good idea!' Freddy agreed.

'Anyway, it's this Colin character who's going to have the awkward questions to answer,' Ricky added. 'If these two blokes are banned from coming into the place, what's he doing having a secret talk to one of them in the garden?'

'And why hasn't he reported it to the police already?' Morris asked. 'Or told Mrs MacDonald this man has turned up?'

'Well . . . we don't know that he hasn't,' Freddy pointed out.

Ricky was shaking his head, as he scrolled through the pictures on my phone. 'Nah, look at his body language. Furtive, that is. He doesn't want anyone to know he's in cahoots with his photofit friend.'

'We'll drive you there, Freddy,' Morris offered sweetly, 'then Juno can get back to work, just as soon as she's finished her cup of tea.'

Sophie was in the shop when I popped in, painting in a vague, abstracted sort of way, a day-dreamy look on her face. 'Any sign of Elizabeth?' I asked.

She shook her head.

'If she does come in, will you ask her to ring me?'

'Anything the matter?' she asked, finally giving me her full attention.

'No. I just need a quick word with her, that's all.' I glanced at my watch. 'I've got to dash.'

From her corner of the shop, Pat's voice drifted gloomily. 'You don't know anyone who's looking for a kitten, I suppose?'

''Fraid not.' I turned to look at her. She was hunched over her table, sewing together some kind of knitted animal, as yet unidentifiable. The end of her nose, as always, looked red with cold. 'Is this kitten one of the new waifs and strays?'

'Him and his four sisters,' she sniffed, without looking up from whatever it was. 'And if you know anyone who'll give a home to a three-legged Labrador . . .'

'I'll keep an ear out,' I promised and made my escape before Pat could go any further down the list of animals looking for owners.

I didn't catch up with Elizabeth until late in the afternoon, when I found her at home. Olly had just come in from school and was sitting on a kitchen chair, eating his way through a slab of fruitcake the size of a house-brick, his bags and coat dumped all over the floor. He grinned when he saw me, brushing a scattering of crumbs from the front of his school jumper. 'I'm starving,' he told me, gesturing with his cake. 'School dinners are a joke. Wouldn't keep a sparrow alive. D'you want some?'

'Did you make it?' I asked.

'Of course.' He glanced slyly at Elizabeth, a twinkle in his light blue eyes. 'I am the master baker around here.' It was true, he was a very good cook. He'd even considered cooking as a career at one time, but like all his career considerations, that had soon been superseded by another.

'I will look after Juno,' she told him. 'Will you kindly pick these things up from the floor and make a start on your revision?' He had exams coming up soon. She frowned at him for a moment. 'I thought you were going into town to get a haircut on your way home.'

'Changed my mind.' He ran a hand over the fair hair at the back of his neck. I realised with astonishment that it was starting to curl. He usually kept it mown so short that it didn't get the chance. 'I thought I might grow it,' he mused, 'go all poetic. What d'you think?'

Elizabeth suppressed a smile. 'I think it's time you stopped cluttering up this kitchen.' She picked up his coat, bundling it into his arms. 'Supper will be in an hour.'

He heaved a martyred sigh. 'Alright, alright,' he grumbled, bending to pick things up. 'See you, Juno,' he called back as he shuffled out of the room.

I waited until I heard him climb the stairs and his bedroom door shut before I dared to speak. 'Did you get my message?'

She nodded. 'Thank you. And the photographs. What I don't really understand is what Ricky's relative was doing at Moorland View in the first place.'

'Looking around the place,' I answered innocently, 'for his elderly aunt.'

She raised a sceptical eyebrow. 'Well, thank him anyway, will you?'

'He's been back since then,' I told her. 'And taken copies of the photographs with him. Mrs MacDonald phoned the police as soon as she saw them. Freddy didn't hang around, but she told him they were sending an officer to interview the member of staff concerned.'

'Was Colin still there?'

'No, he'd gone home. According to Mrs MacDonald, he's working a split shift and is expected back later. She told Freddy she had questions for him herself. He'll be lucky if he keeps his job.'

Elizabeth was silent, her chin resting on one hand as she gazed thoughtfully.

'Do you think Colin will back off once he knows he's been rumbled?' I asked.

'More to the point, will Mr Smith and Mr Jones?' She shook her head. 'Somehow, I doubt it. After all, they are not doing anything illegal in trying to recover George's debt.'

'Doesn't that depend on the way they go about it?'

She laughed wryly. 'It does rather.'

'What are you going to do if they catch up with you?' I asked. 'You said you might go to the police.' I wanted to prod her into doing something. This inactivity wasn't like her.

'Let's just wait and see what happens as a result of this latest development,' she answered with maddening calm.

'And if what happens is that those two thugs turn up at your door?' I challenged her.

'I'll deal with them when they arrive.' She rose from the table as if this was the end to the matter. 'Now, would you like a slice of Olly's cake?' she asked lightly. 'It really is rather good.'

At that moment there was a thundering like a baby elephant tumbling down the stairs and Olly burst the door open. 'I forgot to tell you,' he announced. 'As I was coming home from school, this man in a car slowed down, leant out of the window and asked to be remembered to you.'

'What man?' Elizabeth flicked a sharp glance at me and then back to Olly.

'I don't know. I've never seen him before.'

'Then how did he know who you were?'

Olly shrugged. 'He just said, remember me to your Aunt Elizabeth. Then he drove off.'

'Didn't you ask who he was?'

'Yes, 'course.' He laughed uncertainly as if he didn't know what the big deal was. 'He said his name was Colin.'

CHAPTER EIGHT

'I must say, Juno, you are awfully clever.' Freddy grinned at me as we sat around the table with Ricky and Morris that evening. 'I don't know why I didn't think of this myself.'

Neither, I told him silently, *do I.* It seemed bloody obvious to me. I'd convinced everyone at the table that we needed to do no more at Moorland View, and that the police would take care of things from now on. For Elizabeth's sake I wanted to distract them from the events of the day, not let them persist in asking awkward questions about Colin Smethurst. Which is why I had come up with a scheme to help solve the mystery of what was going on at the theatre with Freddy. I had looked on the theatre's website and into their online booking system; then I had printed out copies of the current booking plans for all matinee performances for the next three months. I spread these out on the table in front of us, each one showing a plan of the auditorium, ticket prices, and which seats had already been booked for that performance. 'The seats that are already taken are coloured dark blue,' I explained. 'The ones that are still available are the pale blue ones.'

I looked around the table to make sure they were all with me. Freddy frowned, prodding the plan in front of him with a finger. 'What are these circles drawn here?' he asked. 'There are four of them in the stalls and another four in the circle. And then the seats around them are marked with an R.'

'They're pillars, you idiot,' Ricky retorted. 'The R stands for "restricted view".' He pointed with a finger. 'It says so there on the plan.'

'Oh, so it does,' he nodded.

'I'm assuming that whoever is listening to your message on a Wednesday afternoon,' I went on, 'makes sure he's got a seat by booking well in advance,'

'He may not always sit in the same seat,' he objected.

Ricky grinned. 'I bet he does. I bet he's found a seat he likes and sticks to it. It makes booking quicker, for a start. Why mess around choosing a different seat every time?'

'He might have a special arrangement with the box office,' Morris added, peering at the booking plan in front of him. 'Always makes sure that his seat is kept free.'

'Yeh,' Ricky chuckled. 'Slip the box-office clerk a tenner.'

'But the beauty of using the online system,' I pointed out, 'is that whoever books the seat doesn't have to have any personal contact with anyone. He can even print off his tickets himself, the box-office staff need never lay eyes on him.'

'So, all we have to do, to work out which seat he's sitting in,' Freddy began slowly, 'is to . . .'

'Is to look through these plans,' I cut in, too impatient to wait for his brain to catch up, 'and find if there's one particular seat that's always booked way in advance on a Wednesday afternoon.'

'Makes sense if we work backwards,' Ricky observed. 'Start with the dates furthest away, 'cos that will have the fewest seats booked so far.'

I passed the plans with the four most distant dates out amongst us. There then followed a brief argument about the best way of going about things. 'Look, I've got the plan for 9th June,' I said, when things were starting to get tetchy. 'Who's got the 2nd?' Morris raised a finger. 'So, Freddy, you've got the 25th May and Ricky the 18th? Right, I'll call out the seat numbers that are already booked on my plan. If you've got the same seat booked for your performance, then write the number down.'

'What if we've got seats booked that you haven't called out?' Morris asked, peering up over his specs.

'Never mind them,' Ricky told him irritably. 'Just stick to the ones that Juno calls out. We can go through the rest later.'

Following this method, we worked our way through the booking plans from June back to the end of April.

'In the stalls, everyone always goes for row F,' Freddy noticed. 'The whole row is nearly full for every performance. And it starts to fill early too.'

'That'll be the first raised row in the auditorium,' Ricky pointed a finger at the plan. 'I bet the seats in rows A to E are on the flat. If you want to see over the head of the person in front of you, go for row F.'

Morris seemed to be looking backwards and forwards between his written list of booked seats and the plans in front of him. 'This is odd. You'd expect the seats with restricted view to be the last to be booked, wouldn't you? But look here, on my lists, there's one that's booked every time. Up in the dress circle. Q7.'

We each checked our own lists. 'And on these,' Freddy said.

'Yup,' Ricky nodded. 'Q7.'

'And on mine,' I added.

Ricky threw down his pencil and leant back in his chair. 'This'll be our mystery man, in Q7. He doesn't care if his view of the play is restricted 'cos he's seen it so many times, and anyway, he's only there to *listen*.'

'And no one will want to sit near him either,' I added, 'because of the restricted view. At least not by choice.'

'So, no one's going to be taking too much notice of him and what he does. He can get up and leave as soon as he's heard what he's waiting for.' Ricky rubbed his hands together gleefully and stood up. 'Time for a little glass of something, I think.'

'But how do we find out who he is?' Freddy asked.

Ricky hovered by the wine rack, considering labels. 'Haven't you got any friends in the box office who could find out?'

'Well, no,' he admitted, sounding slightly superior. 'I'm an actor. Front of house isn't really my area.'

'Front of house,' Morris repeated, frowning. 'I wonder if the same stewards are on for each matinee performance. They get to know regular customers. They might know who he is.'

Ricky returned with a bottle of Rioja and four glasses. He put them down on the table and swiped up the booking plan in front of Freddy. 'Give me that! What time does the box office close? I don't suppose you know that either,' he went on before Freddy could reply.

Morris consulted his watch. 'They'll be in the middle of their evening performance by now.'

Ricky found the box office phone number on the plan, picked up his phone and dialled. 'Good evening, is that the Davenport Theatre?' he began in his best Shakespearean actor's voice. 'I wonder if you can help me. I'd like to book four seats for the matinee performance on Wednesday of next week. Yes, that's right.' Around the table we glanced at one another, listening in silence. 'In the dress circle,' he went on, turning around to grin at us. 'Row Q. Yes, that's right. I know the view's restricted, that's not a problem. I was hoping for 6, 7, 8 and 9.' There was a brief pause while the booking clerk consulted his screen. 'Oh? Q7 is already taken? What a shame! . . . What's that?' There was a moment's pause. 'Oh? We could have Q5 and 6 and Q8 and 9. You don't think this person in Q7 would be prepared to budge up, do you, just to save breaking up a party?' He waited a moment as the voice in the box office responded. 'Unlikely,' Ricky repeated. 'I see. What? Oh, yes of course.'

There was another pause as his hand went to his back pocket. Then we heard him reading out the numbers of his credit card.

'Ricky!' Morris hissed in an under-voice. 'What are you doing?' Ricky just flapped a hand at him to shut him up.

'My God!' Freddy's eyes were round with horror. 'He's actually booking the seats! Well, *I* can't go!'

'That's most awfully good of you. Thank you so much,' Ricky was carrying on at his most charming. 'No, that's quite alright. We'll pick the tickets up when we arrive.' He put the receiver down and turned to us with a triumphant grin. 'Fancy a trip to the theatre, boys and girls?'

'But I can't!' Freddy objected, almost on the point of tears. 'I can't sit next to that man. What if he recognises me?'

'You'll be in disguise,' Ricky told him, brandishing a corkscrew with a flourish. 'By the time I've finished with you, your own mother won't recognise you.' He glanced at me. 'You're up for it, aren't you, Princess?'

Poor Freddy, his face was a picture. I had to stifle a laugh. 'Of course I am.'

'But what's the point?' Freddy demanded.

'Well, for one thing,' Ricky told him, pouring wine, 'we'll get a look at this man who's listening to the messages. For another, we'll know from whatever lines your understudy comes out with, whether or not whatever was going on with you, is *still* going on . . .'

'And we might even be able to follow him and find out who he is,' I added.

'I don't want to know who he is,' Freddy objected. 'I never want to lay eyes on him.'

'Then what are you going to do about your friend with the gun? I asked. 'You can't just hope all this blows over and go back to London.'

'But surely, after a few months . . .' he began.

'Look, whoever these people are who are sending and listening to these messages, they are prepared to spend good money to make sure they get delivered. And it seems they're prepared to shoot you if they're not.' Freddy stared at me, his chin wobbling like baby Noah's when he's going to burst into tears.

'Juno's right, mate,' Ricky told him. 'You'd be a sitting duck in any theatre where you showed your face. And that's assuming anyone will give you a job after you disappeared from this one halfway through a performance.'

Freddy gulped. 'I thought I might try my luck in America.'

Ricky laughed out loud, but whatever sarcastic comment was rising to his lips was cut short by Morris, who was still frowning over the plans. 'You know there's another seat that's always booked on a Wednesday afternoon. S5. What if he is our man?'

Ricky sniffed. 'Well, that's only two rows behind. We'll just have to keep an eye on that one as well.'

Morris sipped his wine, still staring at the table pensively. 'What's on your mind, *Maurice*?'

He pushed his specs up the bridge of his nose. 'I think this Rioja needs a bit of cheese,' he said absently.

'Quite right.' Ricky looked around the table cheerily. 'So, now we're going up to London. How are we going to get there?'

CHAPTER NINE

Elizabeth and I were the only ones in the shop next morning. Sophie had popped out for an hour to arrange the framing of some paintings for a customer and Pat was staying at home because the cold she'd caught had taken a ghastly turn and she didn't want to spread her germs around. I'd rung Elizabeth to ask her to cover for me because I had clients to see to later in the morning. But the real reason I wanted her to come in was because her calmness in the face of approaching danger was worrying me. I might have accused her of hiding her head in the sand, except that she never does that kind of thing. She needed a plan. And if she had one and wasn't telling me, then I wanted to know why.

But we didn't get the chance to talk. She'd barely been in the shop a minute, and was still taking her coat off, when Dean Collins arrived. 'To what do I owe the honour?' I asked, wondering what I'd done this time.

Dean smiled briefly, but his manner was serious. 'As a matter of fact, Juno, it's Ms Knollys I've come to see.'

'Me?' Elizabeth smiled at him with raised eyebrows.

'Is this official business, Constable Collins?' she asked lightly.

Apparently, it was. 'Just a few questions, if you don't mind.' He indicated that she should sit. She cast a mystified glance at me, took Sophie's chair and he pulled Pat's up in front of her table.

'D'you want me to leave?' I asked him. Wild horses wouldn't have dragged me otherwise.

'That's up to Ms Knollys,' he responded, looking slightly uncomfortable. 'As I say, I've just got a few questions.'

'Stay where you are, Juno,' Elizabeth ordered. 'And for heaven's sake, Dean, you know my name. You don't have to keep calling me Ms Knollys.'

'Then, I'll come straight to the point, Elizabeth,' he said. 'Does the name Colin Smethurst mean anything to you?'

'No.' Her single word response was immediate and unhesitating. I glanced at her face but she was looking at Dean and did not meet my eye.

'Colin Smethurst,' he repeated. 'You're sure the name means nothing to you?'

'No,' she repeated crisply. 'Should it?' I felt myself tense up, apprehensive about what might be coming next, but she seemed completely unruffled.

'You don't know him?' Dean insisted.

She shook her head. Beneath the table I felt the slightest touch of her foot against mine, a warning to me to stay silent. 'I've never heard of him.'

Dean reached into his briefcase and took out a

photograph and laid it on the table. 'This is a picture of Colin Smethurst.'

Elizabeth picked it up with a mild sigh. The picture showed a smiling Colin, standing in his front garden, his white cat, Snowdrop, sitting on the wall next to him. 'Well,' she conceded, 'he does look vaguely familiar, I suppose, but if you hadn't told me his name, I wouldn't have known it.'

'You see,' Dean went on, 'police officers called at Mr Smethurst's place of employment yesterday to interview him on a certain matter. When he failed to turn up for his shift, they went to his home. They found him dead.'

'Dead?' The word escaped my lips before I could prevent it. Elizabeth glanced in my direction but remained mute.

'I'm afraid he's been murdered.'

'Murdered?' She spoke now, visibly shocked.

I clenched my hands together in my lap. I dared not look at her.

'How terrible,' she said quietly. She stared back at the photo, appearing to study it, but I knew she was giving herself time to compose her thoughts. When she looked up, her grey eyes met Dean's unflinchingly, 'but as I say, I don't recognise him. I don't quite understand why you're here.'

'I'm here because of this,' Dean placed a different photo on the table in front of her. 'It was found in his wallet.'

She stared at it in shock, her face turning pale.

'Have you any idea why Mr Smethurst would be

carrying a photograph of you around in his wallet, Elizabeth?' Dean asked.

'No. No idea,' she breathed slowly, picking the photo up. 'I've never seen this photograph before.' It had clearly been taken when she wasn't aware of it. She wasn't looking at the camera, but was talking to someone out of shot. It seemed to have been taken at some sort of social gathering, she was wearing a dress and standing with a wine glass in her hand. 'Just a moment.' She pointed at the background against which her picture had been taken - a beige wall with an uninspiring painting of a vase of flowers hanging on it. 'I recognise this room.' She looked up at Dean. 'Was this taken at Moorland View?'

'You know the place?' Dean sounded almost relieved.

'I have visited there,' Elizabeth admitted, without specifying who she was visiting. I wondered just how close to the truth was she prepared to sail. 'May I look at that first photo again?' she asked. Dean slid it toward her. She studied it again, frowning. 'Doesn't this man work there?' she asked innocently. Then she gave an awkward laugh. 'I am so sorry, Dean, I do recognise this man. He works at Moorland View. I'm sure I've seen him there. It's just seeing him out of uniform . . . I didn't immediately recognise him out of context, as it were.'

I had to admire her skill as an actress. If I didn't know better, I'd have believed her.

'That's alright.' Dean smiled for the first time. 'That's not uncommon.'

'But, why does he have my photograph in his wallet?'

He rubbed the back of his head thoughtfully. 'I was hoping you could tell me.'

'I'm afraid I can't, unless . . . you don't think that he . . . ?'

'Was an admirer of yours, perhaps?' Dean completed for her. 'You say you didn't know him on a personal level.'

'I was hardly aware of the man.' She dropped the photo with some distaste.

'And he's never approached you? Tried to get to know you?'

She looked horrified. 'Certainly not.'

Dean sighed as he gathered up the photographs.

'Do you have to keep that?' Elizabeth asked, pointing at the picture of herself.

'I'm afraid I do for the time being.'

'You say this Colin Smethurst was murdered?' I asked.

Dean nodded solemnly. 'That's right.'

'Do we know who did it?'

'Not at this point. Although we have a suspect. A suspicious character was seen hanging around the garden of Moorland View yesterday and it seems may have talked to the victim.'

'How was the victim killed?' I asked.

Dean gave me a slightly amused look. 'I'm afraid I can't reveal that for the moment.'

I hate it when he says that. He always looks so smug.

'I'm sure you understand, Miss Marple,' he added.

I wanted to hit him. The chair creaked ominously as

he rose to his feet. He needed to keep up the jogging, obviously. 'Well, thank you for your time, Elizabeth. Finding your picture in his wallet like that, we had hoped you might be a friend of his, be able to tell us a bit about him.'

'I'm afraid not.' She gave him her most charming smile. 'He can't have been carrying some kind of crush, surely?' she asked demurely. 'Not a woman of my age.'

Dean didn't comment. Perhaps he didn't trust himself. 'Ah, well.' He nodded philosophically. 'If you think of anything.'

'Of course. I'll be in touch.'

He turned to the door and winked at me on his way out. 'See you, ladies.'

I didn't dare look at Elizabeth until Dean was out of sight. She gasped as she collapsed back in her chair, her self-possession deserting her. 'God, Juno,' she breathed softly. 'He's dead. The man is dead.'

'Don't you think it's time to tell the police what you know?' I urged her.

She shook her head. 'They already know as much as we do - that he was probably killed by that man he was talking to in the garden. They can see for themselves he's one of the two in the photofit, a man *not* called Smith or Jones. It's not as if I can give them a name. Or any other information.'

'But they don't know about Colin's attempt to blackmail you, that one of these men had threatened him.'

'I know.' Elizabeth sunk her head in her hands.

'Colin is dead either because he refused to tell them my whereabouts, or because, having told them, they killed him as they had no further use for him. Either way, it's my fault the man is dead.'

'We don't know that for sure.'

'Don't we?'

'It is not your fault,' I insisted, shaking her arm. 'Colin should have gone straight to the police as soon as those men approached him about finding you. But he chose not to. He accepted their offer of money and then tried to get more by blackmailing you.'

'I suppose you're right,' she agreed reluctantly.

'But,' I went on deliberately, 'his murderer may get away with it if you don't tell the police everything you know now.'

'Which is what?' she asked, some of her usual resolution returning. 'All I could tell them is that these men were looking for me because my husband owed them money. I can't tell him who they are or how to find them.'

'And if they did persuade Colin to tell them where you live before they killed him, what then?' I demanded. 'What if he showed them your photograph?'

'I don't think so.'

I wanted to shake her. 'Why not?'

'Because then they would have kept it.'

'You can't be sure of that. You need protection, Elizabeth.'

She seemed to regain her composure and spoke calmly. 'I shall be vigilant.'

Before I could press her to be more sensible, the doorbell jangled announcing Sophie's return from the picture-framers. 'You two look very serious,' she said, staring at our faces. 'Is anything wrong?'

Elizabeth gazed up at her and smiled. 'No,' she assured her, slanting me a warning look. 'Everything's fine.'

CHAPTER TEN

By the time I returned to the shop after dealing with my clients, Elizabeth had gone home, and although I tried to pay attention to Sophie's prattling about Seth and her plans for the next weekend, she was all I could think about.

I phoned her when I got home. Everything was fine, she told me, stop worrying. I tried to talk some sense into her about going to the police but her resolve was armour-plated. She would not go. 'What if Mrs MacDonald at Moorland View tells them that the woman Smith and Jones tried to talk to was your sister?' I asked.

'I haven't done anything wrong in not telling them who I was visiting,' she responded calmly. 'Dean didn't ask me. And it won't help them in finding this Mr Smith or Mr Jones or whoever he is. They've got the photo, they know what he looks like, and I don't know any more than that.'

Which left me wondering whether I should tell them what I knew. I would have to 'fess up to having followed Colin to his house and listened in on his conversation with half of the Smith-and-Jones duo. He'd threatened Colin and mentioned a Mr Shaw. It wasn't much help, as I told Bill when he arrived on my lap that evening. And telling them anything would be a horrible betrayal of Elizabeth's trust in me. For the moment, I didn't know what to do.

The ringing of the doorbell would have been a welcome distraction from my thoughts, if it hadn't been Dean Collins standing on my doorstep. 'I want a word about this morning,' he told me ominously.

'Oh?' I stood back to let him in and we didn't speak again until we were inside the flat, by which time I was on tenterhooks, worrying what he was going to say. 'Cup of tea?' I asked, as he sat heavily on my sofa, next to Bill who didn't look happy about the arrangement.

'If you're making one,' he answered.

I'm never sure if this means yes or no, so I flipped the kettle on anyway. 'How can I help?'

'I'm not sure your friend Elizabeth is telling me the truth,' he said bluntly.

Oh fuck. I tried to look surprised. 'Why wouldn't she be?'

'I don't know.' He settled himself on the sofa, leaning his broad shoulders back against the cushions. Bill dabbed an experimental paw on his lap, then thought better of it and headed off into the bedroom. 'It's just a feeling,' he said, frowning at me. 'I thought you both seemed tense.'

I shrugged my shoulders. 'I don't know what gave you that impression.'

He fixed his eyes on mine. 'I wondered if there was anything you wanted to tell me.'

I stared back, trying to look blank. 'About what?'

'I'm not sure that Elizabeth knows as little about this Smethurst chap as she claims. I mean this business of him carrying her picture around in his wallet. It's odd.'

'Odd?' I repeated. 'It's creepy. But it's hardly Elizabeth's fault, is it? What sort of character was this Colin Smethurst, anyway?'

'Bit of a loner, from what I can make out. Lived by himself. Apart from his cat.'

Little Snowdrop, what would happen to her now? 'Oh, so what happens to that then,' I asked casually, 'the cat – who will look after it?'

He shrugged. 'A constable has taken it up to Honeysuckle Farm.'

Poor Pat, but I suppose one more waif wouldn't make much difference.

'And then there's the fact,' Dean persisted, 'that first of all Elizabeth said she didn't know him, then she said she did.'

'Well, you said yourself, it's not uncommon not to recognise someone immediately when you see them out of context. I didn't recognise the lady from the post office the other day because she was out on the loose in St Lawrence Lane.'

'You just couldn't place her,' he responded. 'That's different.'

'Elizabeth admitted he looked vaguely familiar when she first saw his photograph,' I reminded him. The kettle was boiling and I nipped into the kitchen, glad of the chance to escape for a moment. I put two raisin flapjacks, the latest offering from *Sunflowers*, on a plate in front of Dean as a sacrificial offering when I went back in with the tea.

'Oh, you devil woman!' he murmured appreciatively, his blue eyes twinkling as he reached out to grab one. But if I thought flapjacks were going to distract him, I was wrong. 'So, you can't tell me any different, then?'

'About what?'

'Elizabeth and this bloke.'

'No,' I told him firmly as I watched a second flapjack disappear. 'And any case, if you're not happy with her answers, shouldn't you be asking her?'

'Alright, no need to get tetchy. I expect I will,' he answered cheerfully. 'See, I went back to Moorland View this afternoon, to interview some of the other staff. And I showed the lady in charge the picture Colin had been carrying in his wallet, just to confirm that it was taken there, and she was adamant that Elizabeth's name was not Knollys, but Hunter. You wouldn't know anything about that?'

'No, I wouldn't,' I lied, although I could feel a warm blush rising in a tide up my neck. There was no way Dean wouldn't notice my discomfiture; I felt forced into saying something. 'I think Elizabeth might have been married in the past. She never talks about it, though.'

'That might explain it then,' he agreed, nodding

I urgently wanted to change the subject. 'This man Colin,' I said. 'You said he'd been murdered?'

Dean puffed out his cheeks thoughtfully. 'Well, it'll come out soon enough, I suppose. But you never heard it from me, alright?'

''Course not.'

'He was shot.'

'Shot?' Suddenly I was as cold inside as I had been warm before. 'You mean . . . with a gun?' I added idiotically.

Dean nodded. 'Handgun. One shot in the head, two in the chest. Professional job if you ask me. We think somehow our Colin had got himself mixed up in organised crime.' He stood up and brushed flapjack crumbs from his tie, making ready to leave.

'Why do you say that?' I asked.

'Well, there was no attempt to hide the body or make the murder look like an accident. It was clearly retribution for something,' he added as he reached out for the door handle. 'His body was meant to be found. It was meant to send out a message.'

I couldn't help it. I couldn't stop seeing Elizabeth's manicured hands putting together that old Luger of her father's, seeing the steely determination in her grey eyes; seeing her pulling the trigger. Could she really have shot Colin? Three times. Twice in the chest, once in the head? I had told her where he lived. And he had been killed conveniently before the police could ask him any questions about the mystery man in the garden, one of the two men who had been asking questions about her. And he'd been killed hours after we'd found out that Colin had approached Olly on his way home from school. I couldn't quite believe that Elizabeth had committed murder. But I had no doubt in my mind that she *could* do it if she had to – to protect her sister, to protect Olly. She'd even joked about it. Was her shock at being told of Colin's death, her apparent remorse, just an act? If it was, she had fooled me completely.

In the end, I couldn't rest. I shrugged on my coat and boots and drove up to Daison Cottages where she and Olly lived. A row of four houses originally built for agricultural labourers, they were found on an isolated stretch of road on the way to Owlacombe Cross. I drew up on the opposite verge. There were no street lights here, surrounded as the houses were by fields all around, and by now it was late in the evening, almost completely dark. A few yards in front of me a sleek shape, some powerful car I couldn't identify, pulled swiftly away, its tail lights glowing like two red eyes until it was lost from view around a curve in the road.

I didn't go to the front door, but walked around the side of the house to the back door as I usually did and peered through the window. The kitchen light was on, Elizabeth standing in her dressing gown by the stove. I tapped on the glass. Her head whipped around sharply and I saw relief on her face as she realised it was me. She unlocked the door and stood back to let me in.

'Juno? I was just going to bed.'

'Have you had visitors?' I asked, and turned the key in the lock before she could say another word.

'No,' she answered, looking mystified. 'Why?'

'There was a car parked across the road just now, the driver made off when I arrived.'

'It could have been someone who'd been visiting one of the other cottages,' she pointed out.

'It could,' I agreed. But I didn't think so. And I could tell from the sudden alertness of her demeanour, neither did she.

'Colin Smethurst was shot.'

'Shot?' she echoed.

'With a handgun,' I went on, watching her face intently. 'Twice in the chest, once in the head. The police think it was a professional job.'

'But that's . . .' her voice tailed off as realisation dawned. She stared, her lips parting in shock. 'Juno. You don't think . . . you can't think that *I* shot him?'

'No,' I could hear a tremor in my voice. 'I can't believe it. But I still want you to tell me that you didn't.'

Ice hardened her grey eyes, and her voice when she spoke was brittle. 'No. I did not kill Colin Smethurst.'

'Swear it,' I insisted.

'Juno, you can't . . .' she sighed and shook her head. 'I swear.' She saw my hesitation and added the words she knew would make me believe her. 'I swear on Olly's life.'

I breathed out slowly. 'Thank you.'

The air between us had turned frosty. She stared at me in silence for a few moments, and then shook her head. 'Juno. How could you believe that . . . ?' She began, but a voice interrupted her, calling down the stairs.

'Who's that?'

'It's alright, Olly,' she called back. 'Go back to bed.'

'Who is it? he insisted.

'It's only me,' I called out.

'Juno?' He slopped down the stairs and appeared in the doorway in pyjamas and bare feet. 'What's up?'

'Nothing. I forgot to give Elizabeth a message, that's all.'

'Oh, okay.' He looked as if he wanted to hang around and chat.

'Nice jim-jams,' I said, looking him over. He was growing out of them, too much shin showing and too much bony wrist sprouting from the sleeves. He grinned, suddenly self-conscious, tugged at his pyjama top and gave us a little wave. 'Night, then.' he said, and turned back up the stairs. We heard his bedroom door close.

For a moment Elizabeth and I stared at one another. 'Listen,' I told her, keeping my voice low because of Olly. 'The police think organised crime is involved in this, that Colin's shooting is intended to send out a message. Whoever George owed this money to, they are very dangerous people.'

Elizabeth smiled wryly. 'I realised that this morning when we learnt that he was dead.'

'It's not funny.'

'No. it isn't. And I think we can assume, if you were right about the car parked across the road, that his murderers found out what they wanted to know before they killed him.'

We stared at one another for a moment and Elizabeth reached for the light switch, plunging the kitchen into darkness. Wordlessly we crossed the hall into the living room and stood in the dark, staring out at the road beyond the garden. 'Well, they haven't come back,' she whispered.

Not yet. 'Call the police,' I begged her. 'Please.'

'I'll stay down here tonight,' she said. 'Keep watch.'

'Then I'll stay too.'

'No, Juno. I want you to go home.'

'Not until you call the police.'

She gave an irritated sigh. 'Very well. I'll tell them I saw a vehicle parked outside for a long time with two men sitting in it and I thought it was suspicious. After all,' she conceded, 'unless you have business in one of the cottages here, it is an odd place to stop. I suppose the police might send a patrol car around.'

'Tell them you thought they were dealing drugs. They're more likely to come then.'

She smiled. 'If that will induce you to go home.'

I folded my arms. 'Once you've made the call.'

She sighed again and picked up the receiver.

I didn't drive straight home. What if the driver of that car was watching from somewhere, waiting to see my white van drive away before he came back? Instead of heading back into Ashburton, I drove up to Owlacombe Cross. The road up to Halsanger Common beckoned, to Daniel's house, but I resisted the urge. Instead, I carried on, looping around the valley until I came out at the western edge of town. It was only then that I remembered that I couldn't drive straight through it, because of the road works. With a sigh, I backtracked up the hill again. I didn't see another car.

When I reached Daison Cottages, a vehicle was parked outside the house. But it was a police patrol car, two uniformed officers just being let in through the front door by Elizabeth. As I drove on by, I saw that an upstairs window in the adjacent cottage was lit, a dark shape trying to peer surreptitiously through the curtains. Mrs April Hardiman, the neighbour for whom the words Neighbourhood Watch were invented. I smiled. We could use another pair of eyes just now.

CHAPTER ELEVEN

Maisie was in good spirits, standing in her porch when I arrived at Brook Cottage, leaning on her walking-frame and wearing her pendant alarm like a badge of honour. 'I want you to do the porch,' she announced, sweeping an arm around it before I'd barely got in the gate.

'Well, it's a good day for it,' I called back as I walked up her path. 'At least it's dry.' Maisie's spring-clean of the porch required a dry day. And if the sun kept disappearing behind slate grey clouds, at least there showed no sign of rain. 'Your daffs look nice,' I told her, nodding at a clump in her garden, whose golden heads nodded back in the breeze.

Spring-cleaning Maisie's porch is not a job I look forward to, although it's satisfying in a weird way. First, I cleared away her pots of geraniums and cacti, all of them old and heavy, from the slatted wooden shelves, and put them down in the garden where they could enjoy some welcome fresh air. After I'd brushed and dusted the shelves for withered leaves and the desiccated corpses of insects, I gave them a thorough scrubbing, washed and polished the tiled floor, cleaned the windows and while all that lot was drying, picked dead bits off the plants, dumped those past hope and gave the rest a thorough watering – all under the watchful eye of Maisie, who issued orders from the hallway. Jacko had to be kept indoors to stop him weeing on the plant pots, but he observed the whole procedure from his seat on the living-room windowsill.

'These will need repotting.' I told her, although some of the plants were so pot-bound it was difficult to see how they'd ever be persuaded to come out.

She snorted in disdain. Once a plant is in a pot, it's there for life as far as she's concerned. 'Well, you'll have to do it, then,' she informed me grumpily. 'And get the compost.'

I nodded. 'I'll get some grit as well.'

'Be careful with Frank!' she called out as I began to lift the pots back into their places on the shelves.

Frank is a green cactus, with a squashy-looking skin devoid of prickles, which divides itself into four stubby 'toes' at the top. Maisie and I have named him Frank because we decided that, if Frankenstein ever took off one of his big boots, this is what his foot would look like. Not all of Maisie's plants have names – Mrs Tiggywinkle is a ball of prickles; Margaret, the house-leek, is named after the friend who gave it to her and Grandmama is the spider-plant who has given birth to generations of babies. Each year I pot the babies, so that Maisie can give the new plants to the church to sell at their jumble sale. No one wants them really – spider-plants are as out of fashion as macrame pot-hangers, but it keeps her happy.

Porch completed, I took Jacko for a walk around the lanes which border the churchyard, letting him sniff for messages among the fresh green weeds and bark through the railings at jackdaws strutting among the tombstones. When he's busy and happy, he's as nice as any other dog; providing we don't run into anyone else with four legs, then he swells into a bristling balloon of barking outrage. But I managed to drag him around the shops without him sinking his fangs into anyone and got back to Brook Cottage, avoiding a nasty incident with a cat who was minding its own business sleeping on the bonnet of a car.

After I'd put her shopping away, I left Maisie watching a programme about internet romance fraud on the television and drove off for two hours of delight doing Simon the accountant's ironing. I switched on the same programme on his TV. It was fascinating.

I didn't make it to the shop until late in the afternoon. Sophie was busy at her desk, painting. Pat was back in the shop, recovered from the worst of her cold, although the cuff of her cardigan bulged with stowed tissues. When I walked in, they were deep in conversation about a customer who had just left.

'Why have people got to be so rude?' Sophie was complaining.

'What's up?' I asked.

'There was a woman in here just now who got my

back up,' she said, obviously cross. 'She stood over me for ages, watching me paint.'

Sophie doesn't like people watching her as she works, but she puts up with it as she's learnt it's often a necessary part of the sales process. It's just that some people hang around too long, stand too close, or ask too many questions while she's trying to concentrate. I sensed, from the exasperation in her voice, that this time there was more to it than that.

'She goes on about how beautiful the picture is, and then she says, "Fancy you being able to paint as well as that, with you being left-handed." I mean, honestly! Why are people so rude?'

'My grandma was left-handed,' Pat put in lugubriously. 'At school they tied her hand behind her back.'

'Well, there you are!' Sophie went on, her dark eyes flashing in indignation. 'You'd think things might have moved on, wouldn't you? But Seth says that there isn't a culture in the world that doesn't discriminate against left-handed people.' Seth, Sophie's boyfriend, was studying for a master's degree in cultural and religious beliefs, or something like that. Pat rolled her eyes at me. Since she had started going out with him, Sophie's conversation was peppered with a lot of *Seth says*. 'I just don't understand why people think it's acceptable to be so rude.'

I laughed. 'You want to try being a red-head.' My schooldays had been full of taunts of *ginger* and *carrots* and I'm still amazed at how many adults think saying this kind of thing is hilarious or clever.

'You know, lots of people around the world think red hair is a sign of evil,' Sophie told us enthusiastically. 'Seth says . . .'

'Oh, for goodness' sake, Sophie!' Pat cut in, 'do shut up about what Seth says!'

Sophie blinked, momentarily at a loss for words. She looked seriously affronted, her cheeks turning pink with indignation. 'Well, if you don't want to hear it, I'll shut up!'

'It's not that what Seth has to say isn't interesting,' I put in hastily,' it's just those two words *Seth says* . . . well, you say them an awful lot, Soph.'

'That's right,' Pat nodded, looking a bit uncomfortable. 'That's what I meant.'

'I see.' Sophie rinsed her brush with more vigour than it needed and turned her attention to her work, folding her lips as if wild horses wouldn't drag another word from her.

'Aw, come on, Soph! I want to hear about my evil red hair.'

'No. I feel stupid now.'

'Please!'

She flicked a dark glance at me. 'You're sure? I mean, I don't want to bore you at all.'

'I'm sure.'

'Well, Seth . . . well, *apparently,* in ancient Egypt they used to have this ceremony once a year where a red-haired woman would be burnt alive.' She paused frowning. 'Or was it buried alive?'

'I don't think I fancy it either way.' I'd also have been in trouble in the Middle Ages, where having red hair would have been enough to get me arraigned for witchcraft. I don't suppose living with a one-eyed black cat would have helped much either.

'Plain Jane,' Pat sighed from her corner. We both turned to look at her.

She was knitting, her long, bony hands never stopping in their movement as she talked. 'That's what they used to say at school,' she went on. 'It just meant you were ordinary looking. But they don't say that these days, do they? Plain. I mean, no one has to be plain anymore 'cos of all this mascara and stuff.'

I realised in a moment of sadness that *plain* must be what they had called her, which is why she'd mentioned it. It was true, some of the fairies had been missing at her christening. She was a thin, flat-chested woman with lank hair, pale eyes and a nose whose end was always red with cold.

'Mousey, that was the other thing,' she recalled placidly, 'that's what they used to say about your hair. If it wasn't dark or fair, or red, it was mousey. It just meant brown. 'Course, no one needs to be mousey any more either, do they?'

'Don't you ever wear make-up, Pat?' Sophie asked.

'Me? No.' She laughed. 'I tried it once. Looked like something out of a Punch and Judy show, I did.' She laughed. 'I remember dressing up to go out to a dance with Sue, and my dad saying to me, "You'll never catch a fella. Who's gonna want to get into bed with great big feet like that?"'

I began to wonder if the 1960s had ever actually happened in Pat's family. 'What did you say?'

'Nothin', he was my dad.' She shrugged. 'Back in them days, a man could say anything he liked to a woman. I remember my grandma telling me how in the war she went to work in a factory in Bristol where they made aeroplanes. She had to work off plans and blueprints, and the bloke in charge asked her if she thought she'd be able to understand 'em, and she said, "If I can work my way round a dress-making pattern, I reckon I can handle one of them." And he said, "My good woman, I think you'll find this kind of work requires a cleverer brain than that." And she said, "Right. I'll bring you in a knitting pattern tomorrow, see how you get on with it."'

I laughed. I noticed a copy of *The Dartmoor Gazette* lying on the counter, unopened and wondered if there would be anything in it about the murder of Colin Smethurst. I picked it up while Pat and Sophie carried on nattering.

It was on the inside of the front page, quite a short article with a photo of Colin in his carer's uniform, reporting that his death was being treated as murder and police were investigating. There was a tribute from Mrs MacDonald saying what a considerate and compassionate carer he was. There was very little else, except for a plea from police to anyone with information to come forward.

As I hadn't found the body for once and wasn't

involved in the investigation, there was no mention of my name. But if I thought that meant that no one would connect the article with me, I was sadly mistaken. Ricky arrived a few minutes after I'd finished reading it and stood glaring at me, fulminating wrath in his eye. He gave Sophie and Pat the briefest of greetings.

'A word, Princess,' he said to me, jerking his head in the direction of the back room, and I got up and followed him there.

'What's going on?' he demanded, keeping his voice low in case of listening ears.

'What do you mean?' I tried to sound innocent.

'I mean, you ask us to go to Moorland View and snoop about after this Colin Smethurst bloke because Elizabeth was unhappy about him. We send Freddy, and a few days later this same Smethurst bloke gets murdered, presumably by this geezer in the garden. Freddy's at home having hysterics. What's going on?'

'I don't know. Except that Elizabeth must have been right to have had her suspicions about him. He was obviously mixed up in something nasty.'

Ricky's light-coloured eyes narrowed. 'And why was she suspicious of him? That's what I want to know.'

'I couldn't say. You'll have to ask her.'

'Don't take me for a fool, Princess, you know more than you're letting on.'

'Alright, I do,' I sighed. 'But I'm sworn to secrecy, Ricky. I'm sorry. I really can't say more. And the police are on the case now, so there's no need for anyone else to involve themselves any further.' He grunted in assent, but I could tell he wasn't satisfied. 'You can tell Freddy to calm down,' I added, trying to lighten the mood. 'Anyway, he's got his own gunman to worry about.'

'Gunman?' Ricky repeated. 'This Smethurst character was shot, was he? It doesn't say so in the paper.'

Oh, hell's teeth! Me and my big mouth. 'Look, I got the low-down from Dean but for God's sake . . .'

'Keep it under my hat, I know. It looks as if Freddy got away with his escape anyway.' He picked up a wooden snuffbox from a table, flipping open the lid and sniffing at the inside. 'At least, we haven't had any gunmen in our garden, not as far as we know.'

'So, what about this theatre trip?' I asked, grabbing a chance to change the subject. 'Have we decided how we're getting to London?'

'We're going to go up in the Saab, share the driving.' He looked up and grinned, snapping the snuff-box shut. 'That way we can stop whenever I need to.' He chuckled. 'Every service station along the way.'

'And how are things in that department?' I asked. He might laugh about the condition of his bladder but Morris had told me that he was often in pain.

He pulled a face. 'Okay.'

'Morris is really concerned,' I told him.

'No point in worrying, is there?' he snapped. '*Maurice* is a silly old fool.'

'Only because he loves you.'

'Well, like I said,' Ricky responded, flipping the snuffbox open again, 'he's a silly old fool.'

'I love you too.'

He grinned. 'Don't worry, Princess. I'll be alright.'

I stepped forward and gave him a hug. 'You'd better be.'

'I promise,' he whispered, ruffling my hair.

'Good.' I cleared my throat. 'Now, are you going to buy that snuffbox, sir? 'Cos if you're not, will you kindly stop fiddling with the merchandise.'

Whatever I'd said to Ricky, I was anxious about Elizabeth. The police knew nothing about Colin's attempt to blackmail her, or the fact that he'd been threatened by one of the Smith and Jones duo and there was still the question of the car parked outside Daison Cottages last night. Was the driver really watching Olly's house?

I decided to drive up there as soon as I'd shut the shop. Ricky didn't buy the snuffbox, but he did fall for a propelling pencil in a shagreen case, something for which he probably had no use at all, but which appealed to him aesthetically.

His was my only sale in the shop that day.

As I arrived at Daison Cottages my stomach gave a sickening lurch. A black Audi was parked across the road, low and sleek, the same vehicle I had seen last night, I was sure of it. And the driver was standing outside of Olly's door.

He was dark and sleek like the car: the motorbike rider, Colin's visitor, perhaps his killer. He was staring up at the house and hadn't noticed my arrival. I put the van into reverse and rolled back around the corner, out of sight, then switched off the engine and quietly got out, creeping forward under the shelter of a hedge until I was standing within watching distance. I was in time to see April Hardiman lean out of her upstairs window in the house next door. 'Can I help you?' she demanded, looking down at the stranger.

'I'm here to see Mrs Hunter,' he told her pleasantly. 'She doesn't seem to be at home.'

'Hunter?' April repeated. 'There's no one called Hunter living there.'

The man at the doorstep took a moment to digest this information. 'Are you sure?'

'Of course, I am.'

He jerked a thumb at the door. 'This is number four, isn't it?'

'Yes,' she confirmed with a nod. 'But there's no one called Hunter living there. Or in any of these cottages,' she added before he could ask. 'If I were you, I'd be off.'

'Beg pardon?'

'There's no reason for you to be hanging around here. I saw your car here last night, parked for a good twenty minutes. My neighbour called the police.'

He held up defensive palms. 'Now, there was no need for that. I must have been given the wrong information. Know what I mean?'

'You must have been,' she agreed. 'But if I see you creeping around the back of my neighbour's house, trying the back door handle like you were doing a few minutes ago, I shall be calling them again.'

'Alright! Alright! I'm going.' He hurried off down the

path. 'Nice to have met you,' he flung back sarcastically as he reached the gate. 'Old bitch,' he muttered as he turned away. She stayed at her window, watching, as he opened the car door, simultaneously sliding a phone from his pocket. Before he slammed the door shut, I heard him speak into his phone 'He lied to us. Gave us the wrong address.' And he drove off.

Good old April, she was as effective as a Rottweiler any day. She might have persuaded Know-what-I-mean that Colin had given his killers the wrong address, for the time being. But it was unlikely that he'd be put off that easily. I had no doubt he'd be back. In the meantime, I decided as I hurried to Van Blanc and slid behind the wheel, let's see where he goes next.

CHAPTER TWELVE

I followed him to Owlacombe Cross and up the road to Sigford, passing Birchanger Cross and the end of the lane leading to Colin's house, towards the village of Ilsington, retracing in reverse the route we had taken from Bovey Tracey. It was easy following him along these narrow, winding lanes. I could afford to hang back a little, out of sight, knowing he wouldn't be able to drive fast and get away from me. If we ended up on the A38 and he opened up his throttle, I might have difficulty keeping up. I memorised his number plate, just in case I lost him.

But he wasn't heading for Bovey Tracey this time. Before we reached the town, we turned off on to the road to Moretonhampstead. The river Bovey flows through this valley, and the countryside around is thickly wooded in parts. Here, at the very eastern edge of Dartmoor, the trees hide outcrops of rock as grand and impressive as the famous tors which dominate the open moorland. But they are unknown to many of the moor's walkers and climbers. They are secret, hidden among forest, chunks of granite green with moss and ivy; or they are forbidden to visitors, set on private land. Copplestone Rock is one of these, and Shuttamor Crags and Bowden Tor.

Just past the village of Lustleigh, the black Audi turned off the road and headed down a track. Despite my many journeys up and down this road, it was a turning I'd never noticed before. I pulled in and dug a map from the glove compartment. After some refolding, I found the track on the map. As I suspected, it was a dead end. In my experience, you have to be very careful with dead ends. They may lead you to places you can't get out of. A cluster of buildings was drawn on the map, marked as Raven's Tor Manor. I looked up. There was no sign at the corner of the lane pointing the way, which might mean that whoever lived there didn't welcome visitors.

The sun was already sinking behind the trees on the horizon, it would be dark soon. I checked my watch. If I drove down the track now and encountered the driver of the Audi, I could always play the helpless female and say I was lost. After all, he'd never laid eyes on me. Worth a shot, I decided.

I turned down the track, driving slowly, lights dipped. But before I'd gone more than a few yards I met a vehicle coming the other way, a high-sided, white lorry, its wing-mirrors brushing the hedgerow on either side. There was clearly no room to pass, so I reversed down the lane to the junction and backed carefully around on to the main road to let it out. As it rolled past me, I saw the legend *Devon Garden Services* painted on the side. If I expected a courteous wave or flash of the lights for obligingly getting out of its way, I was to be disappointed. The driver just stared.

I tried the turning a second time, hoping I wasn't going to encounter any more traffic. The lane was not as rutted as I'd suspected it might be, and after a few yards I was surprised to find my wheels rolling over smooth tarmac, as if it had recently been resurfaced. The hedges had been cut back too, and a five-bar gate that opened up a view on my right was made of steel too shiny to have been there very long. The barn behind it had been there much longer, so long that it was almost falling down, bare rafters visible through the red tiles of its roof, a shaggy growth of ivy clinging to one wall, infiltrating tendrils prising the old wooden boards apart. An interesting feature was the black Audi parked outside. I braked and switched off my lights.

I couldn't see the door of the barn, which must have been at right angles to the road, but a few moments later a green tractor chugged out from inside. It was a real rattle-trap, an old fore-loader with a rusty bucket raised up in front and it was only driven a few yards on to a patch of hard standing before it shuddered to a stop. The Audi driver was behind the wheel. Funny, he didn't strike me as the farming type. Then he climbed down and disappeared inside the barn again. It was an odd thing for him to do, I thought, with night coming on, to move a tractor out of a building, just a few yards, then leave it there. What was the point? Unless he needed room in the barn for something else.

He didn't come out again. I checked my watch after ten minutes. What could he be doing in a ramshackle old barn in the middle of nowhere?

The tap on my side window made me jump. A figure was peering in at me, his face half hidden by a beard and shadowed by a fisherman's hat. He didn't look like a fisherman to me, largely because of the shotgun slung over one shoulder, more like a gamekeeper or a poacher.

'What are you doing here?' he asked gruffly.

I wound the window down. 'I think I'm lost,' I told him, holding up the map. 'Is Barton House along here?'

'It's a mile or so along the main road,' he told me, jerking his head in its direction. 'You shouldn't be here, you're on private land.'

'I'm dreadfully sorry,' I apologised. 'Back that way, you say?'

'That's right,' he nodded solemnly. 'You can't miss it.'

'Thank you so much,' I babbled, putting the van into gear and executing a not very tidy turn on the muddy verge, while the man stood solidly blocking the road that led to the manor and watched me. I gave him a silly little wave and retreated the way I had come.

'Well, that was interesting,' I said to no one in particular.

I speculated about Raven's Tor Manor on the way home. Raven's Tor was quite close by, an impressive clump of granite that overlooked the river Bovey. But it lay below the ridgeline of Lustleigh Cleave and could not have been visible to the manor's residents. But then, you've got to name a house after something, I suppose.

Although it was dark, it was still quite early in the evening, and as I was so close to the village of Lustleigh, I decided I'd pay a visit to my friend Margaret, or Lady Margaret Westershall, to give her proper title; or Mags-Bags as Ricky calls her. She lives in the centre of the village, in a house overlooking the cricket ground and knows about most of what's going on locally. Often a useful source of information, she might know something about Raven's Tor Manor.

I walked up the winding path from her garden gate and dogs started barking inside the house. As I rang the doorbell, I could hear them snuffling behind the door. Lady Margaret must be in. Since her bulldog Florence was kidnapped and held to ransom last year, she never leaves either of them behind. If she's going out, she takes them both with her. A light went on inside.

'Quiet, you two!' an imperious voice commanded. 'Wesley, get out from under my feet.'

She swung open the door, an imposing matron in a twinset and tweed skirt, reading glasses on a chain hooked up onto her nose. 'Juno! What a pleasant surprise,' she beamed, as Wesley and Florence snorted excitedly around my ankles.

'I was just passing,' I lied.

She stepped back to let me in. 'I hope you've come to take away some of those boxes in the loft.'

'While I'm here.' The truth was, I'd forgotten all about them. The boxes in Margaret's loft were a source of embarrassment, to me at least. They were full of her dead mother-in-law's porcelain collection and had been languishing up in the attic for years. Margaret had no interest in them and insisted on making me a present of them for the shop. I'd taken a few boxes away with me last year and they turned out to contain some very collectable pieces of Della Robbia pottery which had made an embarrassing amount of money at auction. Margaret had refused to take any part of it. 'I don't want the damn stuff,' she'd told me. 'You're doing me a favour by carting the boxes away. I'm certainly not clambering up that loft ladder to get them down.'

'I was just settling down for the evening with Charles Dickens and a glass of gin,' she explained. 'Would you like to join me, in the gin if not the Dickens?'

'Just a small one. I'm driving.' I let her pour and settle into her chair again, Florence and Wesley lying down next to her slippers. Her idea of a small gin, I noticed, was a lot more generous than mine.

'Well, it's lovely to see you, my dear. To what do I owe the pleasure? I don't suppose you've come all this way to see an old fossil like me.'

'No,' I admitted, 'but as I was in the area, I thought I'd pop in. I took a wrong turning off the Moretonhampstead road and found I was on private land. I got warned off by a man with a shotgun.'

'Took a wrong turning, did you?' Her voice was loaded with scepticism.

I decided to ignore it. 'It's a place called Raven's Tor Manor.'

'Oh, that old place.'

'Do you know who lives there?'

She pulled down the corners of her mouth and shook her head. 'I'm afraid not, my dear. It's been empty for years. Falling down. It's a disgrace, letting an ancient place like that go to rack and ruin. Last I heard it had been bought at auction, by someone from London, I believe. Rumour has it, it might be some celebrity or other – not that I would know who they were – but whoever they are, they're keeping themselves to themselves.'

That was as much as Lady Margaret knew, and after finishing my gin, I climbed the ladder into the cobwebby confines of her loft and dragged another two boxes down into the light of the landing.

'No idea what's in 'em,' she told me frankly, as we opened the cardboard flaps and peered at intriguing newspaper-wrapped objects. I was bursting with unseemly curiosity but resisted the urge to tear the paper off there and then. 'You're welcome to them whatever they are,' she insisted. 'Many more boxes up there, are there?'

'Quite a few,' I admitted. 'But I'll just take these two for now.' I'd parked the van by the village green and they were as much weight as I was prepared to lug in one journey. So, after refusing a second glass of gin, I made my way carefully back to the parking place, staggering slightly with the heavy boxes. I didn't want to trip over my own feet and smash whatever was inside them.

Safely back in the flat, I stoically refused to give in

to temptation, and before I opened the boxes, opened the laptop and Googled Raven's Tor Manor. But first, I'd phoned Elizabeth to tell her about the visitor who'd called while she'd been out.

She already knew about him. 'April told me.' There was a smile in her voice. 'It sounds as if she did a good job of seeing him off.'

'She did. I think she convinced him that he'd been misinformed.'

'So, a reprieve, for the time being.' She sighed. 'But I don't suppose he's going to give up that easily.'

'He might go back to Moorland View, try again with another member of staff,' I suggested.

'With his picture hanging in reception?'

'Or send someone else,' I said. 'I think you ought to stop visiting Joan for the time being.'

'Sadly, I think you're right.'

'I could visit if you like, just to check up on her.'

'That's kind of you, Juno, but there really isn't much point. She won't know who you are, or understand that you've come from me.'

'Very well, then.' I said goodnight. I didn't tell her that I had followed her visitor to Raven's Tor Manor. There were some things she didn't need to know.

Sadly, I didn't learn much more from my laptop than Margaret had been able to tell me. Raven's Tor Manor had been built in the seventeenth century by local gentry and owned by the same family for two hundred years, when the vagaries of fortune forced them to sell it. The original building burnt down some time later and remained an empty shell until it was rebuilt by a Victorian industrialist, who didn't live to complete his work, and once again it lay in a semi-derelict state, until it was bought quite recently by a private buyer, who was currently in the process of renovating it. More than that, I could not discover. What I needed, I decided, was a proper look. But that would have to wait until another day. Right now, I decided, rubbing my hands, it was time to unwrap some of that newspaper.

CHAPTER THIRTEEN

Saturday rolled round again, which meant another day minding the shop. I usually took a turn on Saturday, because I had no dogs to walk and no clients to see to, although I had looked in on Maisie on my way, just to make sure she was alright. She didn't know what day it was and wasn't too pleased when I told her I was just popping by and didn't have time to stop to clean her grill-pan. That greasy conglomeration of carbonised bacon shrapnel and baked-on fat was going to have to wait until my next visit. Meantime, I left it in a bucket to soak.

Saturday was Sophie's day off, but Pat came in to change the display in her half of the window and placed a row of slightly crazed looking hand-knitted Easter bunnies along the window-sill. Each one had buck teeth and floppy ears, wore a coloured waistcoat and carried a little basket of chocolate eggs. It was weeks until Easter. But Pat, like any good salesperson, was getting her stock in well ahead of the event.

I used the day to dust and wax-polish the furniture in

the back room, rub up the brass and silver and wash the glass. Then came the time to set out my new treasures. Most of the items I had unpacked from Margaret's loft I'd left at home because I needed to do some research on them. There were some delicate Chinese tea bowls and a pair of Staffordshire flat-backs, a shepherd and shepherdess to decorate either end of a mantlepiece. I didn't have a clue as to their current value. But I had brought in some Homemaker design plates from the 1950s, and two small Moorcroft dishes that I felt I could price with reasonable confidence.

I was just in the process of labelling them when I heard the shop bell jangle, followed by a loud 'Yoo-hoo!' from within the shop. That deep foghorn voice could only belong to Margaret.

'I'm back here!' I called to her.

She came in, accompanied by Florence and Wesley and sat herself down a trifle breathlessly in a deep-buttoned leather armchair. 'I had to park miles away,' she complained. 'Bloody roadworks!'

'They're replacing gas pipes,' I told her, although the workmen didn't seem to have progressed very far. They'd just moved the hole further along the road.

She tossed back the flap of the tweed cape she was wearing. It was pinned with a Celtic brooch set with semi-precious stones, I noticed. Art Nouveau, probably.

'Coffee?' I offered.

'No thank you, dear. I'm meeting someone in Taylors shortly. But after our conversation last night about that Raven's Tor Manor place, I remembered old Ben Walker.

He owns the adjacent land. And he's had trouble with his new neighbour.'

'What kind of trouble?'

'Ben has a right of way across a corner of their land, so that he can move his livestock from one field to another. I don't know if the right exists legally, it might just be a gentlemen's agreement, but it's been going on for generations. Anyway, the new owner won't have it, has been trying to block off the access.'

'Has he spoken to them about it?'

She shook her head. 'Never laid eyes on them. There's some sort of caretaker type that looks after the place who tries to chase Ben and his cattle off the land whenever he catches them. Waves a shotgun around, apparently.'

'That sounds like the character I met.'

'That's what I thought. Anyway, I gave old Ben a call this morning, to see how things were, and he told me that there's been a lot of digging going on.'

'Digging?'

'A couple of months back apparently. They had a digger in, down by an old barn. Enormous trench, too big to be anything to do with drains or whatnot. Ben wondered if they were creating a lake, although he says it's a strange place to put it. But the odd thing was, the next time he looks, the hole's been filled in again. No sign of it. So, what was all that about?' She blinked at me, as if she expected me to come up with an answer.

'No idea,' I said. 'Perhaps they were burying something.'

'Ben thinks they're up to no good.' She stood up, hauling on the dogs' leads so that they got dragged to their feet with her. 'So, whatever you're up to, my dear, the next time you decide to take a wrong turning, be careful!' She glanced at her wristwatch, a chunky gold one with a wide leather strap. 'Right. Time to go and see the bishop. Don't get up, I can see myself out.'

'Bye!' I called out after her. I didn't have a chance to argue with her about her accepting some money for the loot in her loft. It was an argument we'd had before. She wouldn't accept a penny for herself, or even have any of the profits for her charity, this in spite of the fact that she devoted much of her time to raising money to fight motor neurone disease, the illness that had so cruelly taken her husband. I get around it; I just donate to them anonymously.

I was rewarded for all my waxing and polishing later in the day when I sold an oak chair with a rush seat and a bamboo plant table, together with the decorative chamber-pot I'd placed on top of it. Later on, a customer bought an embroidered linen tablecloth with six matching napkins, and I sold the two Moorcroft dishes, so all in all, it wasn't a bad day. I couldn't wait to get back home though, and work out my plan for Sunday.

Bill and I pored over the map together. I spread it out on the kitchen table, much to his delight, and he lay down on top of it to give himself a wash. I let him carry on with his ablutions whilst I ate my supper: a shop-bought risotto, not as good as anything from Sunflowers, but

I picked him up and dumped him on a chair once I'd demolished a yogurt for dessert.

Raven's Tor Manor might be on private land according to the man in the fishing hat, who must surely be the same shotgun waver that Ben Walker had encountered, but it was not marked as 'private' on my map. I reckoned I could avoid the track on which I'd been challenged the previous evening, if I parked in Lustleigh Cleave and hiked across country from Sharpitor. Then I could approach the manor from the back, and get a good view of the place and its surrounding landscape. I packed up my backpack in readiness, putting in the map, compass and field-glasses. Bill tried to nose his way inside. 'You can't come,' I told him, pulling him back out. 'Remember, curiosity kills cats.'

He blinked his single emerald eye in indignation. And I tried to ignore the voice in my head that pointed out that curiosity might kill me as well.

Sharpitor, near Bovey, on the eastern edge of Dartmoor, is not to be confused with its namesake, Sharpitor, near Meavy, at the western edge. Nor is Sharpitor the only hilltop crag to share its name with others. There are two Hollow Tors, two Hunter's Tors and no fewer than four Sharp Tors, just to make things confusing. Although Bovey's Sharpitor is the bigger and grander of the two, it's far less well-known. Hidden among woods, almost entirely concealed by foliage in summer, there is no distant view of it, and only the occasional glimpse of pale stone among bare trees of winter. Now, in March, before the fresh green leaves of spring began to sprout and fill the sky, it was more visible than it would be in a month's time, though much of the rock was green with moss and scrambled over by thick ropes of ivy.

I'd visited Sharpitor with my cousin Cordelia long ago. We'd clawed up the boulders to picnic on the top and gaze at the far-reaching views of Lustleigh Cleave. I must have been about twelve at the time, home to stay with her for my long school holiday as I was every year. I didn't venture up there today, but spent a few minutes checking out the dry cave hidden beneath the rocks. A rocking stone, or logan stone, known as The Nutcracker, once balanced on the top of the crag. But this was mysteriously 'dislodged' years ago, and an attempt to put it back in place by the army sadly resulted in it rolling further down the slope and shattering into pieces.

I didn't linger at Sharpitor long, but carried on over the ridge and down the valley. I'd started my journey early, conditioned as I am by walking the Tribe on weekdays to wake before six, even on a Sunday. The sun had been shining when I set off, in a clear blue sky. 'Too bright, too early,' Maisie would have prophesied gloomily, and she wouldn't have been wrong. By the time I crossed the river at an ancient stone bridge, and began to climb on the hill on the other side, ominous clouds were piling up on the horizon, and the air that had felt fresh in the sunshine now seemed chilly.

From the top of the hill, I got a view over fields and

scattered clumps of trees, to the road I'd been driving along the other night; and a glimpse between hedges of the track where I'd turned off before I'd been stopped by Fungus Face in the fishing hat. I could just make out the red-tiled roof of the barn. Screened from the road, surrounded by rough scrub that once must have been parkland, stood a crumbling pile of architecture that could only be Raven's Tor Manor.

I took out my field glasses for a closer look. Its eastern wing seemed to be in ruins, empty lancet windows piercing stone walls with jagged corners, roofless rooms open to the sky. But the main part of the building, which seemed to be intact, was caged in scaffolding, in the process of being renovated, presumably by the current owner. Parked outside on a gravel drive was a Land Rover and a black Audi. So, either Mr Smith or Mr Jones was around the place somewhere. Did the Land Rover belong to Fungus Face, I wondered?

I didn't have to wonder for long. He came out of the front door moments later, still wearing his hat, got into the vehicle and drove off, to be lost from view among the trees almost immediately. He was quickly followed by the driver of the Audi, who made sure he locked the door of the manor after him before he too climbed into his car and sped off down the drive. I was just considering the fact that Raven's Tor Manor was now almost certainly empty, and this would be a good time to poke around, when the sun reappeared from behind a cloud and I caught a sudden glint of metal moving between the hedges. The two cars were travelling along the track towards the old barn. I raised my field glasses. I waited, squinting through the binoculars for a minute or two, but neither vehicle reappeared at the turning on to the main carriageway. They must have stopped. The delights of an empty ruined manor house would have to wait. If those two had stopped at that old barn, I wanted to know what they were up to.

It took me twenty minutes to catch them up, walking at a brisk pace and keeping to the shadow of the trees as much as possible. I emerged on the track, a few yards further down from where I'd stopped at the gate two nights before and peered cautiously through the tangled branches of the hedge. The two vehicles were parked outside of the barn but there was no sign of their drivers. The old tractor was parked where it had been before, just outside.

A loud clanging noise came from inside the barn, like a steel door closing, or a sheet of metal being dropped. Stepping across a ditch full of dead leaves, I grabbed a bare branch in the hedge and hauled myself closer, clinging on, my legs straddling the ditch. There was a wide enough gap here for me to scramble through the hedge. But before I could move, Fungus Face emerged, jumped up into the tractor, started it up and began to back it carefully into the barn.

From inside, I could hear the Audi driver's voice yelling at him to *whoa!* and the chugging of the tractor's engine stopped. A few moments later, both men emerged and pulled the wooden door of the barn shut. It was so old it was practically hanging off its hinges, the bottom corner dragging on the ground as it was moved. It barely fit the doorframe, the wood was so warped and rotten with age, but that didn't seem to bother them. They secured it roughly with a plank that dropped into two wooden brackets and left it, heading to their respective vehicles.

Fungus Face asked the Audi driver where he was off to next.

'Torquay,' he responded, laughing.

Fungus Face grinned. 'You going clubbing?'

'I might see what I can pull. But I'll call in on the old Devon Grange first, make sure there's no loose ends left lying about. Got to keep Mr Shaw happy, know what I mean?'

Fungus Face waved as the Audi turned through the gate and headed off to the main road, and then climbed into the Land Rover. Which way was he going? If he followed the Audi out on to the road, I had no problem, but if he turned back towards the Manor then he would have to pass this way and he'd see me.

It would take too long to scramble through the hedge now. I let go of the branch I was clinging to and dropped down into the ditch, groaning as I sank to my knees in a mulch of dead wet leaves and icy cold water. I took off my rucksack, hugged it to my chest, and crouched as low as I could. A few moments later I glimpsed the Land Rover pass by through the stems of the grassy verge. I stayed where I was until it had disappeared around the bend, and then for another painful minute, feeling the increasing burn in the back of my thighs, until I dared to straighten up.

I hauled myself back up on to the road, grabbing at branches in the hedge, my mud-soaked trousers sticking to me, my socks squelching inside my boots at every step. I wanted to take my boots off and pour out the water, but this was not a safe spot to do it. Fungus Face might decide to drive back this way. I tramped, squishy-sploshy, to the five-bar gate, clambered over it into the field and around to the far side of the barn, where I couldn't be seen from the road, then sat and stripped off my boots and socks. Fortunately, experience has taught me always to carry a spare pair of socks in my rucksack. I wrung out the old ones, put them inside a plastic bag, something else I've learnt always to carry, and drying my feet off as best I could, slipped them into the lovely dry socks. My walking boots are good ones, designed to repel water, and lace up fairly tightly, so other than what my socks had sucked up like the wicks of a lamp, there wasn't much water in them, and they didn't feel too unpleasant when I put them back on. Unfortunately, I couldn't say the same for my mud-soaked trousers, which held my legs in a cold, clammy embrace; but there was nothing I could do about those. Shrugging my rucksack back on, I walked around to the front of the barn and took a look at the door.

The plank which barred it fitted into wooden brackets at either end. It was just a question of lifting it out. But it had taken the combined strength of two men to drop it in, so I didn't rate my chances. I gave it a try, but it was heavy, unwieldy, and frankly, I didn't fancy dropping it on my foot, so I wandered around the side of the building, searching for another way in. The wooden walls were in much the same state as the door, the planks warped by age and weather, shrunken and full of gaps. I peered through one ragged hole into the gloomy interior. I couldn't see much. Beyond the bulk of the tractor there didn't appear to be anything in there at all. I looked around outside and found a stout branch, ripped off a tree in a recent storm, and gave the edge of one of the planks a whack with it. The plank splintered in a satisfying fashion and I pulled the crumbling fragments away. A few whacks later I had created a gap wide enough for me to squeeze my body through, although I had to take my rucksack off again to manage it.

The first thing that struck me, once I had wriggled through the gap and found myself standing inside, was that while the walls of the barn might be rotting and there might be holes in the roof, the floor was a layer of pristine grey concrete, and judging by its smoothness and pale colour, only recently laid. I took a turn around the tractor, studying the walls, but I could find no other door, or anything else that might have made that echoing, clanging sound I'd heard just before the tractor had been backed in. Then I dropped to my knees and peered underneath.

There was a steel trapdoor set in the floor, secured by a complicated-looking lock with a keypad attached. It must have been this door closing that had made the noise

I'd heard. The purpose of the tractor, it seemed, was to cover it up, hide it from the view of anyone who might stray inside. And while the barn itself might look as if it could topple over any minute, whatever was hidden beneath that strong steel trapdoor, was very secure indeed. Something underground, something recently dug out, perhaps. The good thing about a tractor though, is that because of the size of the wheels, there is always room underneath. I lay down on my front and squirmed beneath the tractor to take a closer look at the lock. But without knowing the combination for the keypad, there was no getting into it.

Above my head, the warm engine of the tractor was still ticking. Then came a sudden low buzzing sound, a vibration between my chest and the floor. The shock almost caused me a cardiac arrest, but it was just my phone. Cursing, I drew it from my inside pocket. I looked at the display but didn't recognise the number.

'Hello?' I whispered. There was no one around to hear me, but something about lying on the floor squashed beneath a tractor in a barn I wasn't supposed to be in, inclined me not to talk too loudly.

'This is Torbay Health Trust here,' a voice told me. 'Am I speaking to Juno Browne?'

'You are.'

'We have a Mrs Maisie Biddle here at Torbay Hospital,' the voice went on. 'She was brought in by ambulance this morning, I'm afraid she's had a fall.'

I wriggled myself backwards from under the tractor and sat up, just managing not to bump my head. 'Is she hurt?'

'She's fractured her wrist and possibly broken her hip,' the voice carried on. 'We're waiting to give her further X-rays.'

'But who called the ambulance? Who found her?'

'She was wearing her pendant alarm.'

'Oh, thank God,' I muttered.

'The call centre had some difficulty in understanding what the problem was,' the voice continued, 'because of a barking dog in the background, but they sent an ambulance anyway. Maisie's given us your name. We were hoping you could come in.'

'Yes, of course.' I was already on my feet, heading for the hole I'd made in the barn wall, phone glued to my ear as I wriggled through. It was going to be obvious to Fungus Face that someone must have made that hole, but that was just too bad. I had more important things to think about. 'Has anyone informed her daughter?'

'I'm afraid not. Maisie mentioned she has a daughter up north but she couldn't remember the phone number – or her daughter's married name. She keeps asking for you.'

'I'll be there as soon as I can.' I looked at my watch. It was going to take me an hour to walk back to Lustleigh where I'd parked the van, and another to drive from there to Torquay. 'I'll phone Janet, get her to call you. What ward is Maisie in?'

'She's in AEU2 at the moment, but will be moving to a proper ward once we know her position.'

'Thanks.' I pocketed the phone. I wouldn't be bothering with the convoluted route I'd taken to get to

Raven's Tor Manor. My quickest way back to Lustleigh was to march down the main road. My mind was focused on Maisie. If she had broken her hip, she could be facing days in hospital, followed by weeks of rehab. I didn't look back, didn't take another turn around the barn or the field. And that's probably why I didn't notice a modern junction box near the gatepost, some complicated wiring, or the CCTV camera, hidden in the tree above the gate.

CHAPTER FOURTEEN

It was two and a half hours before I made it through the main entrance at Torbay Hospital. I made good time getting to Lustleigh, but when I got back on to the dual carriageway, rain started lashing down in lumps. I felt like I was inside a washing machine, my windscreen-wipers swishing madly back and forth, barely able to keep up with the deluge. I could hardly see the cars in front through the grey curtain of hissing rain. The poor visibility didn't stop some idiots overtaking at speed and the wheels of heavy lorries in the outside lane sent up waves of spray like breakers breaching a sea-wall. By the time I reached Torquay I felt worn out, as if I'd swum there.

Then came the challenge of finding somewhere to park. Major building work was going on at Torbay Hospital and much of the already inadequate parking space was cordoned off. Competition for what remained was fierce, Sunday afternoon being probably the busiest time for families visiting their sick relatives. After driving around and around the various carparks without spotting a single space, I gave up and drove down the hill to the nearest supermarket. Here, fraudulently posing as a customer, I could park for an hour and a half without getting clamped. I hoped. The rain, which had eased off slightly, began coming down hard again as I trudged back towards the hospital.

It was only when I was standing in the brightly lit reception, asking directions to Maisie's ward, and saw other people staring at me, that I gave any thought to what a mess I looked, rain-sodden hair dripping, clumping across the acre of shiny floor in walking boots, a tide-mark of dried-out, muddy water staining my stiffened jeans, brown as far as my knees. Frankly, I couldn't give a damn. I followed the receptionist's directions to the ward, where a doubtful-looking orderly let me in, and looked around until I found Maisie.

Her tiny, frail body might have been easy to miss, among all the other frail little bodies lying in their beds, had it not been for her ridiculous apricot curls shining out against her pillow. Ninety-seven and not a grey hair on her head. The curls were sparse though, I could see through to her scalp, and the hospital gown left her bony neck bare and vulnerable, like a baby bird before its feathers have grown. She seemed to be sleeping, her mouth open, her face gaunt, cheeks sunken, her eyes moving beneath veined lids. Her left arm was in a sling, the wrist tightly bandaged, a canula taped onto the back of her hand. I leant over and planted a kiss on her forehead, then sat down next to her bed and took the fingers of her good hand gently in my own. She half-opened her eyes and stared at me, taking a few moments to register my presence. 'You look a right mess,' she told me, her voice a croaky whisper.

I smiled. 'So do you. I was under a tractor when the hospital called, what's your excuse?'

She chuckled weakly. 'I fell over the dog. Put my hand out to save myself.'

Poor old Jacko, he was getting the blame again.

'What about your hip?' I asked.

'Dunno.' She frowned. 'It doesn't feel broken.'

'That's good, then. I phoned Our Janet. She's driving down. She'll be here by tomorrow night.'

'What's she coming for?' Maisie tutted. 'She doesn't need to come.'

I ignored this. 'I'll pop back to Ashburton and bring you in some things later,' I promised. 'Your nightie and slippers and stuff.'

'Don't bother. I'm not staying.'

'You might be in here for a few days, Maisie, till they get you sorted out.'

'I'm going home tomorrow.' Her bony fingers squeezed mine. 'You'll come and fetch me, won't you?' She beckoned me close so she could whisper. 'And make sure you bring my teeth.'

'I will,' I promised. 'But we'll have to see what the doctors say about when you can come home.'

'But what about Jacko?'

'Don't worry, I'll take care of him.' Though what the hell I was going to do with him, I didn't know. I certainly couldn't take him back to the flat with me. Bill would have a fit; not to mention Kate and Adam.

'Thanks Juno.'

'You just lie here and rest, have a nice nap.'

She gave a docile nod and closed her eyes.

As I walked away from her bed she called after me.

'What the hell were you doing under a tractor?'

I went to talk to the nurse on the desk. It turned out that Maisie had not broken her hip. 'But her wrist will need pinning and that means an operation,' the nurse explained. 'The problem is at her age there's always a risk with a general anaesthetic. We'll need the consent of her next of kin before we can operate.'

'Her daughter can't get here before tomorrow evening.' I knew Janet worked shifts at the weekends. She couldn't just drop everything. She would have to arrange cover.

'Yes, she phoned us after she'd spoken to you. We can keep Maisie comfortable until then.' She looked at her notes. 'She seems very worried about her dog.'

'I'll go back to Maisie's house now and sort him out. And I'll pack her an overnight bag, bring it along later.'

'Could you bring in a list of any medication she's currently taking? She didn't seem too sure herself.'

I promised I would and made my way back down the hill to the supermarket where, mostly to salve my conscience, I nipped in to buy something for supper before I turned for home.

* * *

I was longing for a hot shower and something to eat. But I knew poor old Jacko had been shut in for hours and if I didn't want a nasty mess to clear up, I'd better go to Maisie's first and let him out. He wasn't used to being in the house on his own for long and when I let myself in through the front door, he seemed genuinely pleased to see me, particularly interested in the legs of my jeans. I let him out and while he snuffled his way around the garden, I packed up a bag for Maisie, making sure I included her throat sweets, her reading glasses and some magazines as well as other essentials, like teeth.

I watched Jacko scoff his supper. 'What am I going to do with you?' I asked him. I could leave him here on his own for the evening, but I'd have to come back later and let him out again before bedtime. Then in the morning I'd have to come and do the same early before I walked The Tribe. I couldn't take him with them on their walk because he's too badly behaved. He can't be trusted with other dogs. He'd certainly try to bite one of them, all of them, probably. Janet might be here tomorrow, but she works and wouldn't be able to stay for long, and if Maisie had to stay in hospital for any length of time, we'd have to consider what to do with Jacko long-term.

The doorbell sounded suddenly, sending a snarling Jacko rushing for the front door in full attack mode. I hauled him out of the way and opened the door to find a dumpy lady with short grey hair standing on the doorstep.

'I'm Bev from two doors down,' she told me. 'How's Maisie? I hear they took her off in an ambulance.'

I stepped back to let her come in. By now, Jacko had changed his tune completely, tail wagging in greeting, little whines of excitement in his throat.

'Hello, sweetheart!' Bev bent down to pat him. 'You remember me, don't you? You know where the treats are. Sit then, be a good boy.' To my absolute amazement, Jacko sat up attentively, the very model of good behaviour, while Bev produced a bag of doggie treats from her pocket and gave him one. 'I didn't find out she'd had a fall until I got back from church,' she told me as we went through to the living room, Jacko trotting amiably in front. 'Mr Cooper next door told me. He'd seen the ambulance turn up and came in to see what was going on.'

'Maisie's fractured her wrist and she'll need an operation, so she'll be in hospital for the next few days. I'm going back there now with her overnight bag.'

'I'll pop over to Torquay and visit her tomorrow,' she promised. 'So, if there's anything you forget, just let me know and I can take it in with me. I've got a spare key.'

'Have you?' I was surprised. Maise had never mentioned it. 'Thanks. Janet should be here by tomorrow night.'

Bev smiled and shook her head. 'Poor Janet.'

'I'm just wondering what to do about Jacko.' He was sitting at our feet, his beady brown eyes fixed intently on Bev's treat pocket. 'I suppose he'll be alright here for a few hours.'

'Oh, there's no need for that. I'll take him back with me.'

I wondered if she knew what she was letting herself in for. 'Are you sure?'

'Oh yes. I'll take his nibs here back with me until Janet gets here. It looks to me like you've got enough to do.'

'Thanks Bev. I really appreciate it.' I meant it. If I didn't have to worry about Jacko, and she was going to visit Maisie the next afternoon, that meant that once I'd been back with her things, I could leave visiting her again myself until the following evening. I wouldn't have to cancel any clients, something I'd already resigned myself to doing.

We left the cottage together, me toting Maisie's overnight bag, and Bev loaded up with dog food, Jacko's bowl and his basket. She didn't need to take his lead. He trotted along beside her, tail wagging, and was in her front gate before her, waiting for her at her door. He obviously liked her. She made me wonder what I've been doing wrong all this time. After all, I carry dog treats in my pocket too.

I made it home for that shower, and flung my supermarket lasagne in the microwave. It desperately needed a glass of wine to go with it, but I was forced to resist. After all, I still had to drive to Torbay Hospital and back. I'd been so absorbed with what had happened to Maisie, all thoughts of Raven's Tor Manor and what the Audi driver might have been

159

doing there had been driven from my head. It was only later, back home, my mission to Torbay Hospital accomplished, sitting on the sofa with my feet up, feeling too dazed and exhausted to move, that I remembered what I'd been doing under the tractor before I got that phone call.

I'd better ring Elizabeth, I decided, check that there had been no unwelcome visits from the man who'd been in the garden with Colin at Moorland View. After all, if Mr Smith was still in the area, chances are Mr Jones could be too. Or vice-versa. And either one of them could be Colin's murderer.

'Is everything okay?' I asked, as soon as she picked up the phone.

'Yes, fine,' she responded. 'Tom's here with me and Olly. We're just watching a film.'

This wasn't purely information. She was telling me that she couldn't talk just then.

'In that case, I won't disturb you,' I told her. 'We can chat tomorrow.'

'I'll look forward to it.'

I disconnected, not really knowing what I was going to tell her. She didn't know that I'd followed the Audi driver, or the existence of Raven's Tor Manor. Who did it belong to? Surely not Fungus Face. I couldn't see him as the owner of such a stately, if crumbling, pile. Perhaps the enigmatic Mr Shaw, whoever he was, someone who, according to the Audi driver, was expanding his business down here in the south west; someone who everyone seemed anxious to stay on the right side of.

The phone rang suddenly. I hoped it might be Elizabeth phoning back, but it was Ricky. 'Hello, Princess. What have you been up to?'

I told him about my trips back and forth to Torbay Hospital. I didn't mention the rest.

'Poor old Maisie!' he said. 'If she's going to be in hospital more than a day or two, we'll have to pay the old baggage a visit. Anyway, you haven't forgotten we're going to the theatre on Wednesday, have you?'

I had, temporarily. And right now, what with Maisie and Elizabeth's problems, I didn't care too much about Freddy's. But I had already made the necessary arrangements for taking Wednesday off. We were going to have to leave early in the morning to be sure of making the matinee on time, especially if we had to keep stopping to accommodate Ricky's bladder, so I wouldn't have time to walk The Tribe before we went. I'd arranged for Becky, who runs a mobile dog-grooming service, to walk them for me. She'd done it before when I'd been away and was quite happy to do it this time. As luck would have it, I'd seen her Laundromutt van parked in the street a few days ago, and intercepted her on her way to it.

'What is that?' I'd asked, pointing to the creature on the end of the lead.

'It's Benji. Bloody Cockapoo owners,' she moaned, 'they're all the same.'

I laughed, patting the dog's head. 'What do you mean?'

'They all want their dogs to look like teddy bears,

but they let them get in this mess.' She plucked at the dog's matted coat. 'I'm supposed to wave some magic wand over this lot, bring him home all fluffy and silky. And just look at him!' Benji panted beneath his tangled fringe, tail wagging uncertainly. 'It's not your fault though, Benji mate, is it?' she added with a sigh. 'Come on then, let's get to it.'

'Bye, Benji!' I called as she led him inside her van. 'Nice meeting you.'

Becky would need payment for walking the dogs, of course. And I'd had to cancel my Wednesday clients, so all in all, this visit to the theatre was going to see me out of pocket. Still, there was no point in backing out of the trip now, and I had to admit, I was still curious about what was going on with those altered lines of script and the listener in the dress circle. 'No, I haven't forgotten,' I told Ricky.

'Well, wear something decent, eh? I'm not walking into The Davenport Theatre with a scruff-bag.'

'Is that why you phoned me?' I asked indignantly. If only he'd seen me earlier when I'd walked into Torbay hospital.

He cackled with laughter. 'Nah, I'm only winding you up. Just wanted to be sure you hadn't forgotten, that's all. Freddy's working himself up into a right state about going, terrified he's going to run into that bloke with the gun. He's already trying to pretend he's going down with the flu, so by Wednesday he can say he's too ill to travel.'

I had some sympathy with Freddy's reluctance. 'Are

you sure he's not really ill?'

He dismissed this idea with a snort. 'He's not that good an actor, for a start.'

He can't be much good then, I thought to myself as I put the phone down. Even *I* can fake flu.

CHAPTER FIFTEEN

The next day, Monday, was full on, as it always is, with one client after another, and, as I anticipated, I wasn't able to see Maisie in hospital until the evening. Bev had been as good as her word though, and visited her during the afternoon, taking her news of Jacko, and more magazines, so her day hadn't been too boring. And she'd been sleeping plenty. Not that this stopped her complaining.

'They wake you up so early in here,' she moaned. 'And that one over there,' she added in a stage whisper, pointing at the woman lying in the bed opposite, whose face was as pale as her pillow, 'she's staring at me all the time.'

'Well, you are right opposite her,' I pointed out, 'and she hasn't got anyone else to stare at.' The poor woman's neighbour was hidden from her behind blue curtains and there was no one else in the ward.

'I think she's a bit simple,' Maisie hissed, her whisper louder still. I don't know if the lady in question could hear us, but she smiled and nodded when I turned to look at her.

At that moment, Our Janet walked into the ward, looking drained after her long drive, and worried. At the sight of her I felt a great sigh of relief escape my chest, like the rush of air from a balloon. After we'd greeted one another, I stood up to let her have my chair, leaving her to talk to Maisie. As I looked around for another chair, the lady in the bed opposite called to me softly.

'Excuse me, dear.' I went to her side. 'Do you mind sitting here and having a chat for a few minutes? I haven't talked to anyone all day.'

'My pleasure,' I said, sitting on the edge of her bed. She *had* broken her hip, as it turned out, and in the three days since she'd been admitted, no one had visited. She was a widow and lived alone, she told me, in sheltered accommodation. Her son couldn't take time off work to visit until later in the week. I listened to this sad story with only half an ear. The other was cocked in the direction of Maisie and Janet, whose conversation seemed to be growing louder and increasingly acrimonious. It was the same old argument of course, about Maisie's refusal to leave her cottage and move into a care home near Janet and her family.

'Well, if that's all you've got to say for yourself, you can piss off!' Maisie told her rudely.

'Maisie!' I reprimanded her, hurrying back over to her bed. 'Janet's just driven all day to be here with you, don't be so ungrateful.'

Maisie snorted. 'She's only come to sign my death warrant.'

'Mum, that's an awful thing to say,' Our Janet protested. 'You have to have the operation or your arm won't mend.'

'You're hoping I won't come through it.'

'Oh Mum!' Janet's eyes welled up with tears. She was never a match for her mother.

'Maisie, that's enough!' I told her. At the station, the nurse on duty was craning her neck, trying to see what the fuss was about. 'I think it's time Janet and I left. You're obviously getting over-excited.' I nodded a goodbye at the woman in the bed opposite, took Janet firmly by the elbow and steered her out of the ward.

'C'mon,' I said, tucking my arm firmly into Our Janet's. 'I think we both deserve a drink.'

The following day I didn't get a chance to phone Elizabeth. So, after the shop had shut and I'd cashed up the takings, I drove up to Daison Cottages to pay her a visit. She was home alone. Olly was stopping at a friend's house to work on a school project and we had the place to ourselves. This turned out to be just as well because I'd barely parked my backside on a kitchen chair before the doorbell rang and Elizabeth went to see who was at the front door. A visitor had arrived. Two in fact. The first was Detective Constable Dean Collins. Unfortunately, his chunky, friendly form was followed into the kitchen by the smaller figure of his superior officer, possibly the most unpopular member of our local police force, Detective Sergeant Christine (a.k.a. Cruella) deVille. She stopped short at the sight of me and gave me the benefit of her violet-eyed Medusa glare. She doesn't like me and she doesn't bother to hide it. If looks could kill I would have turned to stone long ago. As she and Dean took their seats at the kitchen table, Elizabeth offered them tea or coffee, but Cruella refused for both of them before Dean had a chance to open his mouth.

'Just a few questions, Ms Knollys, regarding the murder of Colin Smethurst. This is not a formal interview' she went on, returning her eyes to me, 'but you might prefer it if your friend didn't remain.'

'I've nothing to hide from Juno,' Elizabeth said levelly.

Cruella's little mouth twisted in a moue of disapproval. 'Your choice.'

I glanced at Dean who was looking as if he'd rather be somewhere else. I smiled at him and he rolled his eyes heavenward.

'Can you explain to us the precise nature of your relationship with Colin Smethurst?' she asked.

Elizabeth was taken aback. 'I don't know what you mean.'

'No?' Cruella raised a black eyebrow. 'Let's just recap on what you told Constable Collins here. When he showed you Mr Smethurst's photograph, you claimed you didn't know him.'

'I didn't recognise him out of uniform, not immediately,' Elizabeth responded carefully. 'Later on, when I saw the photograph taken at Moorland View, I realised who he was.'

'But you claimed you hardly knew him?'

'That's true. I didn't.'

'Yet Mrs MacDonald at Moorland View tells us that shortly before his murder you had been enquiring about him and when she asked if there was a problem, you praised Mr Smethurst for his care of your sister.'

Elizabeth shrugged. 'So, I might have done. But because I'd observed him at work, doesn't mean I knew him personally.'

'So why was he a source of concern?'

'He wasn't, particularly. I just find men wanting to work in care homes a little strange, that's all.'

'That's rather sexist, isn't it?'

She smiled blandly. 'Blame it on my age.'

Cruella paused, considering her next question. 'Why did you not mention to Constable Collins that you are a regular visitor to Moorland View, and that it was your sister you visited?'

'Because,' Elizabeth returned Cruella's violet glare with her own steely one, 'Constable Collins didn't ask me who I was visiting, or how often.'

'You didn't mention that your sister had been targeted by two men who had got into Moorland View under false pretences.'

'Was she targeted?' Elizabeth raised her brows in surprise. 'Two men got into her room, it's true. I assumed they were thieves or conmen, that their choice of my sister was random.'

'I see.'

'That was weeks ago,' Elizabeth went on, 'and I didn't

mention it because, once again, Constable Collins didn't ask me. I'd forgotten the incident. Mrs MacDonald informed the police at the time and I assumed the matter had been dealt with.'

Cruella tapped the point of her pen on the page of her notebook for a few moments, her little mouth working as if she was chewing something sour. 'Mrs MacDonald seems to think your real name is Elizabeth Hunter.'

'That was my married name,' Elizabeth responded, her fingers touching at one of her gold earrings. 'I'm a widow.'

Cruella gave a jerky nod. 'Tell me, has Oliver ever visited Moorland View?'

'Olly?' Elizabeth frowned. 'Why would he?'

'Well, presumably your sister,' she paused to look at her notes, '. . . Joan, isn't it . . . is his aunt too?'

Elizabeth paused, but only for a moment. 'He would find the visit stressful, as I often do. It's upsetting to see her in her present condition. She wouldn't recognise him anyway so I see no point in putting him through such an ordeal.'

'So, outside of Moorland View, you say you have had no contact with Colin Smethurst?'

'Certainly not.'

'And you've no idea why he was carrying your photograph in his wallet on the day he died?'

'None. I was astonished to discover that he did. I didn't even know the photograph had been taken.'

'During our search of Mr Smethurst's home, we also found this.' She flipped another photograph on to the table and slid it towards Elizabeth. It was a formal photograph of a wedding group, taken back in the 1980s judging by the clothes. For a moment I thought the bride was Elizabeth, then realised it must be Joan, a young and happy Joan. Elizabeth was the bridesmaid standing next to her, a slender young figure in a long, blue dress carrying a small bouquet, her blonde hair piled up in ringlets on her head

'That is you in the photograph, isn't it?' Cruella demanded. 'You and your sister.'

'Yes, but how did he . . . ?' Elizabeth had turned pale. 'Colin Smethurst must have stolen this from my sister's wedding album.' She looked up angrily. 'He must have been rifling through her possessions.'

'And you've no idea why he should have stolen another photograph with you in it?'

'No, I have not,' she rapped back crossly. 'What else of my sister's has he taken?'

'Nothing that we're aware of,' Cruella told her, meeting her gaze. 'But he seemed to be collecting photographs of you.'

'Well, I have no idea why.'

'Are you sure about that?'

'Perfectly certain.'

'I see.' She paused a moment. 'So, you stick by your original statement, that you never knew Colin Smethurst personally?'

'For one thing, I haven't made any statement, not officially, and yes, I stick by the answer I originally gave to Constable Collins. It's the truth.'

Cruella flipped her notebook shut. She clearly wasn't satisfied, but couldn't think of anything else to ask. 'That's all for the moment. If we come across anything else in Mr Smethurst's possessions that we think belongs to you or your sister, we'll be in touch.'

'Thank you.'

'Thank you for your time, Ms Knollys . . . or should I call you Mrs Hunter?'

'I should stick to Knollys,' Elizabeth recommended with a tight smile. 'It keeps things simple.'

Cruella smirked. 'As you wish.' She stood up and Dean rose too, pushing back his chair.

Elizabeth showed them both out and came back into the kitchen, a cry of vexation on her lips. 'What is it about that young woman? She is infuriating!'

'She's smug,' I answered. 'Supercilious.'

'Well, that's part of it, I suppose.' She headed for the living room and came back a moment later carrying a bottle of gin and two glasses. 'I need a drink.'

'I don't suppose you can blame her for wanting to check up on what you told Dean,' I said, watching her pour two generous measures. 'The police often ask the same questions over and over. And you've got to admit, Colin carrying your photo about does look odd. And taking the picture of you as a bridesmaid, that's just creepy.'

She placed a bottle of tonic on the table for me to help myself and then tossed her gin back neat, before pouring herself another.

I laughed. 'Cruella didn't manage to rattle you

though, if that's what she was hoping to do.'

She gave a derisive snort. '"What was the precise nature of your relationship?"' she mimicked Cruella's scratchy voice. 'Was she trying to insinuate that Colin Smethurst and I were having an affair?'

I shrugged. 'They are still looking for a motive.'

'I shot my lover in a rage?' She shook her head in disbelief.

'Stranger things have happened.'

'I thought they were satisfied this was a crime-related killing. One shot in the head and two in the chest hardly resembles a crime of passion.'

'Cruella's just being Cruella.' I took a sip of gin, choosing my next words carefully. 'Do you think Colin might have had a crush on you? Is that why he took that other photograph.'

She shuddered. 'I'd rather not think about it.'

'Dean told me they're still trying to find the identities of Mr Smith and Mr Jones. They are the obvious suspects.' I hesitated. 'Look, you need to know this. They're still around. At least one of them is. Remember that man who was hanging about outside your place and got seen off by April next door? The Audi driver?'

'Yes,' she said guardedly, her glass of gin paused on its way to her lips, her eyes fixed on mine.

'I followed him.'

She thumped her glass down angrily. 'Juno!'

'I followed him to a place called Raven's Tor Manor.'

'Where?'

'Just outside of Lustleigh, on the way to

Moretonhampstead. It's pretty well derelict. But something's going on there, I'm sure of it.'

Her eyes narrowed. 'What kind of something?'

'I don't know,' I admitted. 'But I heard Mr Shaw's name mentioned again. He's definitely the Audi driver's boss and I wouldn't be surprised if the manor belongs to him.'

'Was Shaw the man in the garden with Colin?' she asked. 'The man we think might have shot him?'

'I don't know. I certainly haven't seen him since then. So perhaps that *was* him. But the point is, his friend the Audi driver is still here. I heard him talk about having business in Torquay, so you need to be careful, Elizabeth. He could still be looking for you. He could turn up here again.'

'I'm always careful,' she assured me. 'And you too. You need to be careful. I mean it. I don't want you taking risks for my sake. It's bad enough you following him. Promise me something, Juno.'

'What?'

'That you won't go back to this place again, this Raven's Tor Manor.'

I hesitated. But then Olly burst into the kitchen, breathless from cycling from his friend Marcus's house, and launched straight into telling us about Marcus's dad who had just bought a metal detector. Wouldn't it be a good idea to buy one too, he asked, and I didn't have to perjure myself by promising anything.

CHAPTER SIXTEEN

Stepping through the doors of The Davenport Theatre in London was like stepping inside an egg made by Fabergé. It was a little jewel. From the red plush carpet and gleaming brass handrails of its foyer, to the gilded plasterwork of its three-tiered auditorium, it was a Georgian delight. From my seat in the dress circle, I gazed up into a dome surrounded by painted cherubs blowing trumpets and then down at the velvet ranks of empty seats in the stalls, gradually filling up with audience.

The journey to London had been accomplished in reasonable time, despite one stop for breakfast on the way, and another for petrol, both involving visits to the loo. After paying eye-watering charges to park the Saab in a nearby multi-storey carpark, we arrived at the theatre in time to collect our tickets and enjoy a drink in the tiny, crowded bar; and enough time for another visit to the facilities and a chance to order drinks for the interval.

On the journey, I'd been sitting in the back of the

Saab with Freddy, listening to him bleating about the danger he felt he would be putting himself in by setting foot in the theatre. Ricky ordered him to shut up. He had promised Freddy his own mother wouldn't recognise him and to be honest I think she would have had difficulty. A wig, the addition of a grey moustache and round tinted spectacles had aged him, and a pair of old corduroy trousers, anorak and woollen scarf had given him the geeky look of a trainspotter. No one would have recognised him as dapper actor, Freddy Carstairs. No one would have looked at him twice. Despite all this, he kept his head down during the walk along the corridor that would eventually lead us to our seats, and refused to make eye contact with any of the stewards or programme sellers who greeted us so politely along the way. He tutted whenever Ricky stopped to point at one of the photographs of theatrical greats which lined the walls, which he did on several occasions, declaring loudly 'I was in a show with her once. And him.'

The dress circle was yet to fill up when we went in, the seats mostly empty, but Mr Q7 was already in place, a heavy looking man in a suit and black overcoat. He looked about seventy, his grey hair thinning, thick black-framed spectacles on his nose.

We entered the dress circle from the back. It was steeply raked, the steps down to Row Q, precipitous to say the least. How ladies in their crinolines managed to negotiate them without missing their footing and accidentally tossing themselves over the safety rail into the stalls below, I can't imagine.

Bearing in mind Ricky's warning not to look scruffy, I had dressed very soberly and discreetly, in a calf length brown skirt with knee boots, and a caramel-coloured shirt with a brown velvet jacket.

'Boring!' he had pronounced the moment he'd seen me and had thrown a burnt orange wrap around my shoulders. 'Better,' he nodded approvingly, while Morris rolled his eyes and said it was time to get going.

As arranged in the car, I made a lot of fuss as we went to our seats, squawking loudly about how steep the steps were, and also how beautiful the theatre, and began taking pictures, clicking away on my phone, making sure I got a few good shots of Mr Q7 before I sat down. As I wriggled my way into the seat next to his, he looked up, genuinely appalled. It was clear he wasn't used to having anyone sitting next to him. For a start, he was forced to pick up the Homburg hat he had placed on my seat. He looked as if he might have moved along the row and put distance between us, but by then, Ricky had already hemmed him in by sitting in Q8. I thanked him for moving his hat; he didn't reply, just grunted.

Freddy sat next to me in Q5, his cheeks burning red, and immediately hid his face, pretending to study his programme. As soon as I sat down, I took out my phone again and began shooting off selfies, turning so that I could see Mr Q7 in the frame behind me. There was a tap on my shoulder and I turned.

'I do not wish to appear in any of your photographs, young lady.' His brown eyes were magnified by the lenses in his glasses, like the eyes of an owl, his gaze vaguely malevolent. His voice was low and gruff, containing a twang of the East End and more than a hint of menace.

'Oh, sorry!' I giggled, acting silly.

Mr Q7 meanwhile, turned around to look behind him, as if the situation wasn't to his liking and he expected someone to do something about it. He looked straight at the person sitting in S5. A woman. She hadn't been there when our party had come down the steps and must have slipped in immediately behind us. She was small, a slim, delicate creature a bit older than me, late thirties, maybe even early forties. What I was sure about was that the abundant blonde hair that framed her oval face was a wig. It didn't look right on her, didn't match her olive skin, her dark, almond-shaped eyes. She wasn't a natural blonde. She wore high-heeled leather boots and an emerald-green coat with a fake fur collar. She held my gaze steadily and I realised I'd been staring too long. I looked away. Next to me, Freddy was still gazing intently at his programme. I peered over his shoulder at the cast list. His name was still listed as the actor playing Arnold. I suppose programmes must be printed by the thousand. It was probably too expensive to re-print them just for one cast change. 'Who's playing your part now?' I whispered to him behind my hand. 'Is it still your understudy?'

He shrugged. 'They'll probably make an announcement about it before the start.'

On my right, Mr Q7 was deep into his programme as well, although if he was really the man who came to see the play each week, he must know the cast as well as Freddy did. His attempt to distance himself from his surroundings was interrupted by Morris, who suddenly asked me loudly if I'd like one of his chocolate eclairs.

'Ooh, yes please!' I called back. After all, they were the most expensive sweets I was ever likely to be offered, the theatre confectionary counter charging roughly four times what a bag of the same sweets would have cost in a shop. Ricky took the bag from Morris and nudged Mr Q7 with his elbow. 'Would you mind passing them along to my niece, old chap?' he asked in his best posh actor voice. 'Have one yourself, if you like.'

For a moment Mr Q7's face flushed dark with suppressed fury, then after a moment he said. 'Don't mind if I do. Ta,' and took one. He passed the bag to me. 'Take a few will you, young lady? I don't like rattling bags of sweets being passed back and forth during a performance. It's disrespectful to the actors.'

'Do you come here often?' I asked. It sounded like a cheap chat-up line. 'I mean, do you go to the theatre a lot?' I added hastily. 'Do you see a lot of shows?'

My question took him by surprise. 'I do. I love the theatre,' he told me, with genuine reverence in his voice. 'Now, if you don't mind, miss, I'd like to study my programme.'

I offered the sweets to Freddy. He just shook his head and slumped down further in his seat, so I took two and thanked Mr Q7 politely. He took the bag without looking at me and he passed it back to Ricky, who slid me a sly wink before handing it back to Morris.

Below us the stalls filled up suddenly, a sure sign that the warning bell had rung in the bar; the play was about to start. Not many more people came into the dress circle though, and as the house-lights began to dim, seats Q1 to 4 remained unoccupied. Just before the opening music started a voice announced over the sound system: 'In this performance, the role of Arnold will be played by Jeremy Crowley.'

'Jeremy?' Freddy hissed in my ear. 'He's much too old for the part!'

The curtain was rising. Next to us, Mr Q7 deliberately cleared his throat, which I interpreted as a warning to us to settle down and shut up.

The offending pillar, one of four which supported the tier above us, didn't interfere with anyone's view much except for Mr Q7, and I became so engrossed in the funny, admittedly silly, murder mystery that when the applause finished and the lights came up at the end of the first act, I'd forgotten why we were there.

We trooped off into the bar and found our drinks waiting for us on a tray.

'Anything to report?' Ricky asked. I shook my head. Mr Q7 sat like a graven image all through the first half, barely moving a muscle. Ricky turned to Freddy. 'What do you think about your replacement, then?'

Freddy sneered. 'It's ridiculous, casting a man of his age in that part. He's much too old to be playing Arnold. They must really be scraping the bottom of the barrel.'

'Well, they were getting pretty near the bottom of it when they cast you,' Ricky told him, grinning.

Suddenly a voice like a foghorn cut through the hubbub in the crowded bar.

'Ricky Steiner!' It called out. 'Is that you?' A matriarchal figure with a large nose and an impressive bosom bore down upon him from across the room, her arms stretched out in welcome. 'As I live and breathe! It *is* you!' she declared. 'I haven't seen you since Noah was a boy.'

Freddy turned white in panic and turned his back. 'Oh my God!' he hissed at me. 'That's Lavinia Lamont. I know her! She mustn't see me.'

I tucked my arm in his as Lavinia enveloped Ricky in a scented embrace and steered him out of the bar. 'Come on. We'll go back to our seats.'

As we hurried away, I heard Lavinia demanding to know what Ricky was doing back in London. 'I was in a play with her once,' Freddy confided in a whisper. 'She played my mother. She always plays the most frightful old hags on stage, but actually she's rather sweet.'

Our way ahead was blocked by stewards selling ice creams from a tray. I wouldn't have minded a choc-ice but it would probably have involved my taking out a mortgage on the shop, so I resisted. As we worked our way around the ice cream queue, I caught a glimpse of Mr Q7 standing further down the corridor, deep in conversation with the woman in the green coat from S5. I slid my phone from my bag and took a sneaky photograph. 'You don't recognise them, do you?' I asked Freddy.

'No, of course not. I've never seen either of them before.'

'But if they're who we think they are, they've been coming to see you every Wednesday afternoon. To listen to you anyway. When does the crucial scene come up, the one where you're supposed to alter the lines?'

'It's the first scene after the interval.'

'Not long to wait, then,' I said, as we made it back to our seats. Ricky and Morris stayed locked in conversation with Lavinia Lamont throughout the interval, returning only as the house lights were going down, by which time Mr Q7 was already back in his seat, and a quick look behind me told me that the lady in S5 had also returned to hers. Now we all had to wait, to see whether or not Aunt Drusilla was holidaying in Scarborough this year.

The curtain rose on the brightly-lit stage and Jeremy Crowley, the actor playing Arnold, who from a distance I would have said was no older than Freddy, was trying to tie a bow-tie and making a hash of it. Then the actor playing his friend entered. It was the same actor, Hugh Winterbourne, who had played him when Freddy was acting the part. After a few inconsequential lines during which Arnold succeeded in tying his tie, Hugh asked the fateful question. 'And where is your aunt taking her holiday this year?'

There was a pause as Jeremy seemed to wrestle with himself. As one, the occupants of Row Q leant forward. 'You mean, my aunt . . . Leander?' he managed at last.

Something like a spasm passed across Hugh's face. 'Yes, that's right,' he replied through gritted teeth. 'Aunt Leander. It's usually Scarborough, isn't it?'

'No, no!' Jeremy's voice came out in a squeak. 'This year, it's Branscombe!'

'Branscombe?' Hugh repeated with a sigh like that of a drowning man. 'Are you sure?'

At that moment Mr Q7 turned in his seat and nodded in the direction of the woman sitting behind him in S5. The message had been delivered. A moment later I heard her seat flip up. She was on the move. And I must move too, to find out where she was going. I climbed over Freddy. 'Where are you going?' he hissed.

'To the Ladies,' I hissed back, loudly enough for Mr Q7 to hear. 'I won't be long.'

I hurried up the steps in the dark, trying not to trip. A rectangle of light appeared as the woman in the green coat opened a door into the passageway beyond. It shut a moment later. I followed through the same door and into the passageway's carpeted hush. It was empty, there were no stewards or ice cream sellers about, and no sign of the woman in the green coat. I headed down towards the foyer, thinking I'd catch up with her there, when I heard the soft closing of a door nearby, a whisper of wood against carpet. To my right, a door had a green sign above it, *Fire Exit*. I pulled it open and looked into a bare passageway with plain walls, a steep flight of concrete steps leading down to an outer door at the bottom. The woman in the green coat was standing at the foot of the stairs, her hand on the push bar. She turned and saw me, lingering long enough to give me a dark hostile stare, before shoving the push-bar open, letting in the cold air.

I ran down the stairs after her, through the door and straight out on to the pavement. I blinked, surprised to see it was still daylight outside. The click of high-heels made me turn my head. At the end of a narrow alleyway the woman in green was just getting into a car with its engine running, a car that must have been waiting there for her. I stood helplessly and watched it speed off.

A few minutes later, I crept back into the auditorium, took the nearest empty seat and stayed there until the curtain finally fell at the end of the play. As soon as the applause subsided and the house-lights came up, Mr Q7 followed Ricky and Morris along the row to the far aisle and ascended the stairs to the exit. I pointed him out to a steward hovering near the door. 'That man there in the Homburg, he's a regular visitor, isn't he?'

The steward eyed me askance, as if wondering how I knew. 'He turns up every Wednesday afternoon. He must love the play.'

'You don't know his name, by any chance?'

He shook his head. 'I just call him the Man in the Hat. Tell you one thing though,' he added with a grin, 'he's an angel.'

'If you say so.' He didn't look much like an angel to me.

I caught up with the others in the foyer, just in time to

see the Man in the Hat leaving by the main door. 'Aren't we going to follow him?'

Ricky sniffed. 'Nah. We're going to the pub.'

'Sounds like a good idea to me.' Freddy was twitchy, anxious to leave the foyer, still worried about being recognised by theatre staff.

'We've arranged to meet someone,' Morris added. 'An old friend of mine.'

This was news to me. 'Who?' I asked.

'Someone who knows a thing or two,' was all Morris would say.

We set off down narrow streets that he and Ricky obviously remembered from their misspent youth working in theatreland. I was glad they knew where they were going because I didn't have a clue. Streets full of brightly-lit shops, cafés, and wine bars all looked the same to me. But that's the thing about cities: turn a corner and you're in a different world. Suddenly we were in streets of seedy-looking clubs with darkened windows; we turned another corner and we were out into the bright lights again, pavements crowded with stalls of street food, people rushing by. We passed the entrance to a tube station whose name I didn't recognise, rush hour crowds heading for its brightly lit mouth and I shuddered. I don't like the Underground.

We didn't take the tube, but dived down another narrow street, into a quiet square. Here, away from the crowds, was a place to draw breath. On the corner stood an old pub with smart black paintwork, The Nag's Head picked out in gold above its opaque glass windows, hanging baskets of spring flowers dangling at either end of the sign. Outside the door were two tiny wooden tables with benches for those who liked to drink and watch the world pass by, which is fine if you don't mind the world passing so close that it brushes your knees. The place looked as if it had been recently smartened up by its brewery, gentrified to suit drinkers very different from the ones who used to patronise it back in the days when it was built.

Inside, the dim interior of the pub retained more of its old character with dark wood panelling and shaded wall-lights, and a carpet patterned in red and gold, which was probably responsible for the smell of stale beer. The long, low ceiling was patterned in a mosaic of coloured beermats, the walls hung with yellowed theatrical posters.

We didn't stop at the bar but made our way to a table in the corner. Here sat the individual we were looking for: a hunched old man wearing an overcoat with an astrakhan collar, his balding head freckled with age spots, shaggy dark eyebrows almost concealing his liquid brown eyes. He had the look of a sad walrus, but a smartly dressed one. He was wearing a dark suit beneath his overcoat, and a collar and tie.

'Morris, my old friend,' he said warmly, rising to his feet when he saw us coming towards him. He shook hands with each of us in turn, repeating our names in a soft, croaky voice. Morris introduced him as Monty.

Ricky pointed to the empty pint glass on the table

in front of him. 'What are you drinking, Monty?' he asked.

'That's very civil of you, Ricky,' he responded as we all sat down. 'You're a gentleman.'

'How are you, Monty?' Morris asked. 'Are you keeping well?'

'Not too bad,' he said. 'Peggy's not so good. Memory's playing tricks, you know. And poor old Trevor passed away last week. My brother-in-law,' he explained, turning to look at me.

'I'm sorry to hear that,' Morris said. 'Very sorry.'

Monty shrugged. 'Comes to us all.' He turned to me again. 'We were at school together, you know, me and Morris.' He gestured and I noticed the faint tremor of age in his right hand. 'We learnt our trade together.'

'In the theatre?'

'No, before he got involved in all that nonsense!' he said dismissively. 'Tailoring was our trade, cutting cloth. We learnt it from our dads, who learnt it from theirs. You had to start young in those days. Strictly bespoke, mind.' Monty chuckled. 'Sodom and Gomorrah, that's what his dad thought the theatre was.'

'So, you were a rebel?' I said to Morris. 'Not following in the family footsteps.'

He smiled. 'I've ended up making costumes, so I didn't fall so far from the tree in the end.'

'I used to follow their careers, you know, him and Ricky,' Monty said, looking at Freddy and me. 'Before they retired down into the country.'

'I don't think they've exactly retired,' I said. 'They're very busy.'

He nodded approvingly. 'Better to wear out than rust out, that's what I say.'

Ricky returned from the bar with a tray loaded with drinks and sat down. Monty raised his glass. 'Cheers!' took a sip and settled his pint back on the table. 'Now, what's all this about? You two didn't ask me here to talk about old times, did you? What can I do for you gents?'

Ricky asked me to get out my phone. 'Show Monty those photos you just took.' I passed him a picture of Mr Q7, taken before he realised what I was up to, sitting in his seat and staring straight ahead. 'Do you know who that is?' Ricky asked him.

'Of course I do. That's Lenny, isn't it?' Monty nodded slowly to himself. 'Yeh, that's Lenny.' He studied the picture more closely. 'Sitting in the theatre, isn't he? Wanted to be an actor once, Lenny did, but he didn't get anywhere.' He chuckled to himself. 'Him? Act? He was like a block of wood.'

'One of the stewards called him an angel,' I said.

'He decided to invest money in theatre instead,' Ricky said. 'That makes sense.'

'That's what they mean by "angel" in the theatre,' Morris explained, in case I didn't know. 'It's someone who invests money in shows.'

'Among other things,' Monty added mysteriously.

'Like what?' I asked.

'Just about everything.' Monty leant across the table and lowered his voice. 'You might call him a businessman, an entrepreneur, if you like.'

'But doing what specifically?' I insisted.

He gave the ghost of a smile. 'He's got his fingers in a lot of different pies, our Lenny has. Mind you, he got 'em burnt a while back. Quite a few of the lads working for him got sent down. Long sentences. Very careless with their phones, is what I heard, got themselves tracked or hacked or whatever you call it. Well, they say loose talk costs lives. They couldn't pin anything on Lenny though. Very careful, Lenny is, very old school, set in his ways. He doesn't like all this modern technology stuff.' He frowned a moment, his shaggy eyebrows knitting together. 'Why do you want to know?'

Ricky explained about Lenny sitting in seat Q7 at every Wednesday matinee, and how Freddy, who'd remained silent throughout the conversation and seemed to be trying to blend into the wall behind him, had been paid by an unknown man to alter his lines at specific performances.

'We think that Lenny might have been sitting in the matinee each week to receive some kind of message,' Morris told him.

Monty considered this for a moment. 'Like I said, Lenny's very old school. He doesn't like all this high-tech stuff, doesn't trust it. After what happened with the phones.' He shrugged. 'And if he's put money up for that show, he'd feel entitled to use it for his own purposes. That's Lenny all over.'

I scrolled through more pictures on my phone and

showed him the one that I'd taken in the interval. 'This woman in the green coat that he's talking to was sitting a few rows behind him. Do you know her?' It wasn't a very good picture, most of her face was screened by the blonde wig.

Monty shook his head. 'Can't say I do, but he's got a lot of people working for him. Most of his family are involved in his various businesses. There is his brother for a start, Tony. He's more on the financial side.'

Ricky grinned. 'Cooking the books?'

Monty sniffed. 'Something like that.' He turned to stare at Freddy. 'So, you're the one who's done a runner, right? From this show?'

Freddy looked uncomfortable and cleared his throat. 'Well, yes, if you put it like that.'

He grinned. 'You can't be the one they pulled out of the river, then.'

Freddy's eyes bulged. 'I'm sorry?'

'Last week, police fished some bloke out of the Thames. I saw it on the evening news. Turned out he was some actor that used to be in the same show you just been watching. What's it called?'

'*Murder Weekend*,' he responded faintly.

Monty clicked his fingers. 'That's it. Been missing for weeks. Let me think. What was his name now?'

Freddy had turned white. 'Steven Spendlow?'

Monty was slowly nodding. 'I think you're right. I believe that was the name.' He eyed Freddy speculatively. 'You need to watch it, mate.'

'Why?' He breathed.

'Because you're a loose end, and people like Lenny don't like loose ends.'

'Oh my God!' Freddy breathed in horror. He started to rise from the table. 'I've got to get out of here.'

Ricky's hand descended on his shoulder and pushed him back into his seat.

'Sit down,' he muttered. 'We're not finished yet. So, Lenny's well known to the police?'

'Oh yes. They tried to do him and his brother Tony for money-laundering a year or so back, but they couldn't make it stick.'

'How come you know so much about him, Monty?' I asked.

He smiled and patted my arm. 'He's like a lot of gentlemen in business, my dear. He knows where to come for a good suit. But you know that, Morris,' he added. 'That's why you asked me to come here.'

Morris blushed. 'And we're very grateful for the information, Monty.'

'Anything for an old friend. Just be careful how you use it. He can play rough, can Lenny, and so can his brother.'

'What's Lenny's other name?' Ricky asked.

'Shaw,' Monty told him. 'Lenny Shaw.'

I felt as if I'd momentarily flipped into a different universe. 'Sorry,' I said. 'Did you say *Shaw*?'

'Yes, Shaw.' Monty repeated patiently. 'Lenny Shaw.'

Coincidence! My mind was screaming. This must be a coincidence. Shaw is a common enough name. But in my gut, I knew differently.

Ricky was watching me through narrowed eyes. 'What's up, Princess?'

'Nothing. I was thinking of something else.'

We said our goodbyes to Monty. We had to face the long drive home. It had started to drizzle while we were in the pub, a thin rain that made the cobbles glisten and raised the smell of diesel into the already fuggy air.

We began to trace our steps back to the car park, Freddy babbling all the way about what had happened to Steven Spendlow. 'Do you think he refused to alter some lines too?'

'Well, it looks as if got on the wrong side of someone,' Ricky told him.

'Oh, my God! That man with the gun! If I hadn't managed to get away, I might have ended up in the river too . . . And I've just been sitting two seats away from the man who ordered my execution!' he added dramatically.

'We don't actually *know* that,' I pointed out in an attempt to calm him down. 'Steven Spendlow might have killed himself.'

He shook his head. 'I don't believe that. Well, Jeremy Crowley had better watch out!'

'Do you think he knows about Steven Spendlow?' Morris asked, looking worried. 'Perhaps you ought to warn him.'

Freddy did not pick up on this. 'But you see what I mean about the altered lines?' he prattled on. 'What sort of name for an aunt is *Leander*? It's a man's name, isn't it? Some chap from a Greek myth.'

'He swam the Hellespont so that he could visit his girlfriend,' I told him. 'It didn't end well.'

'It's also a class of frigate,' Ricky put in as we arrived at the entrance to the multi-storey car park, 'or some kind of naval warship.'

'We can't go home yet.' I realised we were about to miss a trick.

'Why not?' Freddy demanded.

'There's someone else we need to talk to, someone who may know more about what's been going on at the theatre than you do.'

Ricky frowned. 'Who do you mean, Princess?'

'The actor who was in the play with Steven Spendlow before Freddy took over his part.'

'You mean Hugh Winterbourne?' Freddy asked, astonished.

'Yes. We have to talk to him. We have to go back to the theatre.'

He made a frightened gobbling noise. 'I'm . . . I'm not going back there.'

I ignored him and looked at my watch. 'There's nearly an hour and a half before the evening performance. Where do you think Hugh will be now?'

'Well, there's a little café he liked to visit between shows, grab a bite to eat, but I don't think —'

Ricky grabbed hold of his arm. 'Just shut up, Freddy and take us there.'

* * *

The Black Tulip was an unassuming little café about five minutes' walk from the Davenport theatre. It had a lace curtain hanging from a brass rail in the lower half of the window, and we had to peer over the top of it to see inside. It looked like a pleasant place, with checked tablecloths, potted palms and chalk boards on the walls announcing the day's specials. Actor Hugh was sitting by himself at a table in a corner, doing the crossword in a newspaper. Although he'd changed into causal clothes and brushed his hair, he looked much as he did on stage, a pleasant looking man in his forties, blonde hair turning grey.

I had to drag Freddy inside, and it was only a shove up the backside from Ricky that finally propelled him over the threshold. We took a table for four by the window and ordered coffee. Then Freddy and I walked over to the corner.

Hugh didn't look up from his crossword until we were standing in front of him. He did a double-take when he saw Freddy and stared at him open-mouthed as we both sat down. Freddy's own mother might not have recognised him, but after staring into his eyes for a moment or two, it was clear that Hugh Winterbourne did. 'Freddy!' he almost shouted. Then looked around him and lowered his voice to a whisper. 'What the hell? Where have you been?'

'Well, um . . .'

'Do you know how much trouble you've caused?' he demanded, 'Just walking out like that?'

'Well . . .' Freddy cleared his throat but Hugh didn't

give him a chance to speak.

'For days we had this fella with a foreign accent hanging around the theatre trying to threaten us all into revealing your whereabouts. Of course, no one knew where you were. You've been declared a Missing Person, for God's sake.'

'I'm sorry, Hugh. I had to make myself scarce. Fast. Jumped into a costume hamper and got transported down to Devon.'

'A costume hamper?' Hug repeated, incredulously. 'Anyway, this thug even went around to your digs and threatened your poor old landlady. She keeps phoning the theatre, trying to find out where you've got to.'

Freddy gaped in horror. 'But that means he found out where I live! Has Ivy told him anything?'

'How do I know?' Hugh gave a weary shake of his head. 'I told you to have nothing to do with that line-altering business. I suppose you've heard that Steven . . . ?' It was only then that he seemed to register my presence. 'Who's this?'

'Juno. I'm a friend of Freddy's,' I said, before he could open his mouth.

I pointed over my shoulder at Ricky and Morris. 'And so are they. We'd like to ask you some questions.'

He raised a defensive palm. 'Look, I'm trying to stay well out of all this.'

'Very sensible,' I agreed. 'But we sat out in the audience this afternoon, and we think we know who's been listening to these altered lines. Jeremy Crowley needs to understand that he could be dealing with some very dangerous people.'

'Jeremy?' Hugh gave a bitter laugh. 'Unfortunately for him, the director was in this afternoon. Jeremy has just had the sack. Lucas is back on for tonight's performance.'

'I think he may have had a lucky escape. But Lucas needs to understand the same thing. Tell me, do you think that Steven Spendlow killed himself?'

'Drowned himself in the Thames?' Hugh shook his head. 'I very much doubt it. Poor Steven. He didn't strike me as the type.'

'But he disappeared.'

'He abandoned the show without so much as a "by your leave", a bit like Freddy here,' he added, flicking a scornful glance in his direction. 'Then, a couple of weeks later, he phoned me. He said he'd got himself into a spot of bother. He asked to meet him, said he'd explain everything. He asked me to bring him some cash. Well, I went to meet him at the appointed place, but he didn't show up. I never saw or heard from him again. Until I learnt last week, he'd turned up in the Thames.'

'And how long had this line-altering been going on before he left the show?'

Hugh stroked his chin as he considered. 'A few weeks. He'd already had one warning about it from the stage manager.'

'Did he ever explain why he was changing the lines?'

'He did when I demanded to know what the hell he was up to. At first, he tried to persuade me he'd just been larking about. But I'd worked with Steven before and always thought he was more professional than that.'

'Did you ever see the man who was offering him money?'

'I didn't share Steven's dressing room. And, as I said, I tried to distance myself from what was going on. It wasn't until Freddy here did a bunk and this thug was wandering about backstage trying to find him, some chap with a foreign accent . . .'

Freddy leant forward, his eyes wide. 'What happened?'

'He came barging into everyone's dressing rooms, hunting for you. The doorman tried to throw him out and when he refused to go, we threatened him with the police. He left then. But he was seen hanging around outside the stage door for several nights afterwards.'

'And it seems that he had already got at Jeremy,' I added. 'Or someone had.'

Hugh frowned. 'And you say you think you know what's going on?'

'Not exactly. We think the altered lines are sending a message to someone in the audience and we might have discovered who. Can you remember any of the lines that Steven altered, any of the places he was told to say instead of Scarborough? Or any of the aunt's names?'

'I remember the first time he did it, because it was such a surprise. He said that Auntie Puffling was going to Watcombe.'

'I had to say that!' Freddy nodded excitedly. 'I had to call her Puffling! And I mentioned Watcombe.' He frowned, trying to remember. 'But were they both at the same time?'

'Maidencombe once,' Hugh went on. 'And I think the name Leander has been used before.'

'So, we know that these various names can be repeated.' I looked at Hugh. 'Will you do something for me?'

'I've told you I don't want to get involved.'

'You don't have to,' I assured him. 'But if you remember any other names, will you phone me?'

He smiled reluctantly. 'Oh, very well.' He opened his newspaper and picked up his pen. 'What's the number?'

I gave it to him. I'd been looking at his crossword, upside down, all the time we'd been speaking, and I pointed at one of the clues. 'I think you'll find that six down is "echidna",' I told him.

Back in the warm safety of the Saab, travelling down the M4, I asked Freddy the same question I'd asked Hugh, if he could remember all of the place names that he'd been told to say instead of Scarborough, the places his aunt was supposed to be staying.

He puffed out his cheeks, remembering. 'Well, there was Torquay. One week it was Slapton and then some place called Maidencombe . . . I don't know even where that is.'

'It's near Torquay,' I told him, scribbling the names down. It was a tiny place, no more than a few houses and a pub, but it had a nice beach. 'Go on.'

'And Puffling,' Morris added.

'No, no,' Freddy corrected him. 'Puffling was the

name of my aunt.'

'Oh yes, that's right,' he nodded.

'Any others?' I asked.

'Dartmouth!' he recalled suddenly. 'And Branscombe. Can't remember any more. Oh yes. Salcombe.'

'Keep thinking,' I told him.

'What's on your mind, Princess?' Ricky asked, glancing at me in the rear-view mirror.

'They are all west country names,' I told him, 'Places on the Devon coast.' *Mr Shaw is looking to expand his business down here in the West country*, I remembered. Could Lenny really be the same Mr Shaw the Audi driver had spoken about? I wished now I'd shown Monty the other photos on my phone; the one taken in the garden at Moorland View, of the man talking to Colin, of the two men in the photofit. Did they work for Lenny? 'It might be significant,' I said.

'So, what are you going to do then, Freddy?' Ricky demanded. We'd stopped for a break and something to eat. We'd turned off the motorway and kept going until we found the first decent-looking pub, and were gathered around the table, awaiting the arrival of our food. We were all starving. 'As I see it, you either go to the police . . .'

Freddy made a weak, whimpering sound and shook his head.

'Which, seeing the kind of people you're dealing with', he went on, 'would be the sensible thing to do. They don't seem like the sort to forgive and forget. Or you change your name, stay out of the West End for the rest of your life and hope to God that they never find you.'

'Stay out of the West End?' he repeated, scandalised.

'You can earn a perfectly good living in provincial theatre,' Morris told him helpfully.

'Or you hop it to America.'

'Do you think, if I paid them back the two hundred?' Freddy suggested. He turned to Morris. 'Perhaps your friend Monty could deliver it to this Mr Shaw.'

Ricky shook his head. 'Freddy, mate, this is not about a measly two hundred quid.'

'What do you mean?'

'Because you didn't alter your lines when you were told to, Lenny Shaw and Co. didn't receive their message and that's probably cost them a lot of money.'

'Don't you understand, Freddy?' I asked him. 'These place names down in the southwest, they all have beaches. Something must be arriving, being landed. Drugs perhaps, or illegal immigrants, something where a lot of money is involved.'

He stared at me. It seemed to take a few moments for him to understand. 'What . . . what . . . about the aunt's names?' he breathed at last. 'Persephone and . . . and . . . Puffling and Kiwi . . .'

'Leander,' I added. 'Those all sound like the names of boats to me. That's what the messages are all about – they tell Lenny where something is coming in, and on which boat. The only thing that your altered lines didn't tell them, is exactly when.'

'Which is why they have to turn up every Wednesday.' Ricky leant across the table, lowering his voice. 'And if these gangsters have missed a shipment of drugs because of you, then it ain't just about the money they've lost. It's about reputation, it's about showing what happens to people who mess them about.'

Freddy looked as if he was about to cry. He gazed around us helplessly. 'What can I do?'

Ricky shrugged. 'I've told you.'

'Go to the police,' Morris urged him, blinking through his specs. 'It's the only way.'

He shook his head. 'No, no. I might have to go to court, be a witness, testify. I've heard what happens to witnesses in cases like that. They get got at.'

I put a hand on his arm, trying to calm him down. 'No one can force you to testify.'

'No, I can't do it,' he insisted.

Ricky sighed, clearly unimpressed with Freddy's lack of courage and good citizenship. 'America it is then,' he muttered, as the first plates of pie and chips arrived.

CHAPTER SEVENTEEN

At this time of year, when I gave The Tribe their early morning walk, I stuck to the lanes and the woods. Too much happens up on the moor in spring: the start of lambing, ground-nesting birds sitting on their eggs, cattle being turned out to pasture and Dartmoor ponies giving birth to spring foals; there are too many ways a dog can get into trouble.

In the woods it was quieter, the signs of spring a little harder to find. It was too early for bluebells and wild garlic. But the yellow, starlike flowers of lesser celandine carpeted the ground where it was damp, and clumps of wild primroses, their pale flowers almost hidden among their wrinkled leaves, dotted the wooded banks. Tiny ferns hid between stones plush with deep, velvet moss and grew in tiny pools of black water between the roots of trees, like miniature rainforests. Above them, blackthorn was in flower, white blossoms appearing on its branches long before the sprouting of its leaves.

The dogs raced ahead of me along a muddy trail,

splashing through puddles, Dylan, Nookie and Boog streaking off into the distance, E.B. sometimes turning to check I was still following, his shaggy eyebrows knitted in a worried frown. I could hear Schnitzel yapping in excitement as he brought up the rear, his short legs barely able to keep up with the others. I couldn't see him, hidden by undergrowth. I just hoped he wasn't rolling in anything disgusting.

If I was walking more slowly than usual, it was because I was thinking of Maisie. She was having her operation that morning, first thing, just the simple pinning of her wrist, but any procedure under general anaesthetic is dangerous for someone her age. Our Janet had promised to phone me as soon as she heard from the hospital.

The other person on my mind was the enigmatic Mr Shaw. I wanted to talk to Monty again, ask if there was anything else he could tell me about him.

But I couldn't contact him without involving Morris, and he and Ricky would want to know what I was after and why. I couldn't tell them without revealing more of Elizabeth's story; and even Elizabeth didn't know everything.

As I walked out from under the cover of trees, my phone buzzed loudly in my pocket. It was Our Janet.

'Mum has come through the operation,' she told me happily as soon as I answered the call. 'But the hospital says not to visit until this evening, because she's suffering from a bit of post-operative delirium. She's complaining about bunny rabbits hopping around the ward.'

I smiled. 'That sounds like Maisie.'

'I'll pop over to Torquay and see her later.'

'In that case I'll wait until tomorrow,' I said. 'Is Jacko still with Bev?'

'Yes, thank heavens.'

'Do you want me to take him for a walk?'

'No, Juno. You've got enough to do. I'm just occupying myself with clearing out Mum's wardrobe. I don't think she's thrown anything away since VE day. She can't possibly wear it all.'

I laughed. 'Good luck with that.' And even more luck with telling Maisie what you've thrown away afterwards, I added silently.

I was busy for the rest of the day, spring-cleaning a house for a client in Buckfastleigh and only making it back to the shop at closing time, just in time to cash up, and to see Dean Collins emerging from the launderette in Shadow Lane, loaded down with bags.

'Our washing machine's broken,' he told me. 'I keep telling Gems not to overload it. Trouble is, when you've got two little 'uns . . .'

'I can imagine.' Noah on his own seemed to keep Kate's washing line permanently filled with babygrows. 'Any news on Colin Smethurst?' I asked.

Dean shook his head. 'We've drawn a blank so far. We've got a photograph of a man he was talking to in the garden of Moorland View – taken by a visitor - which matches the photofit of one of two villains who tried to blag their way into the home a couple of weeks earlier.'

'Oh really?' I decided not to mention the fact that the photo had been taken on my phone.

'But there's no evidence to link this person to the crime,' he went on gloomily, 'and no motive that we can find.'

'Have you been able to identify him then?' I asked, 'The man in the photograph?'

Dean's mouth shut like a trap. 'If we had, you know I couldn't tell you.'

'Yes, but if —'

'The only person we have been able to identify from any photographs,' he cut in before I could speak any further, 'is your friend Elizabeth. We still don't know why Smethurst was carrying her picture in his wallet.' He paused, as if expecting me to speak.

I just shrugged. 'Well, I don't know, and neither does Elizabeth.'

He eyed me balefully as he picked up his laundry bags. 'We'll just have to hope it doesn't have anything to do with his murder then, won't we?'

I smiled sweetly as he thumped off down Shadow Lane and gave him a little wave.

'You don't think this can be the same man, do you?' Elizabeth asked. 'This Mr Shaw you sat next to in the theatre, you think he's the same man that our friend the Audi driver works for? It's too much of a coincidence, surely.'

We were sitting in No.14, a candlelit wine bar in North Street. I'd phoned her and suggested she meet me there. There might be other customers at tables close by but it was one place where we could be sure that Olly's ears wouldn't be wagging. He was at home, up to his ears in revision for his upcoming GCSEs.

'It might not be the same man, but Lenny has a brother, Tony. The Shaws are a big family, apparently. It would be too much of a coincidence if they *weren't* connected, if there was more than one criminal gang in London with the same name.'

'A family business then, with branches everywhere.' Elizabeth raised an eyebrow. 'Some family!' She lowered her voice. 'And you think this strange messaging system is all about drugs?'

'It's about something illegal coming ashore, with a different boat landing at a different beach each time, somewhere down here on the south west coast.'

'Why not stick to the same beach?'

'Too dangerous, I suppose. There's more risk of arousing suspicion if they keep turning up in the same place.'

'And you don't feel inclined to give this information to the police?' she asked.

'We – Ricky, Morris and I – think that Freddy should go to the police in London. He's the one who's involved. If any of us tell the police what we know, they are going to want to question him anyway.'

'True.' Elizabeth thought for a moment. 'But of course, there's no guarantee that if these drug-dealers were caught, it would help me with my little local problem.' She gave an ironic mile. 'Loan-sharking and drug peddling may fall to different branches of the family.'

'I expect the same money is involved.'

'So, the money George borrowed was probably drugs money?' She sighed. 'Thanks for landing me in all this, George!'

There was a tapping on the window just then, and a moment later, Tom Carter opened the door. 'I've been up at the house, looking for you, woman,' he told Elizabeth. 'Olly told me you'd gone AWOL.' He grinned at me, blue eyes twinkling. 'Hello, Maid.'

'Was he revising?' Elizabeth asked, as Tom bent to give her a light kiss on the cheek.

'Well, he was reading a book.'

'That's something, I suppose.'

I stood up to let him have my seat. It was time I went home, and Elizabeth and I couldn't continue our current conversation with Tom there anyway.

As I closed the door, I turned to look back through the window at the pair of them. They had already forgotten me, smiling at each other across the candlelight, holding hands across the table. Why didn't Elizabeth confide in Tom, tell him everything? Did she worry he'd think less of her? I doubted it. But then I thought, if I were in her position, and Daniel was still around, would I tell him? He'd accused me of needlessly and recklessly endangering my life, said I wouldn't do stupid, dangerous things if I valued our love. After the death of his wife Claire, he said he couldn't stand to watch me throw my life away. I'd retaliated by telling him that the truth was he simply hadn't got over her, that he wasn't yet ready for another relationship. Was it the truth? I don't know. But if he was still around, would I tell him everything? Probably not, I decided.

CHAPTER EIGHTEEN

The hospital decided to keep Maisie in until the weekend and so next evening, I found myself sitting at her bedside along with Our Janet, who was visiting again, and Bev from two doors down, who had turned up unexpectedly. They were filling her in on Jacko's adventures during her absence, and I felt surplus to requirements. I was also conscious of the woman in the bed opposite lying there with no one to talk to, so after a few minutes I went to sit by her and we chatted for a bit. Her name was Jane. She'd been born in Torquay, she told me, and had always lived there. She remembered the time when the town had been a fashionable and elegant resort for the well-heeled.

'I know there's a lot of rebuilding going on at the moment,' she admitted. 'They're knocking down old hotels to build flats, but there are still too many shops standing empty, as well as people sleeping rough on the street. Torquay was never like that when I was growing up.'

I murmured the right sort of noises.

'You'd think there was enough money in the place,' she complained, 'when you look at some of those grand houses up around Marine Drive, and some of those yachts in the harbour.'

'I don't think that many of those boats in the marina belong to people who live in Torquay,' I said.

'No, you're probably right,' she agreed, 'they all belong to foreign billionaires. What do they call them, oligarchs? You know, they should never have knocked down the house where Agatha Christie was born. Just think what an asset to the town that would be if it was still standing.'

'The Agatha Christie Festival brings lots of visitors to Torquay every year,' I pointed out. 'They come from all over the world.'

'They can't visit her birthplace though, can they? All they can do is stare at a blue plaque set in a lump of concrete.' Her indignation made me laugh, and after a moment, she joined in.

'Oh, I shouldn't complain. I live in a nice area and I've got super neighbours. But turn around the next corner and it's like a different world, some of the streets look so shabby. Deprived, I call them. And there's nothing for the young people to do except hang about on the street. When I was a girl, there were dances to go to.' She laughed at the memory. 'There was a club called The Bottle Factory, where I used to go with my friends.'

Something clicked in my brain, something I'd heard the Audi driver mention. 'Do you know of a place called The Devon Grange?'

Jane's smile vanished. 'Oh, it was a lovely hotel years ago, The Devon Grange. Of course, like a lot of hotels around here, it suffered when people started going on cheap foreign holidays, and then with the recession, it never really got going again. The owners sold up. It was empty for years. The police raided it a couple of times, I believe, because of illegal parties going on.' She raised her eyes to heaven. 'My son went to one, once. I don't know who owns the place now. It either wants doing up or pulling down, if you ask me.'

'Where is it, this Devon Grange Hotel?'

'At Maidencombe.'

'Maidencombe?' I repeated. That was one of the places that Freddy had mentioned, one of the places where Aunt Drusilla had gone on holiday.

'You can't see the place from the road.' She began to tell me exactly where the old hotel was, but just then I became aware of Maisie squawking in the bed across the ward, complaining about certain visitors who went to visit sick friends in hospital and spent their time talking to other people they weren't supposed to be visiting at all. 'Oh dear, that's me,' I whispered, 'I think I'd better go back to Maisie.'

Jane chuckled. 'Yes, dear,' she said. 'I think you better had.'

I don't know Torquay very well and the one-way system is enough to baffle anyone. As it turned out, a closure due to road works prevented me from taking the easy way home. Bloody roadworks, they were everywhere!

I was forced to follow the yellow signs for diverted traffic, past rows of hotels and guest houses. I didn't feel at all diverted. I found myself driving past ancient Torre Abbey and its gardens, along the road next to a sea that was calm and gunmetal grey, the ropes of coloured lights edging the promenade swinging gently against the darkening sky. Spring holidaymakers were strolling along the seafront enjoying the evening air and gawping at the gin-palaces in the marina; or sitting on benches, gazing at the sea, guarding their bags of chips from marauding seagulls. It was all very pleasant, but it wasn't where I wanted to be heading.

I had no choice but to carry on towards the inner harbour where the tables and chairs of brightly lit bars crowded the pavements at its edge. Across the road stood a row of what had once been expensive department stores. Only one remained open; the rest were boarded up, awaiting development. Beneath an empty store's canopy, which in the daytime sheltered shoppers and bus queues from the rain, huddled a homeless man, bulky as a bloated caterpillar in his sleeping bag, a woollen hat rammed down on his head. A few doorways along, a mound of bedding and carrier bags might or might not have concealed someone sleeping underneath. It was difficult to tell. A gaggle of young women traipsed past them, giggling and screeching, apparently oblivious of their existence. Dressed in pink, tottering on high heels, they were on their way towards the door of the nearest nightclub. Drawn like moths to a flame, they were probably one of the hen-parties that Torquay seem to attract in large numbers.

I turned by the clock tower and headed away from the harbour and its night-time buzz, up the hill past a spanking new hotel that had just been a construction site when I had driven by a few months before. The contrasts in this place were so stark. Jane had said it. Turn a corner and you were in a different world. Now I was driving along a tree-lined road edged by imposing Victorian villas, and while it was quieter and more salubrious here, it was still not where I wanted to be. I tried to cut across town, negotiating the quiet residential areas with no idea of where I was going to end up.

More by luck than judgement, I came to a junction I recognised and found myself rejoining the one-way system that swept past the library and around the town hall. The civic buildings were on my right. The main shopping street sloped back down the hill towards the harbour. A group of kids had gathered around a bench at the top of this hill. They had that look about them, a look of being up to no good, of lingering with intent. Perhaps they were just bored teenagers with nowhere to go; and perhaps they were dealing drugs. The problems Torquay has are the same problems that belong to any other large town, and they are centered around here, a few yards from a church and a hostel for the homeless.

It was in that moment, as I swept past the group gathered around the bench, that I saw him. He was crossing the street, two cars in front of me, a tall, straight-backed figure with a long stride. There was no mistaking him, the way he carried himself, despite the backpack and the shabby clothes he wore, the hood pulled up to conceal his dark hair. He turned towards me and I saw his face. A knife twisted in my heart.

'Daniel,' I breathed. 'Daniel!' I cried out, as he headed off down an alleyway and disappeared. I couldn't stop the van. I was in a queue of traffic and there was nowhere to pull in. Ahead of me, traffic lights had changed to green and the car behind me was already sounding its horn.

I stalled, my hands fumbling stupidly, my vision blurred by a sudden welling-up of tears. I took a deep breath, struggling to get a grip on myself, on handbrake, clutch, ignition. The driver behind me hooted impatiently. 'Fuck off!' I screamed at him, as the van kangarooed into life.

The turning Daniel had taken was a no-entry. I had to drive on across another set of traffic lights before I found a turning where I could pull in, the first place I could park. I climbed out of the van on shaking legs, only remembering to turn and lock the doors as I was running down the road. I crossed in front of lights turning from amber to red, and turned off down the lane where I had seen him disappear. A country lane would have held no fears for me in the gathering dark, but this shadowy, rubbish-strewn alley between blind, windowless buildings was not a place I'd have ventured alone at night. If I hadn't just seen Daniel.

I came suddenly upon a line of people, some leaning their backs against a wall, some squatting on the filthy pavement, queueing for a night in the hostel. Could Daniel have been heading here? He had a home. Why would he be staying in a shelter for the homeless?

I walked along, scanning every face, every bowed head. I couldn't see him. 'How long have you been here?' I asked a girl near the front of the queue, her face, beneath her woolly hat, was pale and pinched with cold, her eyes red-rimmed.

'About an hour.' She nodded at the long line of people behind her. 'Not all of this lot will get in.'

If Daniel had been heading here to spend the night in this hostel, he'd be standing in this queue. And he wasn't. 'I'm looking for someone,' I told her. 'I saw him come this way. Very tall, dark hair, he was carrying a backpack, wearing a hooded jacket.'

She gave me a straight look. 'What's it worth?'

I hadn't brought my bag from the van. I'd been in such a hurry to catch up with Daniel, I'd left it on the front seat. I'd be lucky if it was still there when I got back. I had no money in my pockets to give her. 'All the world,' I said.

She gave a pitying little smile and nodded along the road ahead of her. 'He went that way.'

I ran on along the narrow alley, coming out on to the street, and found myself back opposite the town hall, near the same group of kids clustered around the bench. There was no sign of Daniel. I stood, staring around me like an idiot. There were so many turnings, so many different ways he could have gone. The kids by the bench were watching me, one sitting astride a bicycle. The oldest of them sat on the back of the bench, his feet planted on the seat. They were staring at me speculatively, weighing me up for what I might be worth. I hurried past them, down the road towards the harbour, peering into every shop doorway as I went. A voice called out from the shadows, asking me for spare change. I shrugged an apology and hurried on.

I knew my search was futile. Even if Daniel had come this way, there were too many side-streets, too many alleyways he might have turned down, too many pubs and bars he might have disappeared into. But I carried on around the harbour, weaving my way between kerbside tables, past knots of chattering drinkers enjoying a good night out. I tried in the pubs, asking bar staff if they'd seen anyone fitting his description; but if they had, they weren't going to tell me. A homeless man sitting on the pavement just told me to eff off. I walked along the seafront, its coloured lights swinging, as far as a little rocky promontory that jutted out into the sea, then doubled back on the beach, walking on gritty sand rank with the smell of seaweed, and up steps, to the end of the pier where a few sea-anglers had cast their lines into the darkening sea. No sign of him.

It was nearing midnight before I finally gave up looking and trudged back up the hill to find the van. But that Daniel could be here in Torquay, right now, was a thought I couldn't let go of. I got back in the van and began circling the town by road, slowing down to get a look at any men walking on their own. When I'd caught sight of him near the hostel with the rucksack on his back, I'd leapt to the conclusion that he must be sleeping rough, that depression or illness had overwhelmed him; but perhaps that wasn't true. Perhaps he had somewhere to go. All these months I had thought he might be half a world away, and it hurt, to think of him so far. But the realisation that he might have been here, so close to me, hurt more.

'Oh, my love,' I whispered, as I finally turned the van towards Ashburton, 'why don't you come home?'

CHAPTER NINETEEN

'Are you sure it was really him?' Sophie eyed me doubtfully. 'After all, you only caught a glimpse of him, and you said he had his hood up.'

She was asking the same question I had been asking myself the whole time I was searching for him, the same question I'd repeated over and over during a long, sleepless night. 'It was him,' I told her. I *knew* it was. His features were engraved on my mind's eye, on my heart. It was him.

I hadn't meant to tell her about seeing Daniel. I hadn't meant to tell anyone.

But when I'd walked into *Old Nick's* that morning, she'd taken one look at me and demanded to know what was wrong.

'You look ill,' she'd accused me. It was true I felt shaky. Perhaps it was from the shock of seeing Daniel like that. Or perhaps I was just coming down with Pat's cold. I told Sophie I was fine, but she'd refused to be fobbed off. Now she was staring at me, frowning doubtfully. Since Daniel first broke off our relationship, she has not been his greatest fan. Never mind his reasons, he had hurt me, and for her, that was enough. 'Why would he be hanging about in Torquay?'

'Perhaps he wasn't hanging about. Perhaps he was on his way somewhere, he was carrying a backpack.' Perhaps, while I was engaged in a stupid, futile search for him around the nightspots of Torquay, he had quietly walked to the station and boarded a train. He might have somewhere new to stay, and perhaps, my heart hurt at the thought of it, someone new to stay with.

At least I'd done one sensible thing that morning. I'd phoned the hostel for the homeless, saying I was anxious about a missing friend and asking if they knew him there. They didn't, but tried to be helpful, gave me the name of an organisation that dealt with reuniting missing people with those who are searching for them, and suggested I contacted them.

'What about Lottie?' Sophie asked. 'Was Lottie with him?'

That was another question I'd kept asking. Lottie hadn't been with Daniel last night. She was always trotting at his heels. It was the absence of his devoted little dog, as much as my one brief glimpse of him, that made me doubt whether he was really the man I'd seen. Lottie had belonged to his dead wife, Claire, and she never left his side. She was a miniature whippet, too delicate to survive out on the streets, a timid, little creature, shy and nervous of strangers. I couldn't bear the thought of her shivering in the wet and cold. It horrified me as much as the thought that Daniel might be enduring such a harsh, loveless existence.

A couple came into the shop just then, asking if they could look around, forcing us to break off our conversation. 'How come you're here, anyway?' I asked Sophie, as I watched them wander into the back room. 'How come you're not going to see Seth?'

'He's got to put some work in on his thesis this weekend. And I decided I must be sensible,' she answered loftily, 'and start putting in more hours on my work.'

The idea of Sophie deciding to be sensible was a new one on me, but I was grateful for her company; perhaps she could distract me from obsessing about Daniel for two seconds. The couple in the back room came to ask about the price of a pair of ladder-backed chairs. I had picked them up very reasonably at auction but they'd been sitting in my back-room for a long time. I was ready to haggle.

It was while I was in the back room, busily engaged in getting a fair price, that the shop bell jangled and Ricky and Morris's voices sounded in the shop. I heard Sophie greet them, and an 'Is Juno in?' from Ricky, but after that their voices dropped almost to whispers. I couldn't hear what they were saying. I had a nasty feeling that Sophie was telling them about my seeing Daniel last night but I had to pay attention to my customers, especially as they were also showing interest in a large copper preserving pan. They had no interest in making jam, they assured me, but it would look good on their kitchen dresser. Five minutes later, they went off to fetch their car so they could load up with their purchases and I put a satisfying wad of cash in the counter drawer.

Ricky meanwhile, had draped himself over Pat's chair, clearly waiting for me, while Morris was reading out the details of a cat from Honeysuckle Farm's *looking for a forever home* poster.

'Don't even think about it,' Ricky told him bluntly. 'You know cat fur makes you sneeze.'

'You could always get one of those bald ones,' Sophie suggested helpfully. 'What are they called? Sphinx?'

'You get on with your painting,' Ricky recommended, and Morris turned away from the posters with a little sigh.

'You've got all those grounds,' I chipped in, 'not to mention a field doing nothing, I don't see why you can't take something bigger off Pat's hands.'

I winked at Morris. 'Like a donkey or some goats.'

'You can wind your neck in an' all,' Ricky told me. 'And anyway, the field's not doing nothing, our neighbour is grazing his sheep on it.'

'Have you two actually come into buy something?' I asked, knowing full well they hadn't.

''Course not. We're looking for Freddy. You haven't seen the little blighter, have you?'

'We haven't seen him since last night,' Morris added, looking concerned. 'He said he fancied strolling into town after supper, for a pint in the Exeter. Well, it's quite a haul back up the hill again, as you know, so we offered him the use of the Saab, but he said he'd rather walk.'

'We reckoned that if he was drowning his sorrows till

closing time, 'Ricky added, 'he'd be late getting back, so we didn't stay up, just went on to bed. We'd left the back door unlocked.'

'And he hasn't come back?'

Morris gave an agitated little shake of his head. 'No.'

'We just wondered if anyone had seen him yesterday evening.'

'No. I was in Torquay. Visiting Maisie,' I added, giving Sophie a warning glance.

'And as I don't actually know who you're talking about,' she said practically, 'I wouldn't have recognised him anyway.'

'Sorry, Sophie my love,' Morris took off his glasses to give them a polish on his scarf, 'I didn't realise you hadn't met him. He's Ricky's nephew. He's an actor.'

'You'd know him if you had met him,' Ricky added uncharitably. 'He's a pudgy-faced individual, blinks a lot, talks like he's escaped from a Bertie Wooster novel.'

'I'm rather glad I haven't,' Sophie said. 'I don't like the sound of him.'

'And he's not my real nephew either,' he told her, shooting a glance at Morris. 'In fact, he looks more like *Maurice*'s nephew than mine.'

'And you've no idea where he might be?' I asked hastily, before Morris could retaliate.

'No.' Morris put his specs back on his nose. 'His bed hasn't been slept in.'

'We think he's done a bunk, run off,' Ricky said bitterly.

'Why would he do that?' Sophie asked innocently.

'He's in a bit of trouble, love,' Morris explained. 'He owes money to some bad men.'

Her forehead creased in a frown. 'How bad?'

'Very bad indeed.'

'They've been trying to shoot him.'

Her eyes widened in a stare. 'That is bad.'

'But he's been safely hiding out at your house,' I said. 'Why would he run away now?'

'Because I threatened him,' Ricky sneered. 'I told him, if he didn't go to the police and tell them everything, I'd bloody do it for him. So, he went off, saying he had a lot to think about and a walk would clear his head.'

'Then perhaps that's what he decided to do, go to the police.'

Ricky gave a grunt of derision. 'Don't think so. Besides . . .'

'There's some money missing,' Morris hissed in a whisper and then blushed, as if he hadn't meant to say it.

Ricky nodded. 'The little bastard's stolen a wodge of cash from Morris's bedside drawer.'

'Have you been to see the landlord at the Exeter?' I asked, 'To ask if he actually got there?'

'That's our next port of call.' He looked at his watch. 'As soon as they're open.'

'You'd better try the Silent Whistle as well,' Sophie added. 'And the wine bar.' She frowned. 'You'd have thought he might have left a note or something.'

Ricky gave a short laugh. 'Not Freddy. He's probably on a plane to South America by now.'

Morris shook his head unhappily. 'Oh, I don't think he can have got that far,' he said seriously. 'Not yet. Do you?'

I called in on Druid Lodge after I'd closed the shop to see if Freddy had put in an appearance, but there had been no sign of him.

'We went round all the pubs, and the wine bar. No one had seen him.'

'Do you think he's gone back to London?'

'I don't know and I don't care. He can bugger off and good riddance, take all his damn problems with him,' Ricky told me bitterly, 'but it's his stealing money from Morris that's getting up my nose.'

'Perhaps he's just borrowed it,' I suggested without much conviction.

'Well, he borrowed five hundred quid from me two years ago and I've never had that back either.'

'He might just turn up,' I said.

I was right as it turned out, but not in a good way.

The next morning being a Sunday, with no dogs to walk, no shop to worry about and Janet bringing Maisie home from hospital, there was no better day I decided, to visit the village of Maidencombe. The day was fine and sunny, the grass glistened after a shower of early morning rain, and you could smell spring thrusting its way through the damp earth. Besides, I had to do something. With nothing else to occupy myself, I was tempted to go back to Torquay, trudge the streets, search again for Daniel.

The likelihood of seeing him again was remote and I knew that searching would do me no good. If going to look at his house was like picking at a wound, seeing him unexpectedly had torn it open. It had made me bleed afresh. I had to distract myself from the pain.

There has been a settlement at Maidencombe since the eighth century, part of a small manor which is recorded in the Domesday book. It lies a few miles north of Torquay, and is crossed by the South West Coastal Path. You approach it by turning off the road to Teignmouth, down one of two very steep hills. These wind down the side of a wooded valley, offering occasional stunning glimpses of the sea, and meet at a junction in the heart of the village by the Thatched Tavern pub. Higher up the valley sit exclusive modern houses whose glass walls must offer spectacular views of the coast; but down in the heart of the village, stand houses built of stone and cob and roofed with thatch.

I drove past the pub to the car park, a bare patch of stamped earth and gravel, and parked the van. From here, I could join the southwest footpath, or I could carry on down a series of steep and uneven steps that would take me to the beach; which is what I did.

I stopped on the turn of this stairway to take in my first real sight of the sea, the wide expanse of water coloured blue-grey beneath the pale spring sky. The incoming tide was devouring the curve of the beach, wetting and darkening the sand as waves advanced and retreated, flinging foaming spray against the tumble of rocks that lay at the foot of the surrounding cliffs. These rose up all around, high red rocks topped with trees, their upper slopes lost in a jungle of green. Immediately beneath me, on the next turn of the stair, stood the beach café.

I carried on down the steps, ordered a coffee and sat on the terrace outside. I looked straight out to sea. This was a great place to watch cormorants diving, the occasional bobbing seal, or, if you were lucky, the gleaming backs of dolphins. The beach was popular during the daytime with dog-walkers, swimmers and paddle-boarders. The signs warning of the danger of death or injury from falling rocks didn't seem to put anyone off, despite the fact that just along the coast rock-falls had blocked access to a neighbouring beach. Mad coasteering groups regularly flung themselves off the rocks into this water, not an experience I ever intended to emulate. But later, after the beachcombers had gone home, and the little café had closed its shutters for the day, no one would be likely to observe what went on because, sheltered by the high cliffs around it, this was a beach that couldn't be overlooked. Which makes it attractive, if you're up to no good, bringing in a small boat and landing something illegal on that narrow curve of sand. There were other more secret bays nearby, like Blackaller and Mackerel Cove, but they lacked sandy beaches for landing contraband, and could only be reached by a scramble down a sheer cliff-face. Maidencombe, with its steps, was perfect.

I sat for a while, taking it all in, enjoying the gentle spring warmth. This must be a great place, I decided, to sit and see the sunrise. I saw no dolphins or seals, but watched a pair of cormorants fishing, their dark shapes disappearing under the waves, only to bob up again in a different place altogether.

I clambered down on to the beach to watch the rushing tide fill up the spaces between the rocks with foaming white, making pools that lasted only moments before the water was sucked back out again. A Spaniel emerged dripping from the sea, his ears in ringlets, his nose gritty with wet sand. He raced up to greet me and check on what I was doing. We exchanged a word or two before his owner, walking on the beach, whistled him away.

Fortified by coffee and salt-spray air, I climbed back up the steps, stopping to make way for excited dogs and walkers coming down, and made off towards the signpost that pointed to the coastal path. At the hospital, Jane had told me that the Devon Grange Hotel was not visible from the main road but could be glimpsed from the footpath if you knew the right place to look.

The path crossed green fields that sloped steeply up and down over the cliffs before it disappeared into Watcombe Woods. I turned to look back. The view was stunning. The promontory of The Ness jutted out into the sea, and beyond it, the slender white span of Teignmouth pier. Further away, I could see the red rocks at Dawlish, where the railway line disappeared into a tunnel, and down the coast as far as Exmouth and beyond, until the land was just a blue smudge on the horizon, and Devon had given up and become Dorset.

Ahead of me, the path carried on over fields. To my

right, a smaller track led off into an area of woodland where I could make out the rooftops of secluded houses among the trees. It was standing at the fork of these two paths, according to Jane, that I should be able to spot the Devon Grange Hotel. I lifted the field glasses that hung around my neck and scanned the view. It didn't take long to find, the tallest rooftop among the trees, topped by a distinctive cupola, and set well away from the other dwellings. If I took the path to my right into the woods, I should be able to get close.

I soon realised that the muddy trail through the woods wasn't part of the official route and not one much trod by walkers. I could understand why. The ground sloped awkwardly, and staying on the path involved much clambering over exposed tree roots and wriggling under low-growing branches. It afforded only occasional glimpses of the sea, and in summer, when the trees were in full leaf, most of those would also be lost.

The movement of a bird caught my eye, a small brown bird, not small enough for a wren, a dunnock maybe. I watched it flutter deeper into the wood, landing on the forked branch of a hazel tree. There was something yellow on the branch, unnaturally bright among the greens and browns around it. It was a loop of nylon rope. I let my eyes follow the yellow line down from the branch and found I was looking at a green tarpaulin, suspended by all four corners, tethered to surrounding trees. I turned off the path and clambered across the roots of a leaning oak, to get a better view.

The camp was well-hidden, the tent in camouflage

colours blended into the surrounding wood. Above it the tarpaulin, which would have helped to keep the weather off the tent, sloped in one corner, funnelled into a plastic bucket to catch rainwater. The fire, although it was nothing but grey ash, was laid between stones, a metal grill over the top. The place was tidy and well-organised. And if I hadn't caught the flash of that yellow nylon rope, I would have passed it by and never known it was there. 'Hello?' I called. No answer, just the brooding call of a wood pigeon echoing through the trees. After a moment of standing still, listening, I made my way back to the path.

I didn't get far. My way ahead was blocked, a high wire fence straddling the path. I turned off with the idea of walking around the perimeter, and found signs warning me that the land beyond was private and trespassers would be prosecuted.

Peering through the wire mesh I could see the cracked surface of an old tennis court invaded by weeds, and an area that had once been a formal garden, with paved terraces and a monkey-puzzle tree. This land must belong to the hotel. These were the grounds, according to Jane, that had been invaded by teenagers who held drug-fuelled parties. I could see little of the hotel building itself, just a roof and a few of the upper windows. I needed to get closer.

I followed the fence, wishing I'd had the forethought to bring a pair of wire-cutters. The only tool in my pocket was my little parcel-opening snipe, and I doubted that was up to the job of gnashing through metal. But someone before me had obviously come equipped. The fence had been attacked with cutters. Someone had torn a strip about two foot up from ground level, creating a flap of fence that I peeled back. Handy. This was probably the way the illegal partygoers had got in.

I took off my backpack, got down on my hands and knees and squirmed through the gap, then stood up, looking around as I dusted myself off. I hoped there was no one about. The place seemed quiet, no snarling guard dogs or men waving shotguns to pursue me, but if I met with any hostility, I didn't fancy my chances of scrabbling back through that hole in the fence with any speed.

I wandered through the grounds, past an empty swimming-pool surrounded by rusting garden chairs, dead leaves floating in a foot of brackish rainwater at its deep end.

The hotel came in sight, derelict and sad. I approached a side door and found it covered by a metal shutter and secured by a padlock. I walked around the building. All of the doors were secured in the same way, as well as the ground floor windows. Whoever owned the place, they didn't want anyone to get in. Perhaps they were worried about squatters or arsonists.

I stepped back, shading my eyes against the sun, to peer at the upper windows.

There was something weird about them. Their glass was intact, just the odd cracked pane, but I could see no reflections, no gleam of sun on glass, just blankness, as if the glass had been painted over in a solid, matt black.

Even if I climbed a ladder, if I could have found such a thing handy, and peered through the glass, I reckoned I still wouldn't be able to see inside.

I came around to the front of the building. It was still impressive despite peeling paint and walls stained with damp. When it was built, sometime in the Edwardian era, its wide front door and stepped portico would have looked grand. Now, it was boarded up and shuttered. There was a gravel drive spotted with clumps of weed, where once carriages would have swept in from the main road, a road blocked from view now by the growth of trees. The decorative wrought-iron gates had been taken off their hinges and lay rusting against a hedge, replaced by a taller pair; modern metal gates, padlocked and finished across the top with a tasteful roll of razor-wire.

The place seemed abandoned. Yet, something had been going on recently. Piled at the edge of the drive were unopened plastic sacks of compost, looking as if they'd been delivered by a garden centre. There were dozens of them. It seemed as if some gardening project was about to start, perhaps some mature shrubs or trees were to be shifted to allow building work to start.

I heard a grinding of gears and a hiss of air brakes; a vehicle was drawing up in the road outside. Someone was coming in. I ran for cover, ducking down behind a low wall, and stayed still, watching. A white lorry trundled into view and a man climbed out to unlock the gates. He swung them open, standing aside to let the lorry roll through. He opened up the back and I watched as he and the driver began loading the bags of compost, neatly rubbishing my former theory. These bags hadn't been freshly delivered; they were being taken away. I peered at the green writing on the vehicle's side, *Devon Garden Services*. I'd seen this lorry before, in a narrow lane. I'd been forced to back Van Blanc to let it pass, on the road to Raven's Tor Manor.

CHAPTER TWENTY

'They've taken it away.'

The voice behind me made my heart lurch in panic. I'd been forced to wait in the garden until the men had loaded up their lorry, secured the gates and driven off, before I could safely leave my hiding place and find my way back to the gap in the fence. I'd just wriggled through and picked up my backpack when someone spoke in a low, throaty voice. I swung around sharply. A man was standing a few yards away, a leggy brindled mongrel at his side. He had the look of someone who was out in all weathers, his clothes and boots shabby and well-worn, his skin tanned, reddened, where it wasn't hidden by a grizzled beard. Something bloody hung in a sack at his waist.

He saw the direction of my glance. 'Rabbit,' he explained. 'Bella here caught us our supper.'

At the mention of her name, the dog wagged her tail. Her presence was reassuring. I didn't feel threatened by this man in the wood, but I might have done, if it hadn't been for his dog.

'She's a clever girl,' I said, patting my leg to see if she would come to me.

Her owner grunted. 'She's fast at any rate.'

I looked up at him as Bella and I made friends, me stroking her head, her sniffing my boots. 'You were watching me just now?'

'I found your backpack by the hole in the fence so I knew someone had gone in there. You want to be careful, leaving a good bag like that lying around.' He grinned. 'I thought I'd wait for a bit, see who came to claim it.'

I made a mental note to check its contents later, see if my wallet and phone were still there. He read my mind. 'Don't worry, Bella and I aren't thieves. We haven't taken anything.'

I blushed and moved the conversation on. 'Do you live around here?'

'You found our camp.'

He had been watching me then. Probably since I turned off the main path.

'This wood's not a bad place to camp out,' he went on, 'now that spring's coming on.'

I smiled. 'Plenty of rabbits in the fields there?'

He nodded. 'And good fishing down off the rocks. But we move around. We never stay in one place too long. Do we, Bella?'

He reminded me of Micky, the tramp who roamed Dartmoor with his great dog Duke, only looking for shelter when to stay outdoors would be to invite death. But despite the grey in his beard, this man looked younger than Micky, not much older than me. I wondered how he'd come to be living such a life. He had a badly chipped front tooth, I noticed. What did he do when he needed a dentist? 'You said you'd seen something being taken away from here,' I reminded him.

He glanced at me sideways. 'That information will cost you a cup of tea.'

'Tea it is,' I agreed and held out my hand. 'Juno.'

'Jake,' he responded, and rubbed his own grubby one on the hip of his jeans before he shook mine. We fell into step together and walked back down along the path towards Maidencombe and the beach café, Bella trotting on in front. We walked mostly in silence. I didn't want to scare him off by seeming too curious.

Jake wouldn't sit on the terrace. Too near other people, he said. But he found us a place on a rock overlooking the beach, where we could watch shrieking swimmers wading into the cold water and paddle-boarders practising not falling off. I clambered across the rocks to him with two lidded cups, bags of sugar and three sausage sandwiches; one for Bella.

'I was here a few weeks back, camping in the woods,' he told me, without being asked. 'Lots going on in that place at night. People going in.'

'Inside the hotel?'

He nodded, chewing on a lump of sausage sandwich, intently watched by Bella, who'd scoffed hers in moments and was on the look-out for seconds. She'd already had most of mine. 'They might have blacked out the windows, but there are skylights in that roof. At

234

night you could see light pouring out.'

'But there's no power in there, is there?'

'They had a generator. I could hear the hum.' He stopped talking, coughed and cleared his throat. 'Gone now. They must have taken it away.'

I frowned. 'They?'

'I don't know how many of them there were. But they got spooked when those kids broke in, having their party.'

'Didn't the police go in there?'

He nodded. 'Someone must have tipped 'em off about the kids. They found the hole in the fence, chased a few of them out of the gardens. But the hotel was locked up, wasn't it? All quiet that night. No sign of a break-in so why would they bother looking inside?'

'And after the police left, these people, whoever they were, took everything away?'

He shrugged. 'I suppose so. There are no lights showing at night now. I guess it was too much of a near thing, having those kids and then the police there. That lorry's been up and down that road day and night, taking stuff away.'

'What stuff?'

'Evidence I suppose, of what they'd been up to.' He smoothed the dog's head. 'Bella and I know when to look the other way, don't we, girl? We don't want to be caught watching, if you know what I mean.' He looked at me more directly. He had hazel eyes, green with flecks of brown. 'We don't want to get involved.'

I didn't ask him if he'd mentioned any of this to the

police, because it would have been a stupid question. 'Have you ever seen a boat landing stuff on this beach at night?'

Jake eyed me doubtfully, a sideways glance. 'You ask a lot of questions.'

'So, have you?' I persisted.

'Like I say, Bella and I know when it's best to look the other way. Thanks for the sandwich.'

He made to stand up but I clutched at his sleeve. 'Have you got no home, no proper home I mean?'

'Not in the sense you mean.' My hand still on his sleeve, he sighed and sat back. 'I was in Afghanistan,' he told me. 'Four years, most of the time living in the desert, camping under the stars.' He snorted. 'Sounds romantic, doesn't it? Well, it was a kind of hell, but we got used to it. But when I came home, I found I couldn't live in a little modern house, tiny rooms, walls all around me, looking at more tiny houses across the road. I started camping out in the garden, sleeping there on the lawn. But that had fence panels all around it, so I moved out into the park. My wife . . . well, who could blame her? She'd waited long enough for me to come home and then . . .' He shrugged. 'So, I took to the road.'

'Didn't you get offered any help?' I asked, saddened. 'Any counselling or therapy?'

He gave a sad laugh and reached out for Bella, roughing the fur at the back of her neck. 'The only therapy that's done me any good is Bella here.'

She turned her head, fixing her brown eyes adoringly

on him and he smiled at her affectionately. 'We spend a few nights in a hostel now and again, in the winter. They are good people who run these places. They've tried to help me, get me a flat. They got me the offer of one once from the council. But they won't take dogs. If I wanted the flat, I couldn't take Bella.'

She'd wandered away to sniff at a rock pool and he watched her lovingly for a few moments. 'We've been through everything together, me and Bella. She's the only thing that's kept me going. I'd have cut my throat if I hadn't had her with me. And I'm not being parted from her.' He gave a bitter smile. 'But now I've refused their offer of accommodation, I'm officially off the list, see? I have made myself *intentionally* homeless. So that's it. They don't have to bother with me anymore. You only get one chance. I won't get another.'

'But that's terrible.'

'That's the way the system works. Anyway, how could I live in a tiny flat when I can't live in a house?' He whistled to his dog. 'C'mon Bella. Time we were going.' He stood up and I stood too. 'You've been kind, Juno. But don't think about trying to help me, because I can tell that's what's in your mind. It's written all over your face.' He was right. I'd already been working out a shopping list, like the one I drew up sometimes for Micky: cough medicine, dog food, soap, tea, protein bars.

'And don't come back here looking for us,' he went on, 'because Bella and I will be moving on in the morning.'

237

I could tell he meant it. I felt sad for him and for Bella. 'You take care of yourself.'

'Bella and I look after each other. You're the one who needs to take care,' he told me frankly. He gave me that honest, hazel stare. 'You be careful, asking questions.'

'I will,' I promised.

He grunted as if he didn't believe me. 'Just don't get caught.'

My tatty upstairs flat had never seemed so warm and comforting as it did when I got home. I switched the gas fire on and curled up on the sofa with Bill on my lap, listening to the hum of the fire and cat's gentle purring, grateful I wasn't spending the night in a flimsy tent in the woods. But if I thought I was in for a peaceful evening, I was wrong. First, Our Janet phoned to say that she had not brought Maisie home from Torquay hospital after all. Apparently, she had a high temperature and the hospital were treating her with antibiotics for a suspected UTI. They were likely to be keeping her in for a couple more days. I knew Janet would have to take more time off work. 'I can go and fetch her when she's better,' I told her, 'if you've got to get back home.'

'Thanks Juno', she sighed. 'But I can't leave when she's this poorly. I'll wait and see how she is tomorrow.'

'Well, you know where I am if you change your mind.'

After her call, I settled back down on the sofa. I kept thinking about Jake, about the kind of life he was living.

It's one thing to go camping when you know you've got a warm home and a comfortable bed to come back to at the end of it, but when a tent and a sleeping bag is all there is, with no prospect of any permanent shelter, ever, what must that be like? And these thoughts brought me back to thoughts of Daniel. Where was he now? What kind of life was he living?

The phone rang again, and this time it was Ricky. 'Any news?' I asked.

'Sort of. *Maurice* and I were having a think after we spoke to you, about how Freddy could have got out of Ashburton on a Friday evening.'

'There's a distinct shortage of buses after six o'clock,' I pointed out.

'Right. Which means if he wanted to pick up a train at Exeter or Newton Abbot, he'd have had to have blown some of that money he stole on a taxi. We called the taxi firm, and they told us they'd had a call from a Mr Carstairs, asking to be picked up at Druid Cross on Friday evening. But when the car turned up there was no one waiting. The driver hung around, but after about five minutes he decided Freddy was a no-show and drove off.'

'Where was it booked to take him?'

'Newton Abbot.'

'From there he could have got a train anywhere.'

'Exactly.'

'What time did Freddy phone to book? Did you ask?'

'Yeh. Four in the afternoon, and from our number. The little viper must have made the call while we were out shopping. Apparently, he booked the taxi for seven o'clock.'

'You're lucky he didn't take you up on your offer of the Saab.'

'Nah, he wouldn't steal our car. He knows damn well we'd send the police after him to get it back.'

'If he didn't get the taxi, perhaps someone saw him standing there at Druid Cross and offered him a lift. A lot of people around here would.'

'Well, he couldn't have got far on foot, that's for sure.'

'Did he take anything else with him? Clothes or anything?'

'He's helped himself to an overnight bag, a towel and some shaving things. As yet we haven't discovered if he's raided anything from the wardrobe. Our personal wardrobe, I mean. I don't suppose he's going about dressed as Widow Twankey. But he must have stowed that bag somewhere because he didn't have it in his hand when he walked out of the house. Morris and I are both certain about that.'

'Do you suppose he might have gone to Plymouth?'

'And hopped on the ferry to France? That's too much to hope for.'

'Should you call the police? I mean, technically, I suppose he is a missing person. The point is, where is he? Something might have happened to him.'

'Something will happen to him if I catch the little bugger.'

I heard a voice calling in the background. 'That's

Maurice,' Ricky informed me, 'bellyaching because supper is on the table. Do you want to come up? It's lasagne.'

There was nothing I would have loved more than some of Morris's home-cooked lasagne. But unfortunately, I'd already consumed a shop-bought pasta bake that was lying in my stomach like lead, and I didn't really have the room.

'Another time,' I said.

'Right. Well, as I say, that little toad Freddy can't have got far. So, if you spot him lurking in Ashburton, throw a net over him and give us a call.'

I promised I would, although it didn't seem likely.

I couldn't sleep at all that night. I kept thinking about Daniel, wandering the streets in Torquay. Was he still grieving for Claire? Is that what kept him from coming home? I thought about Jake and Bella, camping in the woods, and about Freddy and where the hell he'd got to and then of course, I wondered about the Devon Grange Hotel, and what might be going on inside.

I could give it a pretty good guess. Those darkened windows concealing bright lights inside, all that compost. They were growing cannabis in there. It was funny to think that while those kids were partying in the grounds, smoking their skinny little joints, there was probably a forest of the good stuff being grown indoors just a few yards away.

But not anymore, according to Jake. The plants had been taken away, together with all evidence of them ever having been there. I tried to remember what I'd overheard the Audi driver saying to his Fungus-featured friend. He'd been going to the hotel to tidy up loose ends, he said. And before that, he'd told Colin that his boss, Mr Shaw, had been forced to move his centre of operations inland, away from the coast. So, was this what had been going on? *Devon Garden Services* had been transporting cannabis plants from the old Devon Grange and setting them up somewhere in Raven's Tor Manor. In which case, that trapdoor in the newly concreted floor of the old barn there, might lead down to something very interesting. Certainly worth another look, I decided.

CHAPTER TWENTY-ONE

Morris was on his own when I called in at Druid Lodge later the following afternoon. I'm not usually free on Mondays, but a client had cancelled, so I thought I'd see if I could help out for an hour or two before I went back down into town to close up the shop. I was so used to seeing Ricky and Morris together, it always struck me as odd when they were apart, even for a short time. Ricky, it seemed, had driven into Exeter to do some banking. Morris had started a cold, and Ricky had persuaded him to stay at home. He was in the hall, surrounded by hampers, busily unpacking the latest batch of returned costumes from a show, and was glad of some help.

'I keep telling Ricky that now you're so busy and can't come here as often as you used to,' he told me, shaking out a petticoat, 'we need to find someone else to help. But somehow, we never get around to it.'

He made me feel guilty. It was true, I used to give them a lot more help than I now did. 'There are plenty of people around Ashburton looking to earn some extra money,' I said. 'It shouldn't be difficult to find someone.'

'Yes, but it's got to be the right sort of someone.' He hung the petticoat on a clothes rail. 'I mean it's not just helping with a bit of sewing and tidying, is it? It's physically quite hard work.'

I was dragging a particularly heavy Tudor dress out of the hamper as he spoke and I could only agree with him. It was made of velvet and brocade, boned, heavily padded and weighed a ton. Getting it on to a hanger and heaving it up on the clothes rail was no job for a weakling. The actress concerned must have got into training to wear it on stage. 'What play is this from?'

'Catherine Howard.'

'Well, as long as we don't unpack another Freddy.'

Morris chuckled. 'No. One was enough.'

'No news of him, I suppose?'

He shook his head. 'I think we should call the police, but Ricky just says good riddance to bad rubbish, and if he turns up here again, he'll throw him out of the door.' He hesitated a moment, as if there was something on his mind. 'Juno, my love,' he began awkwardly, 'I probably shouldn't stick my nose in, but while Ricky's not here, I just wanted to say that . . . well, you know Ricky and I only want you to be happy, don't you, love?'

I sensed what was coming. 'Yes,' I said guardedly.

'It's just . . . well, the other day Sophie told us that you were upset because you thought you'd seen Daniel Thorncroft.'

I knew it. Sophie had been blabbing. I'm going to kill her, I vowed silently. I'm going to wring her neck. 'I did see him.'

'Are you sure it was him, Juno? Sophie says you only got a brief look at him. Are you sure it wasn't just someone who looked like him?'

'Perfectly sure.'

'Only sometimes, you know,' he added, fidgeting with the buttons of his cardigan, 'when we are really longing to see someone, we see what we want to see.'

'Morris, I know you mean it kindly,' I began. 'But . . .'

'I just can't bear to think of you throwing your life away, waiting for someone who may never come back,' he said in a rush. 'You're young, you should be out meeting new people, not . . .'

'Morris, please, I . . .'

'You should move on, love,' he said finally, 'that's all I'm saying.'

'I'm not ready.'

He gazed at me sadly. 'Do you suppose anyone ever feels ready?'

'I don't know,' I admitted.

'You have to start giving other people a chance. There was that nice policeman from Plymouth. He was obviously smitten.'

He meant Mike Swift, from the anti-slavery unit. I met him last year. And he was nice. Too nice, I felt, to be wasting his attentions on a woman who wasn't interested. He deserved better than that. 'Morris, can we just forget this? I appreciate your concern, I really do.'

He held up his hands defensively. 'I won't say any more. We haven't fallen out, have we, love?' he added anxiously.

I smiled. 'Of course not.'

After a slightly awkward moment, we hugged. The grandfather clock in the hall began its pretty half hour chime and Morris drew back to look at its face. 'Ricky's a long time.'

I was glad to change the subject. 'Is he alright?'

Morris turned away with an agitated shake of his head. 'No, he's not. He's up and down to the loo all night, moaning. He's been in terrible pain sometimes, but he's dared me to call an ambulance. When I ask him how he is, he bites my head off.' He sighed. 'He's worried obviously, we both are. He's waiting for this scan. It's been months now.'

I was about to utter something stupid like I was sure everything would be alright, but I was saved by the crunch of gravel outside as the old Saab drew up. Ricky had returned.

'Not a word now, Juno,' Morris hissed in a whisper and we both busied ourselves with unpacking our respective hampers.

Ricky entered like a hurricane. 'Bloody traffic!' he announced as he flung open the door, banging it against the corner of a hamper so that it almost bounced shut again. He stopped it with one hand. 'Hello, Princess!' he grinned, seeing me. He gazed around at the costume hampers cluttering up the hall. 'It's a bit congested in here, isn't it?'

'You've been a long time,' Morris told him, a trifle huffily.

'Well, after the bank, I needed a loo stop, and as the nearest one was in a café, I thought I'd better order a coffee and a tart just to be polite. It was egg custard, before you ask, *Maurice*, but it wasn't a patch on yours.'

Morris dimpled with pleasure. Ricky tried to manoeuvre a route between the hampers. 'Bloody hell, we need to move some of these out of here. Aren't any of them emptied yet?'

'We've done three,' I told him. We didn't often bother to move empty hampers out of the way, because they usually needed filling again straight away, but it wasn't the case this time.

'Let's take the empty ones out to the shed then,' he suggested. 'I don't know why you haven't done that already, Morris, they've got wheels on.'

'My fault,' I told him hastily. 'I've kept him chatting.'

Ricky grunted. 'Well, that's not difficult.'

We lined up, each pushing an empty hamper, in a procession through the hall and down the passage to the back door. There was a shed just outside where hampers were stored. There was already one in there.

It was dark inside the shed and Ricky, the first in line, flipped on the light as we wheeled our hampers in. I had barely registered the faint, sickly smell before Morris uttered a cry and backed away, his hand to his mouth. We all stared at the hamper standing with its lid open, and what was lying in it. We had found Freddy. He hadn't got far after all.

'And when was the last time you saw Mr Carstairs alive?' Detective Inspector Ford enquired, staring at Ricky beneath his sandy eyebrows as he leant his elbows on the breakfast room table.

'On Friday evening,' he responded. He was white-faced, his mouth set in a grim line. He might not have liked Freddy, but he had been the son of an old friend and he'd known him since he was a boy. Like the rest of us, he was in shock. 'At about six o'clock. He said he was going to take a walk down into town and have a pint in the Exeter. He wanted a chance to think, he said.'

Cruella, sitting next to the Inspector, was scribbling all this down. Poor old Dean Collins was out in the shed with Freddy's body, waiting for the pathologist to arrive. I was sitting next to Morris, holding his hand under the table. I could still feel him trembling. It had been terrible, finding Freddy's body like that, lying in the hamper, staring up at us. It didn't take a pathologist to tell what had killed him. If the single bullet wound to his forehead hadn't done the job, it had certainly finished him off.

'But as we found out later,' Ricky went on, 'he'd booked himself a taxi for seven o'clock, to pick him up at Druid's Cross and take him to Newton Abbot station.'

'And you've no idea where he was planning to go from there?'

Ricky shrugged. 'Back to London, I suppose.'

The inspector turned to Cruella. 'See if you can find out if he booked a ticket, will you, Sergeant?'

'Sir,' she said, without looking up.

'So, that narrows the time of death down to sometime between six o'clock and seven,' the inspector went on.

'He didn't have that overnight bag with him,' Ricky told him. 'He wasn't carrying it when he went left here.'

'The bag he was clutching to his chest when you found him?' The inspector steepled his fingers and pondered. 'So, it's possible that Mr Carstairs hid the bag in the shed with the intention of collecting it secretly when he had said goodbye to you, after he was supposed to be leaving for the pub.'

'And his killer saw him doing it and was waiting for him when he went in,' Cruella added.

Suddenly Morris started to speak. 'But . . . but that means he was killed while we were *here*,' he cried wretchedly. 'I must have been in the kitchen preparing the supper, and poor Freddy . . .'

'And you didn't see or hear anything?' Cruella's demand was like an accusation.

Morris shook his head and began sobbing into his handkerchief. I put an arm around his shoulders, exchanging glare for glare with Cruella.

'Please don't distress yourself, Mr Gold.' Inspector Ford leant towards him reassuringly. 'I am relieved you didn't see anything. This looks like a professional job. If the killer had any suspicion that you'd spotted him, it's likely we'd have more than one dead body here to investigate.' He turned to Ricky. 'I don't suppose you have any idea as to the motive for this crime?'

Ricky glanced briefly at Morris and me. 'We do as a matter of fact. It's quite a long story, Inspector. Juno darlin',' he added, turning to me. 'D'you think you could make Morris and the rest of us a cup of tea?'

'So, let me get this straight,' the inspector said finally, after listening to Ricky's story with an increasingly incredulous expression on his face. 'Let's get all the facts here. Freddy Carstairs was employed as an actor in a London show called . . . er . . .'

'*Murder Weekend*,' Cruella supplied for him, glancing at her notes.

'Thank you, Sergeant. And he was receiving regular sums of money from someone unknown, a foreigner, as payment for altering some of his lines?'

'But only on the Wednesday matinee,' I put in.

'And the actor before him had been doing it as well,' Ricky added, 'until he disappeared.'

'Stephen Spendlow,' I said. 'A few weeks later they fished him out of the Thames.'

The inspector looked pained. 'Let's just stick with Mr Carstairs for the moment. At one performance he failed to alter these lines and was subsequently threatened by this foreign man who entered the theatre with a gun, and he was forced to flee for his life.'

'Which is what brought him down here,' Ricky completed for him, 'in a costume hamper.'

'Right.' Inspector Ford sighed like a weary walrus coming up for air. 'So, armed with this information, instead of coming straight to the police, you all decide to go on a jolly up to London to see this show, because Miss Browne here had cooked up some theory that an individual who takes a regular seat for this matinee . . .'

'Q7.' Cruella slipped in.

'Is the intended recipient of some obscure message,' the Inspector carried on doggedly, 'about the places that Aunt —'

'Drusilla,' Cruella uttered.

'Can a man not draw breath, Sergeant?' he demanded, turning to her with an exasperated frown.

Her pale cheeks coloured. 'Sorry, sir.'

He turned back to us. 'An obscure message,' he repeated, 'about the places that Aunt Drusilla is spending her holiday this year.'

'But those altered lines have to be significant,' I broke in, 'otherwise why pay Freddy to deliver them, and why try to kill him when he doesn't do it?'

'Oh, I grant you that, Miss Browne,' he conceded. 'But that's no proof that this person sitting in Q7 is involved in any way. He might be a perfectly innocent member of the public.'

'I don't think so. This has been going on for months. You only have to ask Hugh. And every time it's the name of the aunt that's been changed, and her holiday destination has been altered to somewhere on the southwest coast —'

'Hold on a moment,' the Inspector interrupted, looking baffled. 'Hugh who?'

'Hugh Winterbourne. He's another actor in the play. You need to hear what he had to say about Stephen Spendlow.' I pulled out my phone and began scrolling through the pictures. 'Here,' I said when I'd found the ones I wanted. 'Here's the man sitting in Q7. He's called Lenny Shaw.'

Inspector Ford stared. If the name or face meant anything to him, he did not reveal it. 'And that woman in the green coat and blonde wig,' I added, 'is his accomplice.'

He shot a glance at me beneath his brows. 'May we borrow this phone for an hour or two?' I nodded and he handed it to Cruella. 'Sergeant, get on to the Met, will you? See if they can identify this man, and the woman in the photograph. And find out all you can about this Stephen Spendlow. We also need to speak to this other actor, Hugh Winterbourne.' He glanced at Ricky. 'I suppose we can contact him through the theatre?' Ricky nodded and he went on. 'Also, find out from the booking office if this seat Q7 is booked by the same person for every Wednesday matinee and what name it's booked in.' He was interrupted by Dean Collins' appearance at the kitchen door. 'Yes, Constable?'

'The divisional surgeon says that the body can go to the morgue now, sir.'

The inspector nodded. 'Any evidence of our

perpetrator?'

'Forensics are working on it.' Dean withdrew, without making eye contact with me. I'd try pumping him for information later.

The Inspector looked sadly at Ricky. 'I am very sorry for your loss, Mr Steiner.'

Ricky just nodded. 'Thank you.'

'So, there are two questions remaining here. First of all, how did our killer trace the unfortunate Mr Carstairs to this place? You were a friend of his father,' he added, turning to Ricky. 'Were you the person he usually turned to in time of trouble?'

'He'd come here now and again, usually when he needed money.'

'He was no longer in touch with his father?'

Ricky grunted. 'Not unless he's got a direct line to the afterlife.'

'I see. The other question is for Juno,' he said, looking at me. 'You've got a theory about these altered lines. Sum it up for me.'

'The aunt's holiday destination is always changed to a place here on the coast, somewhere with a beach. The name of the aunt gets changed to something odd, like Puffling or Kiwi. These could be the names of boats. I think this is all about telling the man in Q7 the name of a boat containing an illegal cargo, and where it's being landed.'

'So, if the man in Q7 is the intended recipient of these messages each week,' he asked, 'who do you imagine is sending them?'

'I don't know,' I admitted. 'All we do know is that the man who initially recruited Freddy, the man who ultimately threatened him with a gun, is foreign. Freddy thought Eastern European.'

Cruella sneered. 'It all sounds highly unlikely, sir.'

Inspector Ford favoured her with one of his meaningful stares. 'Just get on to the Met, like I asked you to, Sergeant.'

Because of all this, I didn't get to the shop at closing time as planned. Pat had been there during the afternoon and I knew I could rely on her to lock up for me, so once Inspector Ford let me go, I headed straight over to Elizabeth and Olly's place.

I was worried. Somehow, Lenny Shaw, or the thugs that worked for him, had managed to track Freddy to Druid Lodge. The Audi driver had already traced Elizabeth to Moorland View and from there to Daison Cottages. He'd been seen off by April Hardiman, but I was sure that he'd be back. I was surprised he hadn't been back already. And if Lenny Shaw and the owner of Raven's Tor Manor were part of the same family, they were people who were prepared to kill to get what they wanted. What would happen if they caught up with Elizabeth and discovered she couldn't pay them back the money that her husband owed them? Would they kill her too, just to send out a message? This is what happens when you don't pay up.

Elizabeth tried to maintain her usual calm when I told her the news about Freddy, but I read a flash of alarm in her eyes. 'You think whoever killed Colin also killed him?' she asked.

'How many contract killers do you think there are on the loose in this part of Devon?'

She raised an eyebrow. 'Point taken.'

'And he's very near, Elizabeth. He could be here right now. If you're not afraid for yourself, at least be afraid for Olly.'

'D'you think I'm not?' she hissed. 'I've taken steps,' she added after a moment, evading my eye.

'What does that mean?'

'I've put something together.'

'Elizabeth!' I wanted to scream at her. 'Tell the police! I know you used to shoot, but you know, you and your father's old wartime pistol may not be a match for a professional killer with a more powerful weapon.'

I shut up because the door into the hall opened suddenly and Olly was standing in the doorway, holding out a mobile phone. 'Oh, hello, Juno,' he grinned when he saw me. 'Lizzie, you left your phone in the living room. It's Tom.' He extended it towards her and she stood up and took it.

'Thank you,' she said. 'I'll take it in there,' and she disappeared into the living room and closed the door.

Olly came to sit at the kitchen table. 'While she's in there, I want to ask you something,' he said in low voice. He looked anxious. 'It's about her and Tom.'

'Why? What's the problem?'

'Well, I mean, they're getting on well, right? Do you

think they're in love? I mean, I like Tom. He's great. I like him a lot. But,' he hesitated an added awkwardly. 'D'you think they'll want to get married?'

Whatever I expected his question to be, it wasn't that. I laughed. 'I haven't really thought about it.'

'Only, if they do,' he went on, his face screwed up with concern, 'd'you think Tom will want to come and live here, like?'

'Which is worrying you more, Olly?' I asked. 'The possibility of losing an Elizabeth or gaining a Tom?'

He shook his head helplessly and for a moment he looked almost tearful. 'I just want things to stay the way they are,' he said sadly.

I could tell he was upset. I reached out a hand to him. 'Oh, Olly! Didn't Elizabeth promise you, when she first came to live here, that she would be here for you as long as you wanted her to be?'

'Well, yeh,' he admitted. 'But that was before Tom came along.'

'I really don't think you need to worry,' I told him. 'Tom has his own cottage. It's small and he's got it exactly the way he wants it. I don't think he wants a woman living there with him and I don't think Elizabeth would want to live there, anyway. At the moment, she can come and go whenever she wants. I think you'll find the present arrangement suits them both very well.'

'You sure?'

To be honest, I felt that things might change when Olly left school and went to college or whatever, but that was a year or two off yet. 'As sure as I can be,' I told him. 'For the time being, at least.'

He looked relieved. 'Okay. Thanks.'

I thought I might also take advantage of Elizabeth's absence. 'Olly, has Elizabeth mentioned anything about anyone coming around here, looking for her?'

'Oh, you mean that creep that April said she saw hanging around the back?' He nodded wisely. 'It's a good thing I keep the bike shed locked up.'

'It is, but if you ever see anyone else hanging around here, or anyone hanging around outside your school . . .'

'Hang on. Do you mean that bloke who asked to be remembered to her?' He frowned. 'But he's dead, isn't he?'

'Yes, he is. This would be someone else. If there is anyone asking questions about Elizabeth, will you promise to tell me?'

He looked doubtful, his blue eyes narrowing. 'Shouldn't I tell Lizzie?'

'Yes, of course, but I want you to promise to tell me too.'

'What's all this about then?'

'Nothing, I hope. Just being careful.'

'Alright,' he agreed, looking doubtful.

'You don't need to say anything to Elizabeth about what I just asked.'

He grinned suddenly. 'I won't if you won't.'

We heard sounds of Elizabeth returning. 'Deal,' I told him.

* * *

I didn't need to call Dean Collins because he came knocking on my door not long after I got back to the flat. He'd come to return my phone. He looked a bit down in the mouth, but brightened up when I invited him in for tea and biscuits.

'Gems has got a lock on the biscuit tin at home,' he complained.

I didn't think this was literally true. In fact, he'd lost a few pounds and was looking the better for it, but I imagined she'd be keeping a strict eye on what he ate at home. 'So, what's new then?' I began, casually unwrapping the chocolate digestives.

'I'll tell you what's new,' he responded, looking disgruntled. 'Thanks to you, I've got to drive Cruella up to London on Wednesday so that we can watch this stupid play.'

I felt mildly triumphant. 'To see if the lines get altered?'

He nodded, reaching out for the packet before I'd had time to put the biscuits in the tin. 'And if they do?'

'I can't tell you that,' he mumbled.

'You'll be keeping watch on whatever place is named,' I told him. 'Looking out for the arrival of the boat.'

'No comment.' He made another biscuit disappear.

'But why are they sending you two to watch the play?' I asked, thinking about it. 'Why don't they just send a detective from London?'

'Because the murder of Freddy Carstairs happened on our patch and the boss isn't prepared to hand the case over to the Met unless he has to. We'll share information when we've got something worth sharing.'

'Will you tell me where it is?' I asked. 'The place, I mean?

He snorted and almost choked on biscuit crumbs. 'No, I will not! Last thing we need is you turning up wherever it is.'

I knew that would be his answer. 'It doesn't matter,' I said with an airy shrug. 'I'll just ring the Davenport Theatre and speak to Hugh Winterbourne. He'll tell me.'

'Now, look here, Juno,' Dean began, wagging a chunky finger in my direction, 'I know you and those two old blokes you knock about with thought you were having fun going up to London, but this isn't a bloody game . . .'

'But it isn't fair. I'll miss all the fun.'

'Fair doesn't come into it. Like I said, it's not a bloody game.'

I scowled at him. 'No, you're right there.' I considered trying to snatch my packet of biscuits back, but instead I asked, 'So, am I allowed to know if you identified the people pictured on my phone?'

He grinned then. 'You were right. The man in Q7 is Leonard Shaw. He and his brothers run a criminal gang in London. They're into drugs, prostitution, extortion, blackmail, a really nasty bunch. Originally, it is believed, the family came from eastern Europe, Lithuania to be exact. And it turns out,' he went on, picking my phone up from the table and scrolling through the pictures, 'this pair of charmers here . . .' he pointed at the photofit of Messrs Smith and Jones hanging on the noticeboard at Moorland View, 'is part of the family.'

I didn't feel triumphant now. I just felt a sense of foreboding.

'Who are they?'

He pointed to the older, heavier one, the man that Colin had been seen talking to in the garden. 'This is Vincent Shaw, Leonard's brother. Not very clever, according to the Met, hence he's not very high up the pecking order. And this other one,' he pointed to the Audi driver, 'is Leonard's grandson, Nick – the favourite apparently and most likely to take over the firm from his grandad. He's a really evil little sod.'

'What about Leonard's son, Nick's father, isn't he in the running?'

'He had his jaw shot off in a drive-by killing a few years ago.'

I shuddered. 'Charming.'

'And I'm surprised at you, Miss Browne.' Dean's eyes twinkled. 'Whatever happened to equality?'

'What do you mean?'

'It's Nick's *mother*, not his father, who's Leonard's child.' He showed me the picture of the woman in the green coat.

'That's her?'

'Maggie Shaw. And she's just as evil as the rest of them.'

I could believe it. The glare she'd given me on the

steps of the theatre when she'd realised that I was following her, could have rivalled one of Cruella's.

Dean became serious again. 'These are dangerous people, Juno. I don't want you getting anywhere near 'em. Understand?'

For the moment I was more concerned about them getting near Elizabeth. 'Do we know if the gun that killed Freddy was the same gun that killed Colin Smethurst?' I asked.

Dean laughed. 'Not yet we don't. You've been watching too much television.'

'Can't a ballistics test tell this sort of thing?'

'Yes, but it can't be done in five minutes, you know. These things take time.'

I must have gone quiet, because after a little while I became conscious of Dean watching me. 'What's up, Juno?' he asked me gently. 'Why don't you tell me what's on your mind?'

'Nothing.'

'We're friends, aren't we? You can trust me.' His eyes were searching my face. I felt wretched and looked away.

'No?' he asked sadly. 'Then perhaps you can answer a question for me.' He pointed at the two men on the photofit. 'What are two violent, evil men like these doing at the Moorland View Residential Home in Bovey Tracy, trying to force information out of your friend Elizabeth's sister?'

I wanted to tell him. Instead, I just shrugged.

'And why was Colin Smethurst, an employee at

the home, a man whose life ended violently, carrying a picture of her around in his wallet? What's the connection, Juno? And don't try telling me you don't know, because I won't believe you.'

For Elizabeth's sake I had to tell him. Even now she didn't seem to realise the danger she was in. She didn't really know the kind of people she was dealing with. I drew in a breath. 'Elizabeth was married to a man called George Hunter who was addicted to gambling.' I let the words out in a rush. 'They lost everything because of his debts. When he died, she discovered that he was still massively in debt to some very nasty people . . .'

'He owed money to the Shaws?' Dean asked quickly.

'We didn't know it at the time,' I told him. 'But then these men turned up at Moorland View. They'd traced Elizabeth's sister Joan, somehow. Elizabeth thinks they'd got information from her old neighbours. They got at Colin Smethurst, offering him money to find out where Elizabeth lived. He was trying to blackmail her, threatening that if he she didn't pay him, he'd tell them where she was.'

'Bloody hell, Juno!' Dean exploded, reaching for the phone in his pocket, 'Why didn't you tell me this before?' He got up, heading to the door, the phone to his ear. 'Sir? We need to send a car up to Daison Cottages. Yes, right now, sir. Information received . . .' He turned to look back at me. 'Don't think this conversation is over!' he warned me, and ran off down the stairs.

No, I don't, I mused despondently. Because now I was going to have to tell him about the conversation

I'd overheard between Colin Smethurst and the man I now knew to be Nick Shaw, and that was going to land me in even more shit than I was in already.

I had another phone call around midnight. This time it was Elizabeth.

'There's a police car outside of the house,' she informed me without preamble. 'Apparently, it's there for my own protection. I've also had the pleasure of Dean Collins' company, followed not long after by the wretched Cruella and Detective Inspector Ford – all very keen to ask me questions about George.'

'I'm sorry Elizabeth, I had to.'

'I thought I could trust you, Juno.'

'You can,' I protested, stung. 'Look, all I told Dean was that George owed money to the Shaws.'

'And that Colin had been trying to blackmail me, thus establishing my motive for his murder. Thanks, Juno.'

'Did they say that?' I asked, shocked. 'That you had a motive for murdering Colin?'

'Oh, Cruella came right out with it. Thank goodness, they don't know I've got my father's pistol.'

'They'd soon discover it couldn't be the murder weapon.'

'The Luger is deadly, but I imagine Colin was shot with something more powerful.'

'Just like Freddy,' I said. 'And that's the point. Somehow, these people found Freddy. They almost found you. And look what they did to him and to Colin.'

I heard her give an exasperated sigh. She knew that I was right, she just didn't want to admit it. 'Now, of course, Olly wants to know what's going on.'

'But he's always known about George and his debts. He's not finding out anything about you he didn't know before. And if members of the Shaw gang are still around here, it's good for him to be on his guard.'

'Yes, I suppose you're right about that,' she admitted reluctantly. 'But I haven't forgiven you betraying my secret, Juno,' she warned me. 'Don't think I have.'

'No,' I thought despondently as she put the phone down. That would be too much to hope for.

In the end, I couldn't help myself. Despite everything that was going on, with Elizabeth, with Freddy's murder, with Maisie, even with Daniel, the person I kept thinking about was Jake. Next morning, as soon as I'd dumped the Tribe members back in their homes, I drove back to Maidencombe and headed straight for the woods to find his camp. It wasn't there, just an empty space under the trees, everything packed up and gone, just as he said it would be. The only trace his camp had ever existed was the smear of dead ash where his fire had been. I squatted and raked my fingers through it. It was still warm. Beneath a stone, weighing it down, was a white paper napkin from the beach café. I could see it had been scrawled with pencil and I picked it up.

Juno, I read. *Jake and I are alright. We take care of ourselves. You take care of yourself.*

Bella x

He knew I'd come back. I began to laugh, until, for no reason I could explain, I started to cry.

CHAPTER TWENTY-TWO

Late on Wednesday afternoon, I went to pick Maisie up from Torbay Hospital. She'd been pronounced fit enough to be discharged in the morning, but because of sorting out her prescriptions, the ward didn't release her until the end of the day. Our Janet had been to visit her earlier and say goodbye before she started the long drive back to Heck-as-Like. The poor woman was needed back at home. She'd fixed up with the agency for Maisie's carers to resume their duties that evening, so there would be someone to help her into bed. She just needed picking up from the hospital and I'd volunteered for the job, intending to drive over as soon as I'd locked up the shop.

I couldn't help wondering, throughout the afternoon, how Dean and Cruella were getting on watching the performance of *Murder Weekend*. Was Leonard Shaw sitting in Q7? Was his daughter Maggie in S5? And most important of all, what was Aunt Drusilla calling herself this week, and where was she taking her holiday? I just hoped something was happening. It would be a dreadful disappointment if she was plain Aunt Drusilla after all, and she was only going to Scarborough.

On my way to Brook Cottage I switched on the radio, just in time to hear the local news. *'Fire and rescue crews were called to a blaze in Maidencombe last night at the derelict Devon Grange Hotel. Station Commander Mostyn is reported as saying that in view of the difficulty in accessing and getting water to the site, and as the building was unoccupied and known to be in a dangerous condition, the decision was taken not to commit personnel to tackling the blaze and to let the fire burn itself out. Arson is strongly suspected.'* I bet it is, I thought to myself. Another loose end tidied up.

Tuesday had been a horrible day and I'd been glad to leave it behind. Apart from my impulsive and ultimately pointless drive to Jake's camp, Elizabeth wasn't speaking to me. Her secret kept on unravelling. I found this out from Olly, who seemed to have come into the shop during his school lunch hour specifically to tell me about it. It seemed that Tom Carter had arrived at the house while the police car was outside and demanded to know what was going on, forcing Elizabeth to tell him about her problem with George's gambling past, a fact she had kept to herself when they'd first met and she'd told him she was a widow.

'Was Tom upset?' I asked.

'He says he's more cross than anything, because she's in trouble and she didn't ask him for help. He says she's got too much pride and she should have trusted him.'

He was right on both counts. 'But is he okay now that her secret is out in the open?'

'Yeh, I think so. It's not as if Lizzie's been telling him lies. There's just stuff about herself she hasn't mentioned, that's all. Well, alright, she's not really my aunt —'

'There's no need to tell him that bit,' I put in hastily. 'You haven't, have you?'

'No. 'Course not!' he said indignantly. 'I haven't told him anything. The thing is,' he went on, his face screwing up in a worried frown, 'you know I was worried about him moving in? Well, he more or less has now, because he says he's not going anywhere until all this business gets sorted out. And Lizzie's flown off the handle, because she says there's no point in him being there and putting himself at risk unnecessarily, and anyway there is no risk because the police are there, which Tom says is contradicting herself and isn't that just like a woman?' He sat back, grinning. 'Oh!' he added, tapping the counter with a skinny finger as he remembered. 'And Lizzie said that she wanted him to go away, back to his cottage, and take *me* with him, because I'd be safer there staying with him than I would be with her.'

'And what did you say to that?'

'I said, "This is my bloody house and I ain't going nowhere". And she told me off for swearing and told me what I meant to say was that I wasn't going *anywhere*. And I told her, "Yeh, that's what I just said".'

I couldn't help laughing but the truth was, Elizabeth was right. For the time being, Olly would be safer out of her immediate vicinity. But as neither he, nor Tom, was prepared to think about leaving her to face danger on her own, it wasn't a situation that was likely to arise. The bigger danger was that, unless the Shaws made another attempt to find her pretty soon, the police would be likely to relax their vigilance, seeing it as a diminishing risk, exposing her to greater danger in the long run. She would never be able to stop looking over her shoulder. I didn't mention this to Olly, of course, and he packed himself back off to school before he was late for his afternoon lessons.

I hoped Elizabeth would forgive me eventually.

Maisie was more than ready to come home. 'I've been waiting all day here, just for them to come up with a few painkillers,' she complained, as I wheeled her towards the main hospital entrance in a wheelchair. 'If I'd known that a few paracetamols was all that I was waiting for, I could have sent you to the chemist.'

'Never mind, you're going home now. Jacko will be pleased to see you.' I wasn't actually too sure about that. He seemed to have settled down very comfortably at Bev's, two doors down. He might not be too happy to be forced to return to his previous accommodation.

'Well, at least I'll be sleeping in my own bed,' she admitted. 'It's so noisy in this place, and they get you up too early. They bring you your breakfast before it's barely light. And you have to pay to watch the telly!'

The automatic doors opened in front of us, letting in a blast of cold air. 'It's freezing!' she complained as I wheeled her out of doors.

'It's turned cold again,' I agreed. A bitter wind was sweeping down from the north, more winter than spring.

'Mind you, it was too hot in that ward,' she sniffed disparagingly.

I made the right sympathetic murmuring noises as I manoeuvred her into the front seat of the van. Her wrist was heavily strapped and supported by a sling, so getting her seatbelt done up was a more difficult operation than usual.

'And that woman in the bed opposite that you were so fond of talking to,' she went on as I stowed her bag in the back, 'she went home yesterday and the new one they moved into her bed . . . well!' She shook her apricot curls in disgust. 'Mad as a box of frogs!'

I was only half listening as I did up my own seatbelt and made to turn the ignition. Then I froze, my hand on the key. Two cars away, parked in the zone that was for picking up only, stood the black Audi. And being helped across the pavement to the kerb, was the man I now knew to be Nick Shaw. Except he wasn't going to be driving this time. He was walking with the aid of crutches, his right foot heavily encased in a surgical boot, and was guided around to the passenger side and helped into the seat by the driver. He must have been in some kind of accident. Perhaps he'd come off that expensive motorbike of his. But the real focus of my attention was the man helping him, the man who eventually walked around to the driver's side and slid into the driver's seat. Daniel Thorncroft.

I heard Maisie's voice as if it was coming from a

long way away, barely audible above the sudden rush of blood in my own ears. 'What's the matter with you?' she was demanding. 'You look as if you've seen a ghost. What's up?'

'Nothing,' I breathed, watching the Audi pull away. Every nerve in my body was screaming for me to follow, but I couldn't, not with Maisie in the car. I had to get her home safely.

'Well, why aren't we moving?' she demanded.

I breathed out slowly as I turned the key in the ignition. 'It's alright, we're going now,' I told her, releasing the handbrake.

She was scowling at me, her little face screwed up and fierce. 'About bleedin' time,' she tutted, as the van pulled away.

CHAPTER TWENTY-THREE

Jacko seemed genuinely pleased to see Maisie when she returned to Brook Cottage, wagging his tail and sniffing all around her, even though he did try to leave with Bev when she went home later. Luckily, I don't think Maisie noticed.

Bev had turned up at the door about five minutes after we'd arrived, carrying Jacko's bed and other accoutrements, and stayed for a cup of tea, while Maisie told her what an ordeal staying in the hospital had been, even though all the doctors and nurses had been wonderful.

'There's nothing like being in your own bed, is there?' Bev agreed. I took the chance for a good look around the cottage while the two of them chatted. Janet had given the place a spring clean during her stay, and got in a lot of shopping. I knew Maisie would complain about the brands she had bought and send me out for different ones, but that could wait until tomorrow. For tonight, there wasn't much for me to do except switch on her electric blanket and wait for the agency carer to arrive.

I was desperate to get away. I don't know how we'd got back to Ashburton without crashing. I must have been on auto-pilot, couldn't remember driving home at all. All I could think about was Daniel at the hospital, climbing into the driving seat of that black Audi, next to Nick Shaw. What was he doing? Didn't he know the kind of man Nick Shaw was? 'I suppose you'd like an early night, Maisie?' I suggested hopefully.

'I'm not going to bed,' she told me sharply. 'I only just got here.'

I was afraid of that. I phoned Our Janet, to let her know that her mother was home safely. She wasn't yet home herself, still driving the last few miles to Heck-As-Like, and didn't phone back until about ten minutes later when she'd pulled into the safety of a lay-by. We chatted for a few minutes, during which time Bev let herself out, promising to visit Maisie again tomorrow, and waving a silent goodbye to me with a waggle of her fingers. The television began blaring loudly as Maisie sat fiddling with the remote. She'd abandoned the sling on her arm, I noticed. She'd probably be fine on her own until the agency carer arrived to put her to bed, but I didn't feel I could leave her when I'd just brought her home from hospital. I resigned myself to sitting with her, watching a boring cookery competition with a long, fake, dramatic pause as each of the contestants was eliminated; until the cavalry arrived in the form of Maria from the agency.

A few minutes later I escaped and sat in the van with my forehead resting on the steering wheel, finally giving in to what I'd been aching to do: sobbing. After I'd indulged myself until my throat was sore, I pulled myself together and wiped my eyes. I may not have been able to follow Daniel and his passenger from the hospital, but I could make an educated guess about where they might be going. I turned Van Blanc around and headed off up towards the moor, to Raven's Tor Manor.

It was dark by the time I got there, too dark to do what I wanted to do and approach the manor from the back, hiking over ground from Lustleigh Cleave, as I'd done last time I was here. I wasn't properly equipped. I should have gone back to my flat from Maisie's and collected warm clothes, walking gear and a proper torch. But I'd been in too much of a state to think about it. The only torch I had on me was the one in my phone, and the only equipment was whatever assemblage of odds and ends were in my jacket pockets, which I suspected was mostly old tissues.

Instead, I drove on past the track which led to the manor and parked on the verge a hundred yards beyond the turning, got out of the van and began walking back. There were no clouds, the sky above was clear, the air still; there could be a frost tonight. As I trudged back along the road, a breeze tugged at the hem of my jacket, encouraging me to zip it up. The darkness of the lane closed in around me, the hedges on either side, the bare branches of pollarded trees thrust black fingers upward against the deepening sky. I trod softly. My trainers didn't make as much noise on the smooth, new tarmac as my walking boots.

There was no one about, no one waving a shotgun and challenging my right to be there. I reached the steel five-bar gate and stared across the field at the old barn. There was no sign of the Audi. The old fore-loader tractor was parked on the hard-standing outside, and just beyond it, white in the gloom, was the lorry with *Devon Garden Services* painted on its sides. A light in the barn glowed through crooked gaps in the walls. I heard a metallic clang from inside. Someone was opening or closing that trapdoor. I wanted a closer look. I could climb over the five-bar gate, but it might rattle and give me away. A quieter, but more painful way was to find a place in the hedge where I could squeeze between the bushes; and that's what I did, silently cursing as twigs tore at my hair. I yanked myself free, leaving a tuft of red curls caught on a hawthorn.

From where I now stood, I was facing the back of the barn. There were piles of plastic sacks that hadn't been there the last time I came, rows of them. Probably the same sacks of compost I'd seen piled in the garden at The Devon Grange Hotel had arrived in that white lorry. I scurried across the grass and peered through the gap in the barn wall. The interior was lit by a single dim lamp hanging from an overhead beam; a much brighter light was glaring up through the trapdoor, which lay open. There was no one in the barn, watching, guarding the place. Whoever had opened that trapdoor must have gone down inside.

I crept to the door, tiptoed across the concrete and crouched, peering down the short length of a sturdy wooden ladder. For a moment, I listened to the voice in my head that told me that climbing down that ladder would not be a sensible thing to do. But only for a moment. Whatever lay at the foot of it was sealed off by a curtain of thick, translucent plastic, and I wanted a look. Heart thumping, I climbed down softly, placing each foot with care and then waiting for any sound before I placed the next one. The walls around me were made of rusty blue metal. I was descending into something like a shipping container, buried in the earth. I could hear the hum from a fan or generator. Turning myself around in the small space at the foot of the ladder, I peered through the curtain, my vision blurred by the veil of plastic. It was like trying to see underwater. All I could make out were misty halos of bright light. I peeled back the edge of the plastic with my fingertips, just enough to get a clear view. Light blazed from rows of low-hung lamps and bounced off walls lined with silver foil reflectors. The space overhead was festooned with electric cables, and below the hanging lights, in rank after serried rank, stood dark green plants in pots. The smell was overwhelming; sickly, sweet, sweaty in the humid air. It was not Christmas trees they were growing down here. I dared not take a step through the curtain. Whoever had opened that trapdoor must be here somewhere in this forest. But I could take a photograph. I reached in my pocket for my phone.

A shadow moved above me and startled, I looked up. Fungus Face was aiming his shotgun down the ladder, pointing it straight at my face. 'Evening, Miss,' he grinned. 'We were wondering if you were going to turn up again.'

CHAPTER TWENTY-FOUR

The Audi was parked outside of the manor house, its black metal shape glinting in the light cast from a downstairs window. If my heart had been thumping on the walk up the drive from the barn, the crunch of heavy footsteps just behind me, the muzzle of a shotgun pressed between my shoulder blades, it began thumping twice as hard at the sight of the car that Daniel had driven here. Any moment I might see him. And he would see me. What would happen then?

The front door of the manor opened and I was looking down a long, lighted hall. The person who opened it was just a dark silhouette at first. As I drew closer, I recognised the heavy features of the man photographed in the garden at Moorland View, Nick Shaw's uncle, Vincent. He bore a definite resemblance to Lenny. What was it Dean had told me about him? That he wasn't too bright, wasn't far up the pecking order. I could believe it. The eyes that stared back at me were dull, his face as blank and impassive as a lump of granite. He stepped aside to let me pass. I hesitated on the threshold and got a poke between the shoulder blades from Fungus Face and his shotgun.

'This way.' Vincent led the way down the hall as if he was a butler showing in a guest. He trod heavily. I followed, ever conscious of the muzzle of that shotgun. The walls around me were bare, stripped of old wallpaper, tiny shreds still clinging to cracked plaster, renovation work started but never finished. We passed the open doorways of empty rooms. It was obvious that no one was living here.

But the room we eventually turned into was different. There was a rug on the floor, modern blinds at the windows. A solitary desk-lamp was the only light in the room, the rest lay in shadow. On a table stood a rank of CCTV screens, showing different pictures from cameras around the house. Anyone approaching the place could be seen, coming from any direction. One screen showed the inside of the barn, the bare interior with its trapdoor wide open. Another showed the barn from the outside. And there was a still picture, taken in daylight, of me trying to break in. Sitting in a swivel chair with his back to them all, his heavy surgical boot resting on a footstool like some puppet princeling on a throne, was Nick Shaw. His face looked ghastly in the light of the desk lamp, his skin yellowish, sheened by a film of sweat. His foot must be giving him trouble.

For a moment we stared at each other in silence. Then he spoke. 'We dug up your old picture when we saw you were here again,' he told me, jerking his head at the screen. I was barely listening to him, my eyes roving the corners of the room for a glimpse of Daniel. Someone was standing back there in the shadows; someone I couldn't see. 'You know, you're not bad looking for filth,' Nick's voice went on. When I didn't respond he leant forward and raised his voice. 'I take it that's what you are – filth?'

I thought I'd better pay him some attention. 'I don't know what you mean.'

'Police,' he hissed.

'I'm not police.'

'Then what are you?'

I didn't reply. He sat back in his chair, swivelling slightly. 'I take it I don't need to introduce myself?'

'You're Lenny Shaw's boy, Nick.'

He smiled, pleased with himself and I added, 'You know, you're shorter than I imagined.'

The smile vanished. 'Check her out,' he said to no one in particular. 'Make sure she's not wearing a wire.'

'I'll do it.' Even though I was expecting to see him, his voice sent a shockwave through me. Because suddenly there he was, coming towards me out of the shadows, his face grave, expressionless as a carved statue, his grey eyes as hard. Daniel. For a moment his eyes met mine and I saw nothing but winter. Then he lowered his gaze and I could see only the pattern of his dark lashes as he concentrated on his task, opening the buttons of my shirt, feeling around my rib cage. I trembled at his touch. I'd yearned for the caress of those long fingers. Now I felt sick. 'Nothing,' he said at last.

'Get her jacket off. Empty out her pockets,' Nick

ordered, clicking his fingers, 'Let's see what she's got.' Daniel pulled the jacket off me. I didn't resist. I felt numb, like a creature caught in the headlights of a fast-approaching car. I couldn't take my eyes off him, couldn't move. He rifled through my pockets then handed Nick my phone.

He began to scroll through the messages. It wasn't warm in the room, but I could see the beads of sweat standing out on his brow. 'So, if you're not filth,' he continued without taking his eyes from the screen, 'then who are you, and what are you doing here?' He glanced at me briefly, 'A second time.'

My eyes were still locked on Daniel's face. It was on the tip of my tongue to say 'Why don't you ask *him*?' but some instinct for preservation held me back. I dragged my gaze away and turned to face Nick. 'I fancied one of your pot plants. Thought I might start rolling my own spliffs.'

His laugh was like the staccato rattle of a machine gun. 'I like you. You're funny. But you see, here's the thing. When we found your lovely picture on our security camera a few days ago, I mentioned to the guv'nor that we'd had a tall red-haired woman snooping about here, and he said "That's funny, 'cos I've had a tall, red-haired bint sitting next to me in the theatre, trying to take my photograph. Why don't you send me the picture you've got, in case it's the same woman." And guess what?'

'I don't know what you're talking about.'

'No?' he turned my phone around and showed me

the screen, the picture of Lenny Shaw sitting in the theatre in Q7.

I said nothing. There was nothing I could say.

Nick had resumed his scrolling. 'There's even a picture of you on here, Uncle Vince,' he sniggered, 'taken in the garden at that home we visited, talking to our friend Colin.' He looked up at me. 'Now, why would you have a photograph of Vince and Colin on your phone?'

I couldn't think of a ready answer, all I knew was that if he kept scrolling through the pictures on my phone, he'd find Daniel on there. Instead, I asked him a question. 'Was it you who killed Colin, or was it Uncle Vincent over there?'

'And why should you care who killed him?' His eyes narrowed. 'What was Colin Smethurst to you?'

'Nothing,' I told him. 'Except he was a human being and someone shot him in the head.' Did Daniel know that? Did he know the kind of people he had got mixed up with?

Nick gave a short laugh. 'He was *less* than nothing. He could have been useful to me, but he couldn't keep his promises, failed to deliver. He became a loose end, needed tidying up. Know what I mean?' He held up his thumb and forefinger, pointing the finger at me as if it was the barrel of a gun, and grinned. 'Pow!' he said softly.

A chill ran through me but I tried to look unimpressed. I shook my head sadly. 'Boys and their toys.'

'Funny lady, eh? Well, don't worry, love. You don't have to say anything right now, because as luck would have it, the guv'nor is driving down here this very night, to check on the progress of our operation, and he particularly wants to speak to you. Ask you a few questions.' He tossed my phone aside and looked at me, his voice softly menacing. 'And you'd better come up with something good, because the guv'nor can be quite inventive when he wants answers. Know what I mean?'

I could guess. That smartly-dressed man sitting next to me in seat Q7, talking with reverence about how much he loved the theatre, politely accepting one of Morris's chocolate eclairs, a rather old-fashioned gentleman one would have thought, was an evil monster making money from the suffering of others.

Nick called to Fungus Face. 'Kenny, you and Danny take this lady down to the icehouse, will you? Lock her up. Give her a chance to cool off.'

Danny? No one ever called Daniel, Danny. And Kenny? Fungus Face suited him better.

'Uncle Vince, you better go too.'

Daniel grabbed hold of my arm. I tried to wrench it away, but he tightened his grip, the pressure of his fingers like iron as he dragged me towards the door. I might have fought to tear myself away if it hadn't been for Fungus Face and his gun just behind us. The solid figure of Vincent plodded heavily in front, lighting our way with a torch.

I stared at Daniel's stern profile. How could he do this, how could he be taking orders from a man like Nick Shaw? Had he crossed over to the dark side? Not the Daniel I knew. Could grief over Claire's death have tipped him over the edge? I didn't want to believe it. Yet here he was, stone-faced, dragging me through the darkness.

'Daniel!' I hissed at him.

He didn't answer, didn't look at me, gave my arm a warning squeeze. 'Do you think she'd like what you're doing?' I whispered. 'Claire?'

He didn't answer, his mouth set in a grim line.

'Well, would she?'

'Shut up!' He gripped my arm so tight that I yelped. We'd arrived at a tumble-down brick building, its roof open to the starlit sky. Above us, the full moon wore a ring around it, a halo of brightness. It would have been romantic under other circumstances.

Vincent bent down and I heard the scraping back of a bolt. It sounded rusty and stiff, in needed of oiling. We were standing on the edge of another trapdoor, but not like the one in the barn, an old wooden trapdoor, the planks shrunken and warped with age. Vincent swung it open and shone the torch inside. I stared down a long iron ladder disappearing into the dark.

'Down you go!' Kenny nudged me with the end of his shotgun.

Daniel spoke suddenly. 'I'll go down first. No point in her breaking her neck.' He released the crushing grip on my arm, and I clutched at my shirtsleeve, shivering without the warmth of my jacket. I watched him climb down the ladder into a narrow, brick-lined shaft. Then he disappeared into the blackness, beyond the reach of Vincent's torch beam and I could see him no longer. It was several more seconds before he yelled up. 'Okay!' and clicked on a torch of his own.

I hesitated, staring into the abyss. I'm not nervous of ladders but right now I was trembling, and not just with cold. 'Go on.' Vince's giant hand descended heavily on my shoulder, guiding me towards the edge. I bent down, gripped the top rung with both hands, then placed my foot on the rung beneath.

'Don't worry, Miss,' Kenny sniggered, handing the shotgun to Vince. 'I'll be right behind you.'

I began the descent, feeling with one foot at a time for each of the rungs below me. The iron ladder was thin, but firm, bolted solidly into the brick wall behind it. Kenny had already started to climb down after me, moving faster than I was, as if he was trying to rush me, unnerve me, his kicking boots almost in my face. In the light of Daniel's torch, shining up from below, I could see the walls of the shaft widening out into a chamber. I counted twenty-five steps. The ladder ended about three feet short of the ground and I jumped. As I landed on the stone floor, I momentarily lost my balance. Daniel's arm shot out to steady me, gripping my wrist. The floor sloped towards a drain in the centre, several deep runnels for meltwater carved into the stone. This was where ice would have been stored years ago, in a brick-lined, sunken chamber so cold that it would stay frozen all year.

Kenny landed with a noisy thump next to where Daniel stood. 'Tie her up,' he told him.

'What for?' He shone his torch around the solid

walls of the chamber. There was no door down here. No access. When they'd wanted ice in the manor house years ago, they'd have dug it out from the top. 'She can't go anywhere.'

Kenny produced a short length of thick rope from his pocket. 'Just do it.'

Daniel thrust the torch at him and took the rope. All the time his grip on my wrist never lessened. He dragged me closer to the ladder, looping the rope around my wrist and then twisting the free end around the nearest rung twice. Instinctively I tried to pull back, to twist away. I lashed out with my free hand and caught him across the cheekbone with my fingernails. He barely flinched.

'Behave!' Kenny grabbed my hand and between the two of them they bound the rope around my other wrist, pulling it tight, so that it lay close to the first, separated only by a twist of rope, rough against my skin. He checked the knots and grunted, satisfied. He gestured with the torch at Daniel. 'Up you go, Danny!'

Just for a moment Daniel seemed to hesitate, as if he didn't want to leave me alone with this other man. Then he shrugged and began to climb, without even a backward glance in my direction. I watched him disappear up the ladder and I was left alone with Kenny.

He grabbed my face, crushing my cheeks between his fingers and thumb and peering into my eyes. 'No point in gagging you, Miss. You can scream your lungs out down here. No one will hear you.'

Vince's voice floated down from the top of the shaft.

'What are you doing down there?'

'Nothing.' He released his hold on my face and then put his foot on the first rung of the ladder, his boots narrowly missing my bound hands. 'See you later.' He spoke as if he was looking forward to it and climbed. There was a moment when all three men stood looking down at me. Kenny smirking with a kind of smug satisfaction, Vincent expressionless as a zombie, or maybe as someone who's seen this kind of thing too many times to be moved any longer. And Daniel, what expression could I read in his eyes? He dropped the trapdoor, let it fall shut and I heard the bolt rattle home.

All around me was blackness. Above, a thin ribbon of moonlight defined the ragged rectangle of the ancient trapdoor. Towards the top of the ladder, a few rungs glinted silver in a finger of light. I was shivering with cold. I began to sob softly, but not in despair. I held on to a glimmer of hope as slender as that finger of moonlight. I held on to the object that Daniel had taken from my jacket pocket and, as he'd bound my hands together, pressed secretly into my palm. I could feel the plastic disc, hard, round and flat against my skin, about the size of a fifty pence piece: my little snipe.

CHAPTER TWENTY-FIVE

I was terrified I would drop the bloody thing. It was so hard to hold on to, to work from my palm into a position where I could grip it between my fingers and use my thumb to make the blade slide out, and my hands were so cold. It was frigging freezing down here. I couldn't stop shivering. If I didn't get a move on, I was likely to die of hypothermia before those bastards upstairs could do anything worse to me.

In the blind blackness at the foot of the ladder, I couldn't see. But I didn't need to. Twisting one wrist at right angles to the other tightened the distance between them, but it also brought my little blade in contact with the rope that was looped around the rung. Gripping on to it for dear life, I began sawing back and forth, making one tiny cut after another as I worked through the thick fibres. It was like unpicking stitches. The snipe had been made for cutting string or parcel tape, not for thick rope like this. I prayed the blade wouldn't break.

I had to keep stopping. My sawing hand, fingers bent towards the wrist in an unnatural position, kept cramping up. I longed to flex them, stretch them out, but didn't dare risk losing my hold on the snipe. I would just take few seconds to pause and breathe deeply, before I began the attack again. I had to keep going, to get out of there before they came back for me.

I tried not to think about Daniel, about what he was doing in the company of evil men. What had made him give me this frail weapon? Guilt? Did he genuinely want me to escape, or was this a mercy killing? Did he hope I might cut my throat to save myself from whatever the Shaws had in store for me, and so save him from the disclosure that he and I knew each other? I tried not to think about it, just kept going, one tiny cut after another.

I don't know how long it took. I'd lost all sense of time. Glancing up once, it seemed that the beam of moonlight was striking the rungs of the ladder at a more slanted angle, as if the moon had sunk lower, but I tried not to get distracted. I could feel the steel of the rung through the last fibres of the rope. They parted and the rope's grip slackened. Twisting my hand, I managed to pull it back through the loosened loop. For a moment I transferred the snipe to the other hand so that I could stretch my free hand out, flex my fingers, shake my wrist and feel the agony of returning blood. After a minute or so, when my fingers had enough life in them, I unwound the cut end of the rope from the rung of the ladder and freed my other hand.

My wrists were raw, stinging from rope-burn, but I had to climb. What I was going to do when I got to the top of the ladder was another matter. The trapdoor was bolted. I just had to hope that the bolt was stronger than the rotten wood surrounding it, that I might be able to break through it somehow.

I gripped the sides of the ladder with both hands, found the bottom rung with one foot and tried to haul myself up. For a moment my body swung, dizzy with the effort, my other leg pedalling the air, struggling to find a foothold. When I had both feet firmly on the ladder, I slid my hands upwards, gripped the rung above me and began to climb, up towards the moonlight, the touch of each cold metal rung a step closer to salvation. As I drew near the top, I could see my hand on the rung above me, bone-white where the moonlight struck it, and the cloud of my breath in the cold air. I rested for a moment. Only a few more feet to go.

I climbed until my outstretched fingers touched the underside of the trapdoor. The rotting wood felt damp, slimy and soft. I was sure the ragged edges would be friable, if only I could reach them.

I didn't get the chance. Above my head came the thump of a footstep, the rattle of the bolt being drawn back, and I saw the glow from a torch. I was trapped. I didn't have time to climb back down the ladder. I sure as hell wasn't going to drop off it and risk breaking my neck. There was nowhere to hide in the darkness, nowhere that the probing torchlight wouldn't find me. The door was flung open, I was dazzled. I narrowed my eyes and could see a solitary dark figure but couldn't make out the face of the man holding the torch. Then he spoke. 'You did it, Miss B! I knew if anyone could do it, you could.'

'Daniel?' I breathed.

A long arm was thrust down towards me. 'Here, take my hand.'

I hung back, uncertain if I could trust him.

'Juno, come on!' he urged fiercely. 'Nick is knocked out with painkillers right now, but we haven't got long. You've got to trust me.'

I had no choice. I took his hand and let him help me up through the trapdoor and on to my feet.

'Oh God, you're so cold,' he moaned, feeling my arm. He pocketed the torch. 'I've brought your coat,' he said, picking it up from the ground.

I let him wrap it round me. I felt numb, not just with cold, but stupefied by a tangle of thoughts that felt like barbed wire in my head. I pulled back from him.

'Daniel, what the hell . . . ?'

He grabbed my arm. 'I'll explain everything. I promise. But right now, I need to get you away from here. We haven't got long.'

'I'm not going anywhere with you.'

He stretched out a hand to touch my cheek but I jerked my head away from him. I heard him sigh. 'I'm sorry, my love. So sorry. But I couldn't let them suspect that you and I knew each other.' He took my face between his hands. 'Oh God, Juno!' he murmured. In the moonlight I could see him clearly, his face no longer the stony mask it had been, but the Daniel I knew and loved. Suddenly his lips were on mine. For a moment I let myself be folded into his embrace, felt the warmth of him, felt my body melt against his. Then I swung my arm back and punched him hard on the jaw. Not so fast, Mr Thorncroft.

He staggered but stayed on his feet. Then he raised an eyebrow in surprise and grinned, feeling his jaw. 'I suppose I deserve that.'

I tried to ignore the broken bones in my hand. 'Daniel, what are you doing?' I hissed at him. 'These people are drug dealers. Killers!'

'It's not what it looks like. I'll explain everything,' he promised. 'But first,' he said putting an arm around me, 'we've got to get away from here. Get you somewhere warm.'

Somewhere warm was an old hut in the woods, not much warmer than somewhere cold. But it had to do. I refused to go any further before he told me what the hell was going on. We sat together on the floor, our backs propped up against the wall behind us. I'd let Daniel wrap his arms around me and lean me back against his shoulder but was trying to ignore how good this felt until I'd heard what he had to say.

'I'm sorry, Miss Browne with an e,' he began, sounding genuinely contrite. 'I had to make you believe I was one of them.'

'I wish you hadn't been so damn good at it.'

He looked down at me and grinned. 'I'm hurt you should have been so easily convinced.'

'It's not funny for God's sake.'

'I'm sorry,' he whispered, nestling his face into my hair. 'I'm so sorry. I looked into your eyes just once. I didn't dare look at you again in case my feelings got the better of me.'

'Daniel,' I begged him in a fierce whisper, 'just tell me what happened.'

'Do you remember the last time we spoke?' he asked.

How could I forget? I told him to go away. At the time I thought I'd meant it. Perhaps I didn't really believe he'd go.

'You told me to get out of Ashburton, *out of my space,* if I recall correctly.' He gave a wry smile. 'You obviously felt the town wasn't big enough for both of us.'

'I just couldn't bear you being in my world and not loving me,' I admitted.

'There was never a moment when I didn't love you,' he murmured. 'But you said that a part of me would always belong to Claire, and you were right. A part of me will always hold the memory of her, the memory of the love we shared together. But I did what you asked. I left.'

'Where did you go?'

'I told the firm I wanted to work on a different project, so we agreed I should take over the running of a scheme up in Scotland. But I couldn't forget you, Miss Browne with an e. What was destroying me was not my grief for Claire, but how much I'd hurt you. I'd made such a bloody mess of things. You deserved someone better than me.'

I turned to look at him. 'That's not true. I wish you'd come back. We could have talked.'

He shook his head. 'I wasn't ready. I knew, if I wasn't going to mess it up a second time, I had to pull myself together.' Unconsciously, he had started playing with my hair, gently fiddling with the end of a curl. I decided not to stop him. 'I felt like I was stuck at the bottom of a big black hole. The anti-depressants weren't helping. I chucked them away. Then I chucked in the job.'

'Oh no,' I breathed. His work had always meant so much to him.

'I started travelling around, camping out,' he went on, 'living rough, I don't know for how long – weeks, months, probably.'

I thought of Jake, of the life he was leading, of Bella. 'What about Lottie?' I asked. 'Where is she?'

'What I was doing wasn't fair on her, so I took her to Claire's sister. She's looking after her for the moment.'

'Oh. Poor Lottie.' I knew she would be pining for him. 'I saw you in Torquay, crossing the road by the homeless hostel. I came after you, tried to find you.'

'Did you?' He shook his head in disbelief. 'That might have been the very night.'

'What night?'

'I'd been travelling, for . . . I don't know how long . . . I ended up in Wales, somewhere. I was standing by the side of this road in the middle of nowhere and it started bloody snowing. And it was like waking up from a bad dream. I realised what an idiot I was. And from then on all I could think of was getting back down here, coming home and trying to win you back somehow. I thought, I'll walk all the way if I have to. But I hitch-hiked, got a lift as far as

Torquay, got dropped off and then . . .'

I turned to look at him again. 'Then what?'

'I met Nick.' He spread his hands in a helpless gesture. 'I'd walked into town to look for a cash machine. I took what I thought was a short cut and found myself at the end of an alleyway watching a fight going on. A man was on the ground, being attacked, three or four louts kicking him. One hit him with a crowbar. Another picked up a lump of concrete, ready to drop it on him. I started yelling, running towards them, ready to pitch in.' He laughed. 'If I'd known what kind of man I was trying to help, perhaps I'd have left them to finish the job.'

'No, you wouldn't,' I said.

'No, you're right,' he admitted ruefully, 'I wouldn't. But I thought he was an honest citizen being set upon by thugs. As it turned out, they were a rival drugs gang and he was trespassing on their patch. But I didn't find that out until later.'

'What happened?'

'His attackers ran off. I helped him to his feet, but it was clear he couldn't walk. He couldn't put his foot to the floor and he certainly couldn't drive. I wanted to call an ambulance but he wouldn't hear of it so I got him to his car and drove him to A&E. Several bones in his foot were broken and he had two fractured ribs, as well as cuts and bruises. He spun the hospital some story about having had a fall, which they clearly didn't believe. I stayed with him until the small hours, while they X-rayed him and patched him up.

'Then I drove him to his home, to an apartment block overlooking the sea. He couldn't be left alone for twenty-four hours, the hospital had told me, because of the painkillers they'd given him and in case of delayed concussion. He was pretty groggy with it all and asked me if I would stay, sleep in the spare room.' He smiled. 'I have to confess, the thought of a clean, comfortable bed, not to mention a hot shower and a shave, was enough to persuade me. And I could see he genuinely needed someone there with him.'

'You decided to stay?'

'I thought it would only be till morning. But by this time, Nick had persuaded himself that I'd saved his life.'

'You probably had.'

He shrugged. 'I don't know about that. But the point is, Miss B, he was grateful. He wanted to reward me for my help. I think, even then, I realised what a despicable individual he was. He told me I could have anything I wanted. Drugs, women. He could order me a girl as easily as he could order me a pizza. He tried to give me money. I refused. Then he asked if I wouldn't mind sticking around for a day or two. He could use my help. That part was true. He was in pain and if anything, I was afraid he might overdose on painkillers, he was chewing them like sweets. I felt I couldn't refuse.'

'Did he live alone in this place, wasn't there anyone else there?'

'Not at the time.' He frowned. 'When we were at the hospital, I'd asked him if there was anyone that he wanted me to call and he'd said no. What I've realised since, of course, is that he didn't want anyone to find out he'd been beaten up, especially anyone in his family. He'd made a bad mistake, going where he did, a mistake that could have been fatal. And in his family, letting other people get the better of him meant a loss of face.'

'Where was Vincent during all this?'

Daniel shook his head. 'I get the impression that he'd been sent up to London, which is where I gather most of Nick's family reside.'

'But how come you're *here*?' I asked him. 'Here, now?'

He sighed. 'I helped Nick out for a day or two, mostly driving him to places he wanted to visit. It didn't take me long to piece together what kind of business he was engaged in and I didn't want to be involved in any part of it. The problem was that Nick liked me driving him around. He offered me a job, taking him to the various places where his business was carried on. He had properties in Torquay, Brixham, Exeter, Exmouth – even in Teignmouth and Dawlish. There were people constantly in and out, buying drugs or taking them to sell. Kids a lot of them. I intended to go to the police, tell them everything I'd witnessed, but after that first day we were never alone. Nick always had his cronies around. Then Vincent arrived back from London. To be honest, I felt trapped. There was someone watching me all the time. Of course, by then, I already knew too much. If I made the wrong move . . .'

'Couldn't you have got away?'

'Not as easy as it sounds. But I had begun to plan my

exit strategy, when yesterday Nick asked me to drive him here, to Raven's Tor Manor. And not long after we arrived, Miss Browne with an e, Kenny showed us the lovely picture of you breaking into their barn.'

'Oh.'

'Oh, indeed, Miss B! At first, I tried to persuade myself it wasn't you, but of course, I couldn't disbelieve the evidence of my own eyes. And besides, what other gorgeous redhead round here would be messing about in that barn, poking her nose into things that didn't concern her?'

'They've got a cannabis factory hidden underneath the barn,' I told him. 'In a shipping container.'

'I've been down there,' he told me. 'I've been given the grand tour. In fact, there are *four* shipping containers down there . . .'

'Four?' No wonder they had to dig such a big hole.

'Including one for workers' accommodation.'

'They've got people living down there?'

'Two at all times, who look after the plants. They're youngsters that Nick recruited.'

'My God, do they ever come up for air?'

'I think they get swopped around on a regular basis. He tells them it's part of learning the trade. Anyway,' he said, turning to look at me, 'once I'd seen your photograph, how could I leave? I knew if you came back, you'd be in danger. I had to stick around long enough to find out what you were up to.' His dark eyebrows drew together in a frown. 'What are you up to, Miss B?'

'So, why were you at the hospital today?' I asked, ignoring his question.

'Nick's foot. It's getting worse, not better. They think he's got an infection.'

'Serves him right.'

'Undoubtedly, but you haven't answered my question.'

I told him, in a rush, about Colin's attempt to blackmail Elizabeth, his murder, and how I'd followed Nick here to Raven's Tor Manor; and about the abandoned drugs factory at the old Devon Grange Hotel.

'They've moved it all here,' he told me. 'From what I gather, they're planning to develop it into a much bigger operation. That's why the boss is coming down.' He frowned. 'But what were you doing in that theatre in London, sitting right next to him?'

'That's Lenny Shaw, Nick's grandfather. I went there with Ricky and Morris.'

He groaned at the mention of their names. 'I might have known,' he muttered.

'No, you don't understand.' I told him about Freddy, what had been going on in London, and how Freddy had ultimately ended up.

'And who do you think killed him?' he asked.

'I don't know. It could have been one of the Shaw family, because he hadn't delivered the message telling them where the next pick up was. Although how they traced him to Druid Lodge is still a mystery. But equally, it could have been the man from the dressing room, the foreigner paying him to convey the message.'

Daniel frowned. 'It could have been someone from either end of the supply chain, that's what you're saying?'

'Yes, but the supply of what? It can't be the cannabis they're growing here.'

'Nick is dealing in cocaine.' Daniel nodded to himself. 'That's what the messages must be about. When and where the next shipment of cocaine is coming in.' He grimaced in disgust. 'Cannabis, cocaine, this is quite an empire the Shaws are trying to build. But why the elaborate charade at the theatre? Why don't they just text one another?'

'Lenny's very old-fashioned. He hates modern technology. And we know that the police swooped on of his operations last year and were able to arrest some of his gang because they'd been careless with phone messages.' I had a nasty thought. 'My phone! There are pictures of you on it, of both of us together. If Nick sees them . . .'

Daniel smiled as he slid my phone from his pocket and put it into my hand. 'I'm glad you haven't erased me, Miss B.'

'Don't think I didn't think about it.'

He looked at his watch. 'Listen, Lenny and his entourage are expected to arrive about five this morning, which is why Nick's taken the opportunity for a few hours' sleep. He wants to look sharp for when the boss arrives. The painkillers knock him out, so I don't think he's going to wake up until I shake him. Vince sleeps like a baby and Kenny's gone down in the factory, keeping an eye on the workers. That's how I got the chance to get to you. But you need to get out of here. Away from all this. Where's your van?'

'Parked up on the main road.'

'I've put your keys back in your jacket pocket. I want you to get out now, drive away from here. Call the police . . .'

I began shaking my head. 'I'm not going anywhere.'

'Juno . . .'

'I'm not going anywhere without you. Besides, we've got to wait for Lenny. As long as any of the Shaw family are at liberty, Elizabeth will be in danger. We've got to get as many of them as we can.'

Daniel frowned. 'Then what do you suggest, Miss B?'

'You've been down in the factory,' I responded. 'Is that trapdoor the only way out?'

CHAPTER TWENTY-SIX

Then there was nothing to do but watch and wait. We'd chosen a place under some trees, out of range of any cameras, with a good view of the barn. It was already close on five. The sun wouldn't be up for nearly an hour but the darkness was already thinning like mist, lightening to grey.

Daniel checked his watch. 'I'd better go back. Nick will be expecting me to wake him up around now. If I don't go, he'll be suspicious and the last thing we want is to raise his suspicions right now.'

'Are you sure that Nick will do it?' I asked.

He smiled. 'Trust me, he will. His vanity won't allow him not to.'

I put my arms around him, clung to him hard. 'Be careful. I couldn't bear to lose you again.'

'Likewise, Miss B.' He thrust a hand up through my hair, I drew my head back and he planted a kiss on my lips. 'Don't stir from here until I give you the signal.'

I watched him jog back in the direction of the manor house until he was hidden from me by enclosing trees.

If something went wrong up at the manor house, that could be the last time I ever saw him. I tried not to think about it. But time just dragged. I kept looking at my watch. It was close on half past five and the sky in the east was glowing pink, the promise of the rising sun. Lenny was late. Suddenly Kenny appeared, coming out of the barn with his phone to his ear. I crouched lower, moving forward on my belly and watched him through a screen of weeds and grasses.

'Yeah? Okay, I'll put it back in position.' He swung himself up into the seat of the old tractor and began to back it into the barn. What was happening? Wasn't Lenny coming after all? But as he jumped down from the cab, I heard him speak again. 'Done,' he chuckled, coming back out of the barn. 'All ready for the big reveal. About ten minutes? Alright, I'll hang about down here. See you in five.'

He disconnected and I watched him pacing up and down. It sounded as if Nick had received word of the boss's imminent arrival and was on his way to the barn. A few minutes later the black Audi swung into the field.

Daniel got out of the driver's seat. I let out a breath. Everything must be okay. He helped Nick out of the car. He stood, balanced on his crutches, his overcoat hanging from his shoulders as if he was some minor Mafia don. Vince unfolded himself from the back seat and stood beside him. 'Danny, park the car on the grass over there,' Nick ordered him. 'Leave space for Lenny's car.'

Daniel did as he was told. When he'd parked, he

hung back by the car, leaning against it, arms folded. Everyone was waiting, nervously, as if royalty was about to arrive. Nick kept checking his Rolex.

A dark blue limousine rolled in through the gate and the driver got out to hold open the door for the passengers in the back seat. Two men got out, Lenny, and a man I didn't recognise. He looked a lot like Lenny, perhaps a bit younger, a little taller, he must be his brother. Monty, Morris's old friend, had called him Tony. He hugged Vince and Nick as if they were family, laughing and sociable, as if they'd met by chance outside of a pub and were all going in for a drink. Nick and Vince slapped the driver on the back. I had no idea who he was but he was obviously part of the family.

They chatted. I couldn't catch every word they were saying but didn't dare creep closer. There was obviously talk about Nick's foot. He was all smiles, trying to pass it off as a stupid accident, riding his bike. It was nothing. Daniel was ignored. He was just a worker, a minion, and neither Lenny nor his companion bothered to glance in his direction.

At a gesture from Nick, Kenny suddenly walked into the barn. I heard the old tractor start up, and a few moments later it came chugging out on to the hard standing and stopped. He jumped down and Nick beckoned him over to where he stood with the others. I couldn't catch all of what he said, except it finished with the word *her*. Kenny grinned and set off towards the manor house.

There was only one *her* that Nick could be referring

to. Kenny had been sent to fetch me. It wouldn't take him long to discover I was no longer their prisoner. A few minutes at most. I looked back at Nick and his family. I wished they'd get on with it.

At last, they all began to saunter towards the barn. 'There's no need for you to come down, my son, not with your foot,' I heard Lenny tell Nick, patting him on the shoulder.

'No,' Nick answered, grinning. 'I want to be there when you see this.'

Daniel had been right. Difficult as it would be for him to negotiate the ladder with his injured foot, Nick's vanity wouldn't allow him not to go down it and personally show off his enterprise to his grandfather. He turned to look at Daniel and yelled. 'Danny!'

I took in a breath. If he made Daniel go down first, our plan wouldn't work.

'You stay up here,' he ordered him. 'Hold my coat. And you can take that,' he added, giving him one of the crutches, 'I don't need two of them.'

Daniel took the coat from his shoulders and they trooped into the barn, Nick leaning heavily on Vince. I heard the echo of their voices, the clanging of the trap-doors being opened. I held my breath. It was going to take a minute or two for them all to get down that ladder. Nick could only proceed slowly, encumbered by that surgical boot. His remaining crutch would have to be passed down to him.

I stood up and began to creep across the grass towards the barn. Then I heard the trapdoor very softly close. A moment later Daniel appeared in the doorway and waved. I raced for the Audi and into the driver's seat. The keys were in the ignition where Daniel had left them. He'd lined the car up perfectly. All I had to do was stick it in reverse gear and put my foot down. In the rear-view mirror, I could see him back in the barn, lying down on top of the trapdoor, fiddling with the padlock. He rolled out of the way as I backed the car towards him, stopping with all four wheels resting on the steel trap. It didn't matter if the padlock was locked or not. With the weight of the car on top of it, no one could open that door from underneath. No one could get out. They were trapped, caught in a snare of their own making.

Someone down there had realised the trapdoor had been closed. There was a muffled sound of raised voices coming from below, then yelling and banging on the underside. As we left the barn, Daniel took the car key from me and lobbed it away into the long grass. 'Time for a phone call, I think, Miss B.'

Then we froze. Kenny was standing in front of us, his shotgun levelled. He snarled at Daniel. 'I knew you weren't to be trusted. You!' he growled at me. 'Bitch! Go fetch it! Find that key now or I'll shoot your friend here. You,' he added to Daniel, 'stay where you are. Don't move. This ain't loaded with birdshot. It'll take the head off a fox, and it'll make a very messy hole in your guts.'

I ran across the grass to where I thought the key had landed and fell to my hands and knees, running my hands through blades of grass. I couldn't see it.

'Found it yet?' Kenny yelled.

'I'm trying!'

'Well, you'd better hurry up or Danny boy here is going to get a belly ache.'

I hunted frantically, fighting against a mounting feeling of panic. I dared a quick glance at Daniel. He was keeping absolutely still, staring at the gun. His mind would be racing like mine, desperately trying to work out what to do next. Then I saw a key. Not the key of the Audi, but the key of the tractor, hanging in the ignition where Kenny had left it with the hand-brake on. I could hear the engine ticking over.

'Why don't you let her go?' I heard Daniel say.

Kenny laughed. 'I don't think so.'

'Why not? I can tell you all you need to know.'

Just keep him talking, I urged him silently, as I crept across to where the tractor stood. Luckily it was not one of these new-fangled, computerised machines. It would be just like starting a car.

'The longer I have to wait, the worse it's going to be for you,' Kenny yelled, without turning his head. 'For both of you.'

Holding my breath, I slid into the driving seat. He'd left the tractor in neutral, parking brake on. I dipped the clutch and pulled the lever towards me. Kenny heard the snick as it clicked into gear and turned his head. 'What the f —'

I gave it full throttle, released the brake. He swung around to level the gun at me and Daniel leapt on him, making a grab for it. One barrel fired as it jerked into the air, peppering the barn with shot, ripping out chunks in the wooden wall and sending splinters like daggers flying. The tractor jerked forward. Kenny jabbed the butt of the gun in Daniel's face, knocking him to the ground. He took aim, then as the wheels began to roll, turned to fire at me. I pulled a lever and the fore-loader swung down in front of my face like a visor. I heard the second barrel fire, the shot spattering, ricocheting off the metal bucket and pinging into the grass. I couldn't see where I was going. I just put my foot down and charged.

CHAPTER TWENTY-SEVEN

'Would you describe all that for me once more, Sergeant? From the beginning?'

Detective Inspector Ford looked like a man suffering from a migraine, sitting in the interview room with his eyes closed, pinching either side of his nose with his forefinger and thumb. Cruella's scratchy voice can induce a headache in no time and she had been speaking for nearly an hour.

'Acting on information received from a member of the public . . .' she began. By a member of the public, she meant me.

'Yes, yes. You can skip that bit,' the inspector broke in irritably. 'Just start when you arrived at Raven's Tor Manor.'

Cruella glared at me across the table and began again. 'The scene was in considerable disarray, sir. The tractor had crashed into the barn, partly demolishing it, and timbers had collapsed on to a male we later identified as Kenneth Rudd, wanted by police in Cornwall and Somerset for drug-related offences. He was unconscious when we found him, clutching a shotgun, both barrels of which had been discharged.'

'I don't suppose that the barn collapsing on him did him any good,' the inspector commented. 'Do we know his current condition?'

'His injuries aren't considered to be life-threatening, sir.'

The inspector took his hand away from his face and favoured me with one of his steady stares. 'And your reason for being at the wheel of this tractor, Miss Browne?'

'I told you. Kenny was trying to kill Daniel. They were fighting over the gun. He'd already fired once, I had to stop him before he fired again. The thing is, I'm not familiar with the controls of a tractor and the bucket on the front came down, and I couldn't see where I was going . . .'

For a moment I saw the slightest smile tug at the corner of the inspector's mouth. 'I see. And how is Mr Thorncroft?'

'He was treated by paramedics at the scene, sir, for a minor head injury,' Cruella told him, putting a heavy stress on the word *minor*. 'But he declared himself fit and able to be questioned.'

'Excellent. Carry on, Sergeant.'

'The armed response unit had been called in, in response to Miss Browne's call, and they carried out a search of the premises. Following the removal of a parked vehicle, they opened a steel trapdoor and descended a ladder. They found cannabis plants in commercial production spread through four underground shipping containers, with a sophisticated ventilation system powered by generators. They also found seven males, one of whom was found to be armed with a handgun. Shots were exchanged but there were no casualties. Two of the males were juveniles. The others were identified as brothers, Leonard and Anthony Shaw, their nephew Vincent Shaw and Leonard's grandson, Nicolas. They are all known to Scotland Yard, sir, on a variety of charges, including drug offences, extortion and blackmail, aggravated assault, money laundering and attempted murder. But for a variety of reasons including the suspected intimidation of witnesses, only Vincent and Anthony have ever been convicted.'

The inspector actually smiled. 'Well, we've got them bang to rights now.'

'Yes, sir. One of those present,' Cruella continued impassively, 'was a Mr Brian Beckett, a London resident, who claims he was only employed as a driver and had no idea, when he descended the ladder under the barn, what he would find.'

'Has Mr Beckett got any form?'

'Tons of it, sir. He's a well-known associate of Leonard Shaw.'

'Right, then. Where is Mr Thorncroft at present?'

'With Collins next door, sir, giving his statement.'

'I need to speak to him.' He turned back to me. 'Right, Juno, you can go.'

'I want to wait here for Daniel.' I hadn't seen him since we'd arrived at the station. We'd been kept apart so that we couldn't influence each other's statements.

'I'm afraid he's going to be with us some time. Now listen to me,' he said before I could protest. 'We've caught a nest of vipers this morning, and confiscated drugs with a street value of God-knows-what. So far, so good. But I'm afraid it's not yet over. This operation is on-going and it's vital that no word of what happened this morning gets out. If I could, I'd lock you up.'

Well, there's ingratitude for you.

'Fortunately for you,' he added, with the slightest twinkle in his eye, 'the cells here are full just at the moment. But you are to go home and speak to no one about this. I'll arrange a car to take you back to your flat.'

'But —'

'Stay there!' he warned me with a raised hand. 'You look exhausted. Go to bed.'

'But you're not arresting Daniel?' I asked, horrified.

The inspector sighed. 'That depends on what he has to say.'

It was close on one o'clock the next morning before I heard the soft knocking at the door that I had been listening out for. I had gone to bed but I hadn't slept. I just lay awake, listening to the pattering of rain on the window. I flew down the stairs in my bare feet and opened the door. Daniel was standing there, looking shattered, raindrops glistening on his hair. He stepped inside and we clung to one another, my face buried in his shoulder. 'I thought they would never let you go,' I muttered.

'It's all fine,' he told me. 'Nothing to worry about.'

I pulled back to look at him. He looked pale and exhausted, hollow-eyed. There was a dark bruise on his temple where Kenny had hit him with the butt of the shotgun and a cut on his cheekbone that a paramedic had stitched.

I reached up and touched at it gently. 'You might have a scar.'

He smiled. 'I'll say I earned it in a duel.'

'Pistols or sabres?'

'Sabres, definitely.'

'Fighting for my honour?'

'The only thing worth dying for,' he murmured and pressed a kiss on my forehead.

Over his shoulder I could see a police car parked by the roadside. The two uniformed officers were both staring in our direction; gawping might have been a better word for it. 'Aren't they going?'

'No, I think they're staying.' He pulled the door shut behind him and we climbed the stairs. 'Inspector Ford told me that we must consider ourselves under house arrest for the time being,' he said, collapsing on to the sofa with a groan. I poured us both a glass of whisky while he kicked off his shoes and stretched out his long legs, resting his feet on the coffee table.

'House arrest? Can he do that? We haven't been charged with anything. And I've got dogs to walk in the morning.'

'I'm afraid you haven't. It's for our own safety, apparently, although it shouldn't be for long. The inspector says that we are witnesses and he has a duty of care towards us.'

'But you're not really under arrest?' I handed him his drink and sat next to him.

He stretched out an arm, pulling me in close. 'No. But they wanted to know every detail of my time with Nick – who he had spoken to, where we had been. The same questions over and over.' He tossed back the whisky and shuddered. 'I have to go back to the station later, take police officers to all of the places I drove Nick.'

'They'll try to mop up some dealers?'

'I think so.' He closed his eyes. 'In the meantime, we have orders to stay here.'

I heaved a sigh. 'And I wanted to go out on the town.'

'Another time, Miss B.'

'May as well go to bed, then.'

He opened one eye and looked at me. 'You know, that's the nicest thing anyone has said to me in . . . forever.'

'Then let's go.'

'That's the second nicest thing,' he said, struggling to his feet.

Clinging on to one another, we staggered to the bedroom and collapsed on to the bed. The springs bounced. Bill, who'd been sleeping on the duvet, meowed in protest and slid off on to the floor.

'You know, Miss B . . .' Daniel began loudly.

'Sssh!' I whispered. 'We mustn't wake baby Noah.'

'Right,' he whispered back. A moment later, he was asleep. And a few moments after that, so was I.

'You know, Miss B,' Daniel murmured next morning, pulling me towards him and dropping a kiss on my mouth. 'I could get used to this house arrest stuff.'

'Is the police car still there?' I asked.

'It was a moment ago when I looked out of the bathroom window.'

'Those two have been there all night.'

'I'm sure another team will relieve them soon.' He rolled over on top of me, kissing me hungrily. 'But never mind them.'

'Just be serious a minute,' I said, pushing his hand away from the place where it had found itself.

'I'm deadly serious Miss B.'

'You told me you'd thrown in your job.'

He sighed, giving in to the inevitable and sat up. 'So I did.'

'But I thought Re-Wilding UK was your company.'

'I founded it, along with Mark, my business partner. But we had a fundamental disagreement.'

'What about?'

'Two things, really. First of all, this was the first year we've made any profit. He wanted to give our shareholders a dividend, I was all for investing it back in the company and giving our staff a rise. Neither of us was prepared to compromise. Then we disagreed profoundly on Natural England's proposals for the future management of Dartmoor.'

'Well, what . . . ?'

He laid a finger on my lips. 'Quiet. You really cannot expect to lie here in this bed, naked, warm and ravishing, and expect me to talk about protecting farmers' grazing rights. It's my own grazing rights I'd rather concentrate on.' He gazed down at me, traced my lips with his finger. 'You are beautiful, Miss Browne with an e.'

'Do you really think we need police protection?' I asked.

'No, not for a minute. Ford just wants to keep us out of the way for some reason.'

'I think I know what that might be.'

He crooked an eyebrow at me. 'What?'

'I'm willing to bet,' I smiled, sliding my arms around his neck, 'that Aunt Drusilla, or whatever she's calling herself, isn't taking her holiday in Scarborough this year.'

CHAPTER TWENTY-EIGHT

As it turned out, it was Aunt *Diane* who decided to take a holiday, and she took it at Exmouth. The beach there had been staked out by Border Force police since Dean and Cruella had returned from the theatre with this information on Wednesday evening. So, when the crew from the *Diane* came ashore with several kilos of cocaine, they were welcomed by a reception committee. Not only had the police bust open the Shaw's cannabis growing operation, they confiscated cocaine worth two million and arrested two more members of the clan in the process. The *Diane* had come across the Channel from France. The cocaine had travelled much further, from Lithuania. Which is also where the information about the places the drugs would be brought ashore had come from; delivered in an envelope by an unknown Lithuanian to the backstage noticeboard of The Davenport Theatre.

'They wouldn't have caught any of them without you,' Daniel told me, buttering toast. We had been released from our captivity and were in Sunflowers café treating ourselves to a very large, very late breakfast. Adam had delivered our order with a sideways glower at Daniel. 'You're back, are you?' was all he said, before he stomped back into the kitchen.

Daniel just grinned. 'Nice to see you too,' he called after him. He cast a glance at me. 'Why so down in the mouth, Miss B?'

I sighed, 'Because we still don't know who murdered Freddy, or Colin.'

'Not yet we don't,' he agreed, spearing a mushroom with his fork. 'But we will.'

'Inspector Ford says that the Shaws never confess to anything.'

'Maybe not. But I bet every one of them would rat on the others if they thought it was worth their while.'

'I don't suppose we'll ever know now. They're all being transported to London today. Inspector Ford says Scotland Yard will take over from here.'

'He'll still get the brownie points though.'

To be honest, I was more than a little pissed off with the Inspector. I understood that it was vital that the arrests at Raven's Tor Manor weren't leaked to anyone who could warn the other branch of the Shaw gang before they landed their cargo. But who did he think I was going to tell? If he wanted to imprison people who were likely to blab things to all and sundry, he should have locked up Ricky and Morris. Or Sophie, for that matter.

'Hello, who's this?' Daniel raised his eyebrows as Kate wheeled Noah's buggy into the café. He hadn't yet met her son. He tickled the baby's trumpet-blower cheek and made all the right noises about what a bouncer he was. Noah just pouted. He might have inherited his mother's dark eyes and hair, but he was looking more and more like his grumpy dad.

'Oh hello, Daniel!' Kate cried in surprise. She rolled her eyes at me in a way that was supposed to be significant. She looked from me to Daniel and back again, clearly not sure what to say. In the end she said nothing, just wheeled Noah into the back of the café where she began exchanging furtive whispers with Adam, simultaneously craning her neck to keep staring at us over the cake display. Kate doesn't really do subtle.

'My return seems to be causing some speculation among your friends, Miss B,' Daniel observed wryly.

'Well, it would.' I didn't add that most of them wanted to thump him. I decided to change the subject. 'What are you doing after this?'

He looked at his watch. 'I'm due at the police station in an hour.'

'For your drive around the drug dens of Devon?'

'Yes. And you?'

'Apart from the half dozen phone calls I've got to make, apologising to people for not turning up to walk their dogs this morning, I need to go to *Old Nick's*. But before anything else, I must check up on Maisie and see if she's okay.'

We agreed to meet up later and went our separate ways. Outside of the café Daniel pulled me into an embrace and whispered, 'My God, that's a fearsome-looking baby!' before kissing me and striding up off the street.

I stood watching his tall, dark figure for a few moments, giving Kate the opportunity to shoot out of the café door as if she'd been fired from a cannon and hiss at me. 'Juno! Are you two . . . ? I mean, sorry, it's none of my business . . . only . . . Daniel, well, is he back for good this time?'

I glanced his retreating back and smiled. 'I certainly hope so.'

'Where the bleedin' hell have you been?' Maisie demanded as I let myself in to her cottage, deterring a snarling Jacko from attacking my ankle with the offer of a specifically purchased pig's ear. 'You haven't been here for months!'

'It's actually been two days, Maisie,' I told her as Jacko snatched the ear and hurried off with it to his basket. 'Today is Friday. I brought you home from hospital on Wednesday evening. Since then, I've been a bit tied up.' To be fair, I couldn't believe it was only two days ago either. It seemed like a lifetime since I'd driven up to Raven's Tor Manor.

'Our Janet's been trying to phone you.'

'I know I missed her call, but I couldn't answer the phone. I'll call her back in a minute.'

'Your hair's a mess. What've you been up to?'

'You wouldn't want to know. How are you?'

'Bearing up,' she sniffed, in a tone of noble suffering.

'At least Bev's been popping in to see how I am. She got some shopping for me.'

I refused to be drawn. 'That's good, then. So, you don't need anything at the moment.'

'I do! I've run out of marmalade.'

'I'll get some. How's your wrist?'

She fingered the dressing and scowled. 'No worse, I suppose.'

I bent down to look at it. 'Do you think you might be well enough to go out for a cup of tea?' I asked solicitously.

'I don't know.' She shook her head and then sneaked a glance up at me. 'What now, like?'

'It's a lovely day,' I swept an arm in the direction of the window. Lovely day might be an exaggeration. There were grey clouds blotting out patches of blue sky, but at least it wasn't pouring with rain. 'I could drive you up to the café in Widecombe. There are new spring lambs up on the moor.'

Widecombe was her favourite place but Maisie waggled her head as if she had a tough decision to make. 'And they sell lovely marmalade in the gift shop,' I added.

After a moment's more struggle she gave in. 'I suppose I could manage a cup of tea,' she conceded reluctantly, 'as long as there was a bit of cake to go with it.'

'That's settled then,' I said, patting her shoulder. 'I'll get your coat.'

Later, after I'd closed the shop, I let Daniel drive me up to Daison Cottages in the van to see Elizabeth. I couldn't wait to tell her the news, that she didn't have to worry about the Shaws anymore. They wouldn't be coming around demanding their money back. It was only seeing the relief on her face, the anxiety falling away from her, that I realised how strained she'd been looking before. We opened a bottle of wine and chatted for a long time.

'I'm going to see Joan on Sunday,' she told me. 'Why don't you come with me? I'd like you to meet her. Not that she'll know who you are, of course. Would you mind?'

'No, of course not,' I assured her. 'I'd love to meet her.'

On the way back, Daniel pulled the van up at Owlacombe Cross. We could turn one way for Halsanger Common, the other road would take us back into town. 'Which way?' he asked. 'Caravan or flat?'

'It's too late for the caravan. And it'll be freezing, you haven't lived in it for months. Let's go back to my flat. Bill will have been missing us.'

'There's only room for one man in your bed, Miss B,' he told me sternly.

'Then it's a good job he's a cat.'

Daniel frowned. 'The thing that worries me,' he admitted, turning the wheel back towards town, 'is that I'm not sure he knows he's a cat.'

I smiled. Actually, Daniel was not a problem for Bill. His long, wicked fingers had already found the sweet spot on his spine that could reduce him to purring idiocy. It was when Lottie arrived that the problems would start.

CHAPTER TWENTY-NINE

'What's Daniel doing with himself today?' Elizabeth asked as she drove us towards Bovey Tracey on Sunday afternoon.

'He's gone to see Claire's sister,' I told her. 'It's quite a long drive.'

'And you didn't want to go with him? You could have, you know. I didn't mean to deprive him of your company.'

'It's alright. He doesn't think that she's ready to meet me yet.'

Elizabeth smiled wryly. 'Or anyone else replacing her dead sister?'

'That's about it.'

We arrived at Moorland View and checked in at reception, signing ourselves in the visitors' book. It was the first time I'd actually been inside the place. It was clean and comfortable and the décor was pleasant in a flowery beige way. I noticed that the photofit picture of Nick and Vincent Shaw was still pinned up on the wall behind reception. 'I think it's safe to take that down now,' I told the receptionist.

We went to see Joan. Her room was bright, with French windows opening on to the gardens. She was sitting in an armchair gazing through it into the beyond. But whether she saw the daffodils or the blossom on the cherry trees raining pink petals in the wind, I could not tell. Her face was vacant of all expression. Perhaps it was having seen the photograph of her as a bride, so young and attractive, but the sight of her made me sad. She was an older, fatter version of her sister, her heavy body sagging in her chair, hands hanging limply in her lap. She wore a blue floral print dress and slippers, her grey hair brushed back tidily and kept in place by a band. She was obviously being looked after, but she had the pallor of someone who lived indoors. This was the lady who used to keep herself fit, who used to swim every day.

Elizabeth kissed her cheek and drew up a chair to sit next to her, taking her hand. 'Hello, Joan darling.' I drew up a chair on the other side of her armchair, but not so close. 'This is Juno,' she went on. 'My friend.'

Joan did not answer. Her hand did not return the pressure of her sister's fingers. She just carried on gazing. Elizabeth began to tell her of Olly's latest exploits at school, and how hard he was studying, and how Tom had begun to teach her fly-fishing. But to be honest, there was no way of telling if Joan realised her sister was in the room.

Elizabeth kept this one-sided conversation going nobly but after about half an hour began to struggle to find things to say. 'Shall we go for a turn around the garden?' she asked Joan brightly, looking around her. 'Now, where is your wheelchair? It should be in here. I wonder what they've done with it.'

'Shall I see?' My own inadequate attempts to keep the conversation going had failed miserably, and despite my honourable intentions, I was glad of an excuse to escape the room.

'Would you mind, Juno? Just ask in reception.'

I slipped along the corridor. I couldn't see any wheelchairs, so I waited at the reception desk while the member of staff behind it was on the phone. For a few moments I gazed aimlessly at the view in front of me, looking down a side passage that ended in a door marked Fire Exit. I experienced a strange moment, a sort of what's-wrong-with-this-picture moment, as if I was seeing something that shouldn't be there. I was staring at a row of lockers and hooks where the staff obviously hung their outdoor coats. There was a smart, emerald one with a fake fur collar, hanging on one of the pegs that caught my eye. I realised what was wrong, I'd seen that coat before.

'Who does that belong to?' I asked the receptionist as she put down the phone.

She turned to see what I was looking at. 'Oh, the green coat? It's lovely, isn't it? It belongs to Mary, she's our newest member of staff. She only started yesterday.' She lowered her voice and added confidentially, 'She's Colin's replacement.'

'Mary?' I repeated blankly.

'Yes.' She frowned.' Is anything wrong?'

'Where is Mary now?'

She looked confused. 'Um, I'm not sure.'

It didn't matter. I could see her, coming out of a door at the far end of the passage. In the street I might have passed her by. She wasn't wearing the blonde wig and for a moment I didn't recognise the slim woman with the straight dark hair, dressed in a carer's blue uniform. Then she glanced in my direction, and I was back on that flight of steps in the Davenport Theatre as she turned to glare at me, her hand on the push-bar of the Fire Exit.

'Maggie Shaw!' I called out. Her lips parted in astonishment, then she pushed the bar and was out through the fire-exit door and into the garden.

I set off after her. 'Call the police!' I yelled back at the receptionist.

'What?' I heard her mutter, but I was already out of the door after Maggie.

Outside, there was no sign of her, just a collection of recycling bins against a wooden fence and a path that led around the side of the building. I followed it, my eyes searching the nearby bushes for any movement. It led me to the garden at the back of the house. Daffodils, cherry trees, petals scattered like confetti on the path, this was the view from Joan's window. Her open window.

Maggie stepped forward from behind the tree that had concealed her. She took aim, directly through the window, her arms stretched out straight, both hands around the gun, its barrel fitted with a silencer.

'Elizabeth!' I screamed in warning.

At the sound of my voice, Maggie turned towards me and fired. I felt the bullet scorch the air near my right cheek. She turned back towards her target and I flung myself on her, my weight knocking her sideways, the gun firing into the air as we fell struggling to the ground. We rolled on the path. Her face was a snarling, spitting blur close to mine. But she was a small, delicate creature compared to me, and I pinned her down. She squirmed beneath me, writhing like an angry snake, her teeth sinking into my arm. I closed my fingers around her slender wrist, and banged the back of her hand against the ground repeatedly until she let go of the gun, sending it skittering across the path. We both reached for it, but my reach was longer. I grabbed it by the barrel and rolled away from her. I'd never held a loaded gun before. It was heavier than I thought. I hated touching the thing. I manhandled it clumsily, my fingers all thumbs as she began crawling towards me: Maggie Shaw, Lenny's daughter, Nick's mother, the family member we'd forgotten, as evil as the rest of them. I turned the gun around, got the business end pointing towards her, and she stopped in her tracks. She sat up, breathless, brushing back the hair from her eyes. Her face twisted into a contemptuous smile as she watched the gun barrel wavering in my shaking hand. 'You won't shoot me,' she spat. 'You don't even know how to fire the thing.'

'She probably doesn't,' a calm voice answered as

Elizabeth came through the open door. She bent to take the gun from my trembling fingers then turned to point it at Maggie and smiled. 'Fortunately, I do.'

'There aren't any more of them, are there, Miss B?' Daniel asked me, after listening in horror to my account of the afternoon. 'There are no psychopathic great-aunts waiting in the wings to avenge the family honour?'

'I don't think so.' It was after midnight and we sat together in my flat in the glow of the gas fire. Bill, tart that he was, had forsaken my lap for Daniel's. I raised my head from the sofa cushions and took a sip from the glass of whisky we were sharing. 'But that's what it was about, avenging the family honour. Someone has to pay, that's what Maggie kept saying. No one could be allowed to get the better of the Shaws because their enemies would see that as a weakness.'

'And because Elizabeth couldn't pay her husband's debts, they were going to kill her?' he asked incredulously.

'But Maggie wasn't aiming at Elizabeth. She was aiming at Joan.'

'Joan?'

'You know, working there at Moorland View she could have killed her so easily, smothered her with a pillow or given her a drug overdose, and probably got away with it, made it look like an accident. But she wanted Elizabeth to suffer by seeing her sister murdered in front of her.'

Daniel was wearing a deeply troubled frown.

'I'm alright,' I assured him.

He reached out to touch my face. 'I love you, Miss B. I just don't want to lose you because of evil people like the Shaws.'

I thought I might as well tell him the next bit, because he was going to find out anyway. 'The police are pretty sure that it was Maggie who killed Freddy. Apparently, he was killed with the same kind of weapon that she was using today. They're carrying out a ballistics test on it. Also, she was *here*. Mrs Macdonald says that she applied for the job as soon as they advertised the vacancy. The day Freddy was shot was the same day she came for the interview. She had excellent references, forged of course, and she told Mrs Macdonald that she lived in Torquay.'

'I'm getting confused, Miss B. Wasn't she at the theatre with Lenny on Wednesday afternoon?'

'Apparently not. I didn't find this out from Dean until today, but when he and Cruella attended the matinee there was a young man sitting in S5. They don't know who he was, probably just a minion, but when he left his seat, Cruella followed him out of the theatre. He got into a waiting car, just like Maggie did. But Maggie was already in position down here, ready to start the job at Moorland View. She knew that Elizabeth would turn up to see her sister sooner or later, she just had to wait.'

'But how did she find Freddy?'

'The police don't know yet. She's not talking until

her lawyer arrives from London.'

'What about the man she replaced, in the job, Colin? Do we know if she was the one who killed him?'

I shook my head. 'Dean says they have DNA evidence putting Nick at Colin's house. It doesn't prove he killed him, that he was there on the day that Colin was murdered, but it's enough to put pressure on him. They're hoping they might get a confession. We don't know that bit, of course.' Daniel looked confused and I added, 'that information about Nick. I didn't get it from Dean.'

'You mean, he didn't tell you and you haven't passed it on to me?'

'Correct.'

He sighed. 'This is all highly irregular, Miss B.'

'And driving a drugs dealer around isn't?' I asked lightly.

He slid an arm around my shoulders and pulled me closer towards him. 'Now that you mention it, it seems that any possible charges from my activities in Torquay are likely to be swept under the . . . er . . .'

'Oh, yes?'

'In view of the information I've been able to give the police, helping them with their enquiries.'

'I see.'

'But you didn't hear that from me.'

'No?'

'And I didn't hear it from Inspector Ford.'

'Of course not.'

'I'm glad that's settled.'

I touched his cheek. His black eye was starting to fade, turning yellow around the edges. He took the whisky glass from my other hand and set it down on the table as I lay back on the cushions. Bill, dislodged from his lap, padded off into the bedroom in disgust.

I was in a happy place. Warm and heavy, as if I'd sunk into the bed and become part of it. It was blissfully quiet. Daniel's voice came to me out of the not quite light of morning.

'You know, Miss B, I'm going to have to start looking for a job very soon.'

My eyelids felt heavy. I opened just enough to see his face up close to mine, dark hair and eyebrows but otherwise a bit blurred. 'What?' My voice sounded husky, like a little frog.

'Truth is,' he admitted. 'I'm broke.'

I cleared my throat, blinked myself into wakefulness. 'But what about your company? You helped to found it. Didn't your partner have to buy you out?'

'Yes, but breaking up a business is like going through a divorce. It takes time and there's a lot of legal stuff involved.'

I thought for a moment 'What you mean is, you haven't had the money yet.'

'Exactly, Miss B. And what's more, I don't know when I'm going to get it.' He was quiet a moment. 'And I probably haven't helped matters.'

There was a ruefulness in his tone and I raised myself up on one elbow to squint at him. 'Oh?'

'Mark and I quarrelled. I told him to go to hell and walked out.'

'And slammed the door?'

'Metaphorically.'

'And you call me reckless.' I bit back a smile.

He crooked a dark eyebrow at me. 'What?' he asked suspiciously.

'Nothing.' He'd behaved like a typical Scorpio. I could almost hear Cordelia laughing. What a pity, I thought sadly, that the two of them would never meet.

CHAPTER THIRTY

'So, it was Maggie who shot poor Freddy?' Morris shook his head sadly.

We sat in the workroom, fiddling with repairs and alterations from the last batch of returned costumes. My usual Monday afternoon client was away, so I took the opportunity to bring the occupants of Druid Lodge up to date with recent events. The ballistics test had proved that the gun that killed Freddy was the same one that Maggie Shaw had used to try to shoot Joan and Elizabeth. And one of her black hairs had been discovered caught in the wicker of the costume hamper we had found his body in. I didn't get this information from Dean, obviously.

'But how did she know where to find him?'

'You remember Hugh Winterbourne, the actor we met in London?'

Ricky looked up from his work and grinned. 'The poor sap who had to ask where Aunt Drusilla was taking her holiday this year?'

'Never knowing what answer he'd get.' I nodded.

'That's him. Apparently, Maggie approached him in the theatre bar and started chatting him up. He had no idea who she was, of course. She acted like a real fan, told him how much she loved him in the play and spun him a story about having seen the matinee several times and having been puzzled about the changes in names.

'He starts to tell her the whole story, including Freddy coming back to London and Hugh seeing him with us in the café. If you remember, Freddy told Hugh how he escaped the gunman in the dressing-room by climbing into the hamper. Hugh didn't remember the name of your costume company, but Maggie only had to go to the theatre next door and make a few enquiries about where they got their costumes from. I think Hugh realised afterwards that he'd said too much, but it was too late then.'

'So, Maggie gets our address from the theatre and comes here and shoots Freddy?'

'She's utterly cold-blooded. Just like the rest of them.'

'And we never even knew she was here,' Morris cried, agitated. 'Didn't see her or hear her.'

'She'd have taken great care to ensure you didn't see or hear her,' I told him. 'And remember what Inspector Ford said, if either of you had spotted her, she'd probably have shot you too.'

'And who was the mystery gunman in the dressing room?' Ricky asked, frowning. 'Do we know that yet?'

'No. The police think he's Lithuanian, someone who worked for the drug cartel on the continent, the place where the cocaine was coming from.'

We were quiet for a while, inwardly digesting all this information, then Ricky asked. 'Where's lover boy today?'

I glanced up at him. 'If you mean Mr Daniel Thorncroft,' I answered with a slight edge to my voice, 'then he's gone to London for an interview.'

'What?' he frowned. 'For a job?'

'To an agency that specialises in jobs in sustainability and ecology.'

Morris blinked at me, surprised. 'I thought he had his own company.'

'Well, he did, but he's left them. Difference of opinion. What he'd like to do in the long term is set up his own consultancy, advising firms on environmental issues. But at the moment, he just needs a job that pays him a regular salary.'

Ricky took a pin from between his lips. 'Doing up that old house must be costing him a fortune.'

'The problem is,' I went on, my heart sinking every time I thought about it, 'there aren't many jobs in ecology. At least not around here.'

Morris sounded surprised. 'I thought councils and energy companies employed ecologists now. I saw it on the television.'

'Well, they do. But not at the salary he needs.'

'Where is this job likely to be then?' he asked.

'I don't know. I don't think Daniel knows either

until he's had an interview. The agency will put him forward for any vacancies they think he might be suitable for. With any luck, there may be more than one.' Perhaps the truth was that he didn't want to discuss with me where any jobs were likely to be until he knew whether or not they had anything to offer him.

'Let's hope it's not too far away,' Morris said brightly, after I'd been quiet for a few moments.

Suddenly Ricky made an announcement. 'You'll be glad to know, both of you, that I haven't got cancer.'

Morris and I looked up from our work. 'What?' he asked softly.

'I haven't got cancer.' Ricky beamed at the pair of us. 'My prostate. I've had the results of my scan. It's not cancer. My prostate is enlarged, which is what's been causing all the trouble with my waterworks. But they can fix that. Just a very simple procedure . . .'

A rush of relief surged through me and I jumped up to give him a hug. 'Oh Ricky, that's wonderful!'

'What do you mean, you've had the results?' Morris's quiet voice cut through our celebratory laughter. 'You haven't even had the scan yet. We're still waiting for a date.'

Ricky looked vaguely uncomfortable. 'Well, I have, as a matter of fact, *Maurice,* I had the scan three weeks ago.'

Morris stared at him, baffled. 'When? When did you go to Exeter?'

'It was the day you went on that trip to that National Trust place with the U3A. I told you I didn't want to go. It's because I had an appointment. I'd had a letter.'

'I didn't see any letter.'

Ricky grinned. 'I made sure you didn't.'

Morris looked stunned. 'But I was going to come with you.'

'There wouldn't have been any point,' he responded evasively. 'You couldn't hold my hand. They don't let people come in the room with the scanner. You'd have just been waiting about outside, getting in a flap.'

Morris blinked through his gold-rimmed specs, digesting this a moment. 'When did you get the results?'

'Last Monday. The hospital phoned, asked me to go in. I popped in there when I went to Exeter to do the banking.'

'But you didn't know what the result would be when you went?'

Ricky cleared his throat. 'No, I didn't,' he admitted. 'I thought it was going to be bad news and that's why they'd asked to see me. But it was only to discuss what happens next with this procedure. It's called a Transurethral Resection of the Prostate and . . .'

'You thought it was going to be bad news,' Morris repeated, his voice still very quiet. 'And you didn't want me to go with you?'

'No, I didn't!' Ricky snapped. 'I had enough

trouble dealing with my own nerves without having you there getting hysterical.'

'And you've known since last Monday?' Morris insisted. 'All this time? You didn't think it was worth telling me the results utill now, with Juno here? After all I've been through worrying about you, sitting up with you night after night, you couldn't come home and tell me straightaway?'

'When I got home last Monday, you may remember, *Maurice*, I had barely got in the door, before we discovered poor Freddy's body. It didn't seem like the right moment.'

'That's true,' Morris admitted. He gave a deep sigh, took off his spectacles and began to polish them, slowly, on the edge of his cardigan. He spoke quietly, steadily. 'We've been together for over thirty-five years. Did you honestly think I wouldn't have understood if you'd told me that you'd rather go to the hospital on your own? It's true I get emotional,' he added, without looking up from his polishing. 'But that doesn't make me a fool, and I wish you'd stop treating me as if I was.' He hitched his specs back on his nose, his eyes very bright and shiny, turned and left the room.

'*Maurice*!' Ricky yelled after him, as we heard his soft footsteps pad along the landing and the bedroom door close quietly. '*Maurice*, don't be such an idiot.'

'Shut up!' I grabbed Ricky's arm as he made to follow him. I was ready to slap him. 'Don't try to make a joke out of this. You can't always solve everything by being funny.'

He gazed at me for a moment, then collapsed back into his chair, obviously distraught. 'I just didn't want him to worry.'

'He was already worried.'

'He gets himself in such a state. I just didn't . . . I couldn't cope with his feelings as well as my own.'

'He gets in a state because he loves you.'

Ricky shook his head. 'I was trying to protect him in case it turned out badly.'

'You heard him. He's not a child. He doesn't want protection from you, he wants honesty. He wants the truth.'

Ricky sat with his head in his hands, running them through his silver hair. He looked shattered suddenly, and old.

'I'm going to go now,' I told him. 'Leave you to it. And you'd better think of the right thing to say to him, Ricky, because he is really hurt.'

He nodded sadly. I took pity on him then, put my arms about his shoulders and hugged him hard. 'I'm so glad the news is good,' I whispered. 'You know I couldn't bear to lose either of you.'

He took my hand and kissed it. 'Two silly old queers?' he asked, managing a smile.

'Two silly old queers,' I nodded.

He stood up and took a deep breath. 'God, I should have done this years ago!' As I let myself out, he was standing outside of the bedroom door. He winked at me as he knocked, but I could see that he was nervous. 'Morris,' I heard him say softly. 'May I come in? There's something I want to ask you.'

'Norway?' I repeated, scandalised. 'Fucking Norway?'

'Don't shout!' Daniel glanced around him. We were sitting at a candlelit table in No.14, the wine bar in North Street, enjoying a glass of Chardonnay, and some lovely figs and cheese. Fortunately, it was early in the evening and we were their first customers, the place was empty. It would fill to capacity later.

'Don't panic, Miss Browne with an e, I'm not going to apply for the job. I went to Oslo once before, if you remember, for a conference. The agency saw that on my CV and thought I might be fluent in Norwegian. I had to assure them I'd only picked up a smattering, certainly not the level of fluency I would need for the job.'

I relaxed slightly. 'Anything else?'

'A couple of things. There is a vacancy for a flood risk consultant. They need someone with my experience. It's mostly interpreting flood data, writing technical reports. It might be deadly dull but the pay's good and it's a fixed term contract. Only six months.'

'Where?' I asked suspiciously.

'Yorkshire.'

My heart sank. 'Well, it's closer than Norway, I suppose,' I conceded grumpily. 'Are you going to go for it?'

'I might.' He paused a moment. 'There is an alternative.'

'Which is?'

'You remember I worked on a peat restoration project a while back?'

I nodded. 'In Ireland.'

'Well, there's an opportunity to go there again. The Rivers Trust in Inishowen are looking for a Senior Project Officer. My previous experience would be invaluable. I'd almost certainly get the job. And the money's good. And it's another fixed term contract.'

'How long?' I asked, my heart sinking.

'A year.'

'Isn't there anything in Devon? Dartmoor has plenty of bogs of its own.'

'Well, yes, there are jobs but not at the same kind of salary.' He leant close across the table. 'Look, you know there's nothing I want more than to be here with you. But if I take this job in Ireland now, I'll be in a much better position when anything does come along.'

I sighed. 'You need an income. I understand.'

'I do if I'm ever going to finish the damn house, if I'm ever to stand any chance of living in it.' He gestured helplessly. 'I suppose I could just sell it as it is. At least then it would be off my hands. And I wouldn't be the one having to find money for putting in a damp course and getting that fractured beam in the kitchen replaced.' He took a sip of wine. 'Not to mention dealing with the dry rot.'

'Dry rot?' I hadn't heard that before. 'Where?'

'Didn't I tell you? The builders only discovered it the yesterday. It's behind the wainscot in the living room.'

'Isn't there anything left of your aunt's money?' I asked tentatively.

'I'm afraid the new roof and the re-pointing and the damp course have taken care of all of that.' He rubbed a hand across his face. 'I wish the old girl had left the place to someone else.'

'No, you don't,' I told him. 'Don't sell it. You'll regret it if you do. And you'd only get a fraction of what it's worth. You've already spent a fortune on it. And it's a beautiful house, or it will be.' I leant across the table and took his hand. 'You must take the job in Ireland.'

'I could go for the job in York.'

'You'd be bored.'

'But it's not so far. I could get down here every weekend.'

'Shut up and listen. This isn't about money. It's about you, who you are and what you're trying to do to help the environment. It's about your life, your career.'

'Not my career,' he interrupted. 'My future. *Our* future. One day, Miss B, I . . .'

I cut him off short, laying a finger on his lips. 'You can still visit. It's only a short hop away on a plane. Besides,' I laughed, 'you love messing about in those old peatbogs. You know you do.'

He smiled at me across the candle flame. 'You are as wise as you are beautiful, Miss B.'

I gave that silly laugh that women give that is supposed to dismiss such flattery as nonsense.

Actually, he could say it again if he liked.

'So, when's this interview for the Irish job?' I asked.

He gave an apologetic smile. 'The day after tomorrow,' he said.

CHAPTER THIRTY-ONE

Ricky, it seemed, had found the right thing to say to Morris. They'd done all the legal stuff the day before, at the registry office. Today was pure celebration. And if I say so myself, I looked stunning in the cream silk dress that they had made me for the occasion. The marquee in the garden of Druid Lodge was decked with flowers in shades of cream, yellow and gold, the interior glowing in the May sunshine. Almost everyone I knew seemed to be gathered in that marquee; most, like Lady Margaret Westershall and Amanda Waft, sitting on elegant golden chairs; the rest, like Dean Collins and the members of Dartmoor Operatic Society, standing up at the back. I was down at the front of course.

Ricky and Morris were dressed in identical grey morning suits, each with a gold silk waistcoat and a yellow rosebud in his buttonhole. I glanced across at Daniel, looking dangerously sexy in a dark suit, Lottie, a gold ribbon around her elegant neck, sitting quietly at his feet. Michelle, the celebrant, complimenting the colour scheme in primrose silk, cleared her throat and a hush fell. The happy couple turned to face each other and the ceremony began.

'I Ricky, take you, Morris, to be my lawful wedded husband, my best friend and my love. I have loved you since I first laid eyes on you almost forty years ago,' he went on, smiling. 'You were the prettiest chorus boy I'd ever seen and I am so grateful that you also turned out to be a brilliant chef, and that you are the one who's gone bald and not me. I love you, even when you nag me for trying to have a fag before breakfast. I promise I will love you till the end of my life, however long that may be. I give you the gift of this ring . . .'

Michelle gave me the signal and I hastily thrust the little ring cushion I was carrying into her hands.

'I give you the gift of this ring,' he continued, putting it on Morris's finger, 'as a pledge of my love and faithfulness. As I give you my hand to hold, so I give you my life to keep, for you alone I trust with it.'

I glanced across the aisle at Daniel, who grinned at me and winked.

'I, Morris, take you Ricky, to be my lawful wedded husband, my best friend and my love,' Morris began, a slight tremor in his voice. 'When you walked into that theatre forty years ago, you were the handsomest man I'd ever seen. There wasn't a woman in the place who didn't want you. Quite a lot of the men too. And I have to say, it was a good three weeks before you even noticed me. Thank you for still loving me, even though I have gone bald. I love you, even when you call me *Maurice* just to wind me up. I promise I will always love you, whatever we have to face together. I give you the gift of this ring as a pledge of my love and faithfulness. As I give you my hand to hold, so I give you my life to keep, for you alone I trust with it.'

'Thank you.' Michelle turned her radiant smile on them both. 'You are now husband and husband. You may share a kiss.'

Tumultuous applause and cheering broke out all around the marquee, with lots of hugging and shedding of happy tears. Pat's eyes were suspiciously shiny and poor Sophie was awash, sobbing into her hanky, while a grinning Seth attempted to enfold her in a hug. Would they be next ones to tie the knot, I wondered? I had to wipe away a tear myself.

The wedding march started up and the newly-weds led us out of the marquee and across the garden to the house, where the wedding breakfast would be served in the dining room. I linked arms with Daniel and we walked together with Lottie trotting happily by his heels.

There were no formal speeches at the reception, but plenty of people had stories to tell. There were songs, and music and a few turns. Olly and Tom, on penny whistle and squeezebox respectively, played a jig. Digby Jerkin and Amanda Waft, recently returned from holiday, each read a poem. Amanda performed a Shakesperean sonnet. Digby, in his deep mellifluous tones, read from a poem on marriage by Kahlil Gibran.

'. . . let there be spaces in your togetherness . . .'

I grinned at Daniel. We had spaces in our togetherness alright. He had been working in Ireland for five weeks now. That mean part of me, the part that hoped he might not get the job, or that he'd hate it and come home, had been stifled. He was obviously loving it, loving Ireland.

'Make not a bond of your love,' Digby continued. 'Let it rather be a moving sea between the shores of your souls.' In our case it was the Irish sea.

Daniel was chatting to Seth, with Sophie, Pat, Elizabeth, Tom, Olly and me all at the same table. What had started as an enquiry from Seth about his new job had morphed into a discussion about the bodies thrown into bogs by ancient civilisations and found centuries later in a remarkable state of preservation. It might have been an odd conversation for guests at a wedding, but it was fascinating. Olly was listening, wide-eyed. I sensed that archaeology might be the next career on his list. I glanced at Elizabeth and she smiled.

Under the table, Lottie stared up at me from soulful eyes. She'd been ecstatic to see me when she'd arrived with Daniel the day before, dancing up and down on her tippy toes in excitement. Now she laid her muzzle on my knee and sighed, as if she knew we'd be parting too soon. I stroked her smooth head. 'Lovely Lottie,' I whispered and the tip of her tail wagged.

The day after the wedding, I drove Daniel and Lottie to Bristol airport so that they could catch their flight. I've never actually been to Ireland. I'm looking forward to going in a few weeks, to stay with them for a short holiday in Inishowen in the beautiful county of Donegal. I may, in future, have to wrestle Sophie for weekends off.

'You will be careful, won't you Miss Browne with an e?' Daniel asked as we kissed each other goodbye. By now, he should know that such a request is a waste of breath. As I've tried to tell him before, I don't go looking for trouble. It finds me by itself.

Bill, it had to be said, had been less ecstatic to see Lottie over the weekend than she had been to see him. She was so pathetically desperate to be friends, sniffing at him eagerly, the end of her tail wagging. He had buffeted her around the nose, claws out. But Daniel had brought Lottie's bed with him. It was made of pink corduroy and lined with fluffy sheepskin, very warm and cosy. Bill stared at it for a very long time, giving it serious consideration. He even dabbed at the fluffy lining with an experimental paw.

The evening before the wedding, we went out to dinner. When we came back, both Bill and Lottie were curled up in it together, fast asleep. It didn't stop him from attacking her the moment he woke up, but I suppose it's a start.

ACKNOWLEDGEMENTS

Thank you to Ian Wellens of The Cheese Shed for pointing out to me that Juno had never been to Bovey Tracey and for letting me sample all that lovely cheese. Thanks to the wonderful Michelle Parfitt, celebrant, for sharing her knowledge about civil weddings. I'm also indebted to Max Piper, for his excellent book *East Dartmoor's Lesser-Known Tors and Rocks*. I'd like to thank Teresa Chris, my agent, for her unflagging enthusiasm for my work and for her advice always being right. Thanks go to my editor, Fiona Paterson, for her care and attention. Thank goodness one of us knows which day of the week it is! Thanks to Susie Dunlop and the rest of the team at Allison & Busby. Thanks, as always, to my friend Di, to Sue Tingey and the rest of the Devon crime-writing community. Things never seem so bad after a lunch. And lastly to Martin, who has accepted with grace and fortitude the changes that my decision to 'become a writer' has wrought in our lives.

STEPHANIE AUSTIN has enjoyed a varied career, working as an artist and an antiques trader, but also for the Devon Schools Library Service. When not writing she is actively involved in amateur theatre as a director and actor, and attempts to be a competent gardener and cook. She lives in Devon.

stephanieaustin.co.uk